Peril, Passion, Peru

by

Eve Dew Crook

Peril, Passion, Peru

The Wild Rose Press, Inc.
PO Box 708
Adams Basin, NY 14410-0708
Visit us at www.thewildrosepress.com

Publishing History
First Crimson Rose Edition, 2015
Print ISBN 978-1-5092-0242-3
Digital ISBN 978-1-5092-0243-0

Published in the United States of America

The gleam of gold

reflected in the flashlight's beam. Jill freaked, forgetting her vow to leave. Reaching in, she pulled out handful after handful of precious objects. A necklace in spun gold. An intricate nosepiece of electrum—she was beginning to recognize that odd amalgam of gold and silver. A huge chunk of rock crystal dangling from a heavy silver chain. Ear spools. Pendants. Bracelets. She was breathing so hard she had to sit down.

Legs spread out on the cold rock, forgetful of danger, Jill took piece after piece of fine metalwork out of the sack. How collectors would covet these works of art! Well, she had her answer. She had to get out of here. It was too dangerous to hang around any longer. With a deep sigh, she picked up her flashlight and got to her feet.

Suddenly, a noise.

A footstep.

Terrified, Jill glanced wildly about. The sacks weren't tall enough to hide behind. The evidence of her presence was strewn upon the ground. There was no place to conceal herself.

She had only one chance. As the footsteps came closer, she switched off the flashlight and loped over to the tunnel entrance, skidding to a stop at its side. Raising her arm, she held the flashlight high, ready to strike.

Dedication

To Ken, always.
~*~

To Phyllis, without whom this book would not have
been written.
~*~

To Estelle, who brought me to Peru.
~*~

To Ally, my wonderful editor.
~*~

And to all those in Saguaro RWA and GV Writers who
helped with advice and encouragement.

Chapter 1

Manuel held his breath. The jar was almost clear. He scratched at the dirt with his fingers, afraid to use a tool. So far, he hadn't uncovered a crack, or even a chip. In the glow of his lantern, the pictures were so bright they could have been painted yesterday, not a thousand years ago. He alone had discovered this Moche tomb, carting away the fallen rocks night after night to find the cave entrance. If the jar came out of the damp soil intact, his family would eat very well at *Navidad*—indeed, throughout *el año nuevo*. He knew *el profesor* who would pay handsomely for it.

Hands trembling, he lifted it from the soil and blew lightly to clear the surface. As he turned the jar to follow the pictures around, his ears caught a faint tinkling sound. The mouth was just wide enough for his hand, so he pressed his thumb into his palm. Squeezing his hand into the jar, he used the tips of his fingers to pull out the contents. The sudden flash of gold made him blink. *Oro!*

Manuel's lips spread wide, a toothless smile matching the guile in his eyes. No more digging for *los gringos*. The gold would not be offered to the man who loved pots, however. He would take this find to the one who was losing his hair.

****

The relentless *pat-pat-pat* of raindrops against the glass wall of her office gnawed at Jill's nerves. She swiveled her desk chair and rose to gaze out the window. Madison Avenue had morphed into a sea of colorful umbrellas, jostling and bobbing along the sidewalk, but they couldn't dispense the gloom. Although it wasn't yet four, lights were on in the older building across the avenue. The distorting rain turned the lighted windows into runny egg yolks—a Salvador Dali scene.

Amused at the turn her imagination had taken, Jill returned to her desk and picked up the faxed newspaper clipping that slid from the humming machine. "BANDITS ATTACK TOURISTS EN ROUTE TO CUZCO," the headline shouted. "American Kidnapped, Held as Hostage."

She raised an eyebrow. The news covered only three columns. These days, kidnappings were so ordinary, it took a celebrity to rate a banner. Now, if it had read, "TOM CRUISE MISSING…" Tragic but true, and wasn't she getting cynical? Frank's nasty convictions had reached out to engulf her for too long. The divorce was almost final, yet there were times she wasn't sure she liked her new self.

Why did *Abuelita* keep faxing her these clippings? Frank's excavating in the danger zone must be giving her grandmother malicious pleasure. The woman had never cared for him, barely hid her disdain, yet his smarmy attitude had corrupted her, too.

The machine hummed again, and Jill reached for the fax. No headlines, thank goodness. This message came from Harry Lang, Frank's team leader in Peru.

Her eyes narrowed as she read it. "Flanders

missing from the excavation five days. Have you heard from him? If he is not back at work on Monday, we will call the police."

Hell. The bastard had absconded from the site. Without coming home to sign the final divorce papers. Jill had been counting on Frank to visit his mother for Thanksgiving. In all the years she had known him, *Francisco* had never missed returning when Mama had crooked her little finger. Yet Thanksgiving had come and gone and so had Frank. His mother had even called her to see if she had heard from Francisco. How that must have galled. To the sanctimonious woman, Frank's news of their divorce would have been devastating. If she weren't so angry herself, Jill could almost feel sorry for her.

Damn. Damn. Damn. She wouldn't let him get away with it. She'd put up with him long enough. Needed to feel free. But without his signature, the divorce wouldn't be finalized. An overworked judge could delay the case for months. The rat must have known that when he'd scurried away, taking her brand-new laptop with him.

Leaning back in the chair, she tapped the fax against her teeth. When she'd told him she was getting a divorce, Frank had been furious. He'd stormed out of the apartment, taking nothing...or so she had thought. Surely, he would return for his clothes and books, his precious hunting gear. But no, Frank had been more eager to get back at her, spiteful man. Thank goodness she'd backed up the laptop before he grabbed it.

She sighed. So much easier to concentrate on the little things and ignore the vital one. She had to get those divorce papers signed. Who knew where Frank was now? On some beach with a bouncy bimbo and a bottle of booze? Probably celebrating the divorce, once he got used to the idea.

If she were ever to feel truly free, she'd better fly down and see what she could learn from the police. The troubling possibilities were endless. A new idea struck, and Jill bit her lip. He could have run into bandits down there. If Frank were poaching on their patch, they'd tear him apart. For a brief moment she recalled the once captivating man she had married, now perhaps in mortal danger. But the image faded as her anger rose.

She had no desire to become a widow before she had a crack at being a divorcée. That role had much more cachet. Oh, hell. Mean thought. She was becoming as shallow as Frank. The cynicism served well as protective covering, but it eroded her spirit. She had to think positive.

If she flew down, maybe she could help. The guys at the dig wouldn't miss a tiny pottery shard, but they'd step over a body to get to it. Nothing interfered with that. She'd bet no one at the site had taken the trouble to learn Spanish, but she was fluent, could assist the police and act as interpreter.

Her gaze returned to the window. It would be warm and sunny in Peru. She'd accrued lots of vacation days, and the office was quiet right now. The boss might even let her stretch the leave through Christmas. It would be fun to see how *Navidad* was celebrated in summer. She could picture Santa sliding down the chimney in an old-time, two-piece red swimsuit, his belly button lighting the way, like Rudolph's nose.

Chuckling, Jill jumped up and hurried down the hall. Another quick decision, but she liked it that way.

A trip to Peru was the right move. When the philandering "Cisco Kid" showed up, she'd insist that he sign the papers even before he answered questions. Then she'd say goodbye to him for good. Break all the ties with that conniving bastard. Live it up as the gay divorcée—too bad it wasn't PC to call herself that.

She'd send his clothes to Goodwill, offer Tim his pick of what was left. Her little brother would go for the weird mementoes Frank had brought back from his excavations, especially the piece of skull with red hair still attached. She grimaced, turned her thoughts to travel plans.

Reaching the door, she paused for a moment, hesitating. Then she straightened her shoulders, gripped the doorknob, and marched into the main office.

****

In the airport's cavernous waiting room, framed posters filled the empty spaces between souvenir shops. Jill passed racks of paperbacks, skimming their titles as she rolled her carryall along. T-shirts, sunglasses, duty-free perfumes. A poster caught her eye. She wheeled her luggage closer, stared for a long moment, then began to laugh.

"Stop that," she chastised herself. "Just because they're a thousand years old, it doesn't mean the people carved on those pots and vases didn't have the same urges we have today."

The poster touted, "Erotic Art through the Ages," and featured pieces from Peruvian galleries, but the text for a Lima museum exhibit listed entries from all over the world. *What a delightful idea. All of us prurient art lovers can compare...* Her gaze lingered on the image of a seated man with legs spread to reveal a huge, jutting phallus. She smirked. Apparently, men have boasted about their package since the dawn of time. She'd save a day to see the show before leaving the country.

She looked at her watch. Still a few minutes before her flight would be called. Once again her glance flew to the tiny lifelike figures. What was it about naked people acting out their fantasies that brought on a guilty laugh—even when they were only five inches high and made of clay? Sex on display made her uncomfortable, and what did that say about her? More than she cared to admit in today's permissive world.

Jill stepped back, squinted. The faces were so solemn. None of the wild abandon one would expect from the poses. Perhaps that was what bothered her most. They didn't seem to be enjoying themselves. To modern eyes, the lack of emotion was unsettling.

Face it. All that explicit coupling—twosomes, and singles, and even some threesomes—were disturbing, but exciting her, too. Stirring up feelings she'd rather suppress. Especially now.

She scanned the images. Was coupling the right word? Perhaps tripling for some poses? Singling for a few? At the thought, she couldn't stop her giggle from slipping out. There she went again…self-conscious and always editing. Turning those thoughts into a joke was a great cover for her own hidden emotions. Well, whatever catastrophe she'd be involved in once she reached the dig in Peru, she could look forward to being diverted by this exhibit.

Her flight was called. Jill hurried to the boarding area, wheeled her carryall up the ramp and found her seat. She lifted her luggage into the compartment above, waiving the offer of help.

As she fastened her seat belt, five plainly dressed, dark-skinned women stepped into the cabin. Each carried a doll as big as a six-month-old baby, garbed all in pink from bonnet to bootees. The visual was so bizarre, for an instant Jill felt she'd stepped onto the set of a TV reality show. She shook her head to clear the vision, but the dolls were still there.

They must be Christmas presents. Her favorite uncle had given her one like that on her ninth birthday. Jill smiled at the memory. She'd sassed him that she was too old for dolls, but had hugged it to her when he tried to take it back.

Now, these dolls were being stuffed into the overhead storage compartments. There was something macabre about the scene. A young flight attendant, his officer's cap tilted at a rakish angle, walked along the aisle banging shut the compartment doors. She shuddered with each bang. Her overheated imagination fancied little coffin lids dropping.

The cabin was too warm. Jill dabbed lightly at her forehead. With a last look around she settled back, her mind once more dwelling on the problem in Peru. Where was Frank now? Back at the dig, sated with sex, or… She had to stop imagining the worst scenarios.

The day had been exhausting, and the flight would be long. She gripped the seat arms as the plane revved for takeoff, but once it lifted and began its monotonous throbbing, Jill slipped in and out of a light doze.

A soft-spoken *"¡Qué mamacita!"* snapped her awake. The flight attendant was peering at the spot where a pearl button had popped open on her white silk blouse to expose a wisp of lace and satin. She would have sworn she saw his lips purse into a kiss.

****

In the Lima airport waiting room at Callao, Dex Conroy sat rubbing a tight muscle in his thigh. All those hours of non-stop driving, and now the plane was late. He should have brought his notes. Why did Harry have to send him to meet the woman? And what bad timing—right after he had gotten his hands on the Moche pot with its fantastic paintings. If he could decipher their meaning, what a find it would be. Universities would be begging him to lecture. He'd have it made.

Blinking in the glistening light the setting sun spilled into the room, Dex glanced impatiently at his watch. Crazy idea—a woman traveling alone to a macho country like Peru. If Flanders' wife was dumb enough to come all the way here to look for her sleazy husband, she could damn well get to the dig by herself.

He could imagine what she was like. An aging Clairol blonde, judging from the type he'd seen Frank Flanders latch onto. Big boobs. Too much makeup. A Tiffany maybe, or a Veronica, with a shrill, carping voice. She had stayed married to him for several years, hadn't she?

The woman would get nowhere with her inquiries. She'd disrupt everyone, make a nuisance of herself. Flanders had surely run off with one of those nubile volunteers at the site. Or else he was on his way back to the States, his pockets stuffed with Moche gold. Dex sneered, his gut telling him Flanders was in cahoots with the looters. But how could he prove it?

Unaware that he was venting his annoyance, he scowled at an elderly couple sitting across the aisle. The woman cringed, and the old man put his arm around her, staring back at Dex with pathetic menace. But the archaeologist only glanced again at his watch.

He'd have to get hotel rooms. The plane's ETA was so late, by the time they made it through customs it would be dark. Nothing would be available in Callao now, so that meant a night in Lima with Frank's wife, plus another night on the road. He groaned at the thought of being away from his Moche pot for three more days. Why couldn't Harry see that was more important?

Rising, Dex paced the waiting room. A runny-nosed Quechua Indian child in a dirty striped shawl, her feet wrapped in rags, pulled at his arm. "Chiclets," she whined, *"Mariposas."*

He looked down at the battered cigar box in her tiny brown hand. It held a few packets of gum and small wooden frames with iridescent butterflies, her *mariposas,* mounted on cardboard. Smiling at her, his irritation already fading, he took some *soles* from his pocket and threw them into the box. With a pat on the skinny arm, he turned down her offered souvenir.

At last he caught the rapid, muffled Spanish announcing the plane's arrival from New York. He walked over to Gate Two, certain he would spot the woman the moment she stepped onto the ramp. As he watched the passengers descending, Dex noticed with amusement the large pink dolls so many women carried in their arms. *Feliz Navidad.* Christmas wasn't far off. No white Christmas for him this year, and he was glad. Even with bandits roaming, it was more peaceful here, far from his uptight family.

Where was she? His eyes scanned the crowd

walking across the tarmac. Floodlights had been turned on, but he saw no one who fit the description in his mind. In fact, only one woman among the bundled passengers looked like a classy New Yorker.

She was tall. Long, shapely legs caught his attention. As his glance rose higher, he became aware of a slender body moving sensuously in the short-skirted suit with its man-tailored jacket—a deep, rich, ruby port red. A carryall dangled from her shoulder, and she wheeled an overnight case. His gaze rose to reach her face, and his pulse skipped a beat. A heart-shaped face. *Dolce de leche* skin, smooth as the honeyed ice cream. Glossy dark hair pulled tight in some kind of complicated braid. And those eyes. Green. Gleaming with anticipation. Did he see an invitation there?

Dex checked a grin. He must be hallucinating. This couldn't be Flanders' wife, but he wouldn't mind a quick tumble with this one. Maybe not so quick. It had been a while, and she had his pulse jumping.

Forcing himself to turn away, he scrutinized the crowd once more. The plane finally emptied, and the flight attendants emerged. No frowzy blonde—he must have missed her. Shaking his head in disgust, Dex turned back toward the waiting room. With one foot forward he stopped, caught his breath and stared. The passengers had all gone for their luggage. The only person left was the green-eyed woman.

****

Jill walked toward the waiting room, wondering if Harry Lang had come to meet her. When she'd been introduced to him in New York, he'd come across as a typical scientific nerd—too easily distracted to be let loose in Manhattan. She could picture Harry kneeling on the ground, blade in one hand and brush in the other, so absorbed in rescuing a protruding artifact he'd be unaware of a bandit's knife pricking his neck. But Harry wasn't here—surely he had sent someone to meet her.

She frowned, then caught sight of a tall, rangy, heavily tanned man who didn't look at all Peruvian. The sun had bleached his hair the color of sand, for his short, curly beard was a darker gold. She liked the look—dusty jeans tight across narrow hips, a cotton shirt, laced at the throat, straining across broad shoulders. Behind black-framed glasses, his eyes appeared dark.

He must have been sent from the dig, but who was he? Could Harry afford to send an archaeologist? They must be shorthanded with Frank gone. Yet there was something about this man. He moved with the loose, confident walk women found attractive. As he came toward her with an endearingly hesitant smile, Jill felt a stirring of awareness, a little blip of anticipation.

Tired and irritated at her unexpected reaction to a stranger, she forced the thought from her mind. She was here in Peru to help find Frank and to get her divorce papers signed. Whoever this man was, she'd keep her distance.

He stopped in front of her. "Ms. Flanders?" he asked, his voice deep and resonant.

His eyes were a startling dark blue in his tanned face. The intensity of his gaze brought on a flush. "I'm Jill Flanders." She covered her embarrassment with a cool smile. "Did Harry Lang send you?"

"Yes, ma'am. I'm Dex Conroy. We'll drive into

Lima and I'll take you to a hotel as soon as we get out of the airport."

Ma'am, Jill thought in disgust. Did the flight tire her out that much? Just how old did he think she was? She caught herself staring, felt the color rise again in her cheeks.

His lips quirked. "I'll grab your luggage while you're having your passport stamped. It's too late to head for the Pyramid of the Stars tonight, but we'll get an early start in the morning. We've got a lot of driving to do."

"How early?" Jill asked, all at once overwhelmed by fatigue.

"Best we head out at sunup."

A groan escaped. After her sleepless night and the long flight, she had been counting on eight hours' rest to catch up. She glanced at Dex. Was he laughing at her? Her guard must be down if he could read her that easily.

Fumbling, she removed her passport case from her carryall. "I checked a suitcase through—green, with red wool wound around the handle." She handed him the ticket stub.

He left her at Immigration. Jill stood in a line of overdressed people, prepared for a northern winter instead of a southern summer. She could smell their sweat and cringed at the ear-splitting babble.

At last her turn came. The official stamped her passport quickly when she told him in Spanish that she was a tourist, here to see his beautiful country. Dex had still not returned with her luggage, and Jill leaned against the counter. She shut her eyes, tuning out the hubbub.

A hand grabbed her arm. Her eyes flew open, and she clutched the strap to her carryall.

"Did I scare you? Sorry. I found your bag." Dex nodded toward her suitcase but continued to carry it.

Jill glared, then gave in to his lopsided grin and returned a wan smile. No woman could resist it.

"On to customs." He propelled her. "This will take time."

The line didn't seem to be moving. "What's going on?" she asked. She had eaten little on the plane, and her stomach was rumbling.

"There's always confusion here." With a resigned shrug, he explained. "Drugs and artifacts being smuggled out. Guns and hot money coming in."

He inched her forward, their turn next. Suddenly, a skinny man with a drooping mustache broke from the line. His suitcase hit her leg, almost knocking her down as he dashed for the counter and jumped over it. Shouts and screams began, then escalated. The din became a roar. The crowd pushed forward, crushing her against the counter.

Dropping her suitcase, Dex grabbed Jill and held her close, protecting her from the mob with his body.

A shot. Another. Trembling, Jill closed her eyes. She felt the strength of his arms around her and leaned into him for protection. She could feel his heart beating rapidly...or was that hers?

It was all over in moments. Two policemen dragged the man from the room. He shouted something Jill couldn't make out in the melee but, miraculously, her luggage was still there. Dex swung the suitcase onto the counter.

The customs agent gave Jill an admiring glance, his

gaze roaming over her body while she waited, gritting her teeth. She was too tired to be flattered, barely able to be annoyed. Her forbearance was rewarded, for he stamped her cases without opening them.

"What was all the excitement about?" she asked as they finally reached the parking lot.

"El Rio Flujo, the Flowing River, smuggling in guns. Have you heard of them?"

Her eyes opened wide. "They're terrorists, aren't they?"

"That and more. Thank God they weren't bombing the airport today." He hustled her over to a dusty red pickup truck. "It was reckless of you to come to Peru on your own, you know. This isn't a safe country."

Exhausted as she was, Jill resented his tone. Women didn't need to be bubble wrapped. She started to retort but stopped. There would be time enough to tell this arrogant man just what she thought of his idea.

Brushing aside Dex's arm, Jill took the high step into the closed cab on her own. Her short skirt hiked up to her hips, and she felt the night breeze ripple across her pink silk panties. She heard an appreciative smacking of lips and swore under her breath. He was as bad as the rest of them. Men.

Just you wait, Dex Conroy. There'll be a reckoning before I leave Peru.

Chapter 2

They drove in silence through Lima's dark streets. Ignoring Dex's scowl, Jill rode with her eyes closed. At a sharp turn, she slid into him. Her lids flew up and she glared, but he continued to stare stonily ahead. Only when they reached the ancient, ornate Hotel Balboa did he crack a smile. It was closer to a smirk as Jill, one hand trying vainly to hold down her skirt, allowed the doorman to help her from the truck.

The paunchy clerk at the front desk eyed Jill with raised brows. Her French twist was coming apart, and a dark curl nestled on her collarbone. One end of her white silk blouse was untucked. Her skirt had twisted halfway around. She had eaten off her lipstick, and her mascara was smeared.

"¿Una habitación con cama matrimonial?" he asked, beaming at her.

One room with a marriage bed? She didn't need any more ideas. Jill saw Dex wink at the clerk, but before he could say a word, she raised her voice. *"Dos habitaciónes sencillas.* Two single rooms."

The night clerk hesitated, glancing at Dex, who shrugged.

What were they, buddies? *"¿Hay un problema?"* she snapped. *"Digame.* Speak to me."

Hands fluttering, he hastened to reassure her. "No

21

problem, madam. *Perdón, por favor.*"

He handed her the key, and Jill marched over to the elevator. "Why do women have to put up with men and their stupid macho ploys?" she fumed.

Dex stood at her side, his glance teasing now, despite the provocation. "I like your style, Madam Executive."

It was too much. Jill forced herself not to melt as his lips curved into a rueful smile. He was making fun of her.

"Want to get a bite to eat?"

"I've lost my appetite," she lied, refusing to allow the attraction to undermine her resolve. "All I want to do is sleep."

"Coffee shop opens at five a.m. Be ready." The scowl was back as he walked away. Had she offended him? Too bad. She was too tired to think about it now.

Turning the key, Jill pushed open the heavy door and stepped into an opulent room of red velvet and black walnut. She wanted to flop down on the bed but felt too hot and dirty. Luckily, she didn't have to face a time change, only flight fatigue. A shower would feel good.

When she stepped into the bathroom, however, Jill saw only a big old-fashioned tub with claw feet, black cracks running through its chipped enamel. With a sigh, she started the water running.

Hanging up her suit, Jill stripped and hurried back. She passed the room's full-length mirror without a glance. What would be the point? Frank had convinced her she couldn't compete on the erotic level. Men admired her, but they all played the same game. Sexual hockey, she'd named it. Conquest was the goal, love, the penalty box. And if she carried the analogy further, women were the pucks. Hearing the words in her head, Jill giggled. She hadn't intended it to sound like a dirty joke.

While the tub filled, she unpacked a filmy blue nightgown, wondering again why she had packed something so impractical. Well, it made her feel good— so what. A little thing like that took away the loneliness for a night.

Oh, whom was she kidding? She poured a travel packet of camellia-scented foam bath into the tub, stepped over the high porcelain side and lowered herself until her shoulders were immersed in bubbles. She closed her eyes. After all those hours cramped into the plane's narrow seat, the warm water was a caress.

She stroked herself slowly with the soap-filled sponge the hotel had provided. Her sleepy mind kept returning to that tall, disturbing man with the hard chest and steely arms holding her so tightly, so protectively, when violence erupted at the customs desk.

A laugh bubbled up. She was hallucinating. A woman her age in a strange country lying in a tub, having erotic thoughts about a man she had just met—a bossy, irritating man who scowled at everything. Another archaeologist, and pure Anglo to boot—her anathema. The poster in the airport must have affected her brain.

What was his job at the site? The sifters were usually college kids. He must be one of the leaders, but he wasn't at all like Frank. There was something exciting about Dex. Something decisive. He was different from the few men she'd had a drink or a meal with since she started divorce proceedings. Crazy thought, but she liked his scent. Clean and fresh underneath the sweat. Male. It sparked the airport memory of being in his arms.

Closing her eyes, she ran the sponge in lazy circles around her stomach and breasts. She was so tired. As she started to nod off in the soothing water, Jill shook herself awake. Scolding herself, she climbed out and toweled vigorously. Enough fantasizing. She was a woman on a mission, here in Peru to help find her wayward husband and get his signature on the divorce papers. There would be other times for sensual yearning—with men who stayed longer, she swore. No more philandering types.

What had Frank said the site was? A Moche Indian *huaca*, a ruined fortress-pyramid between the mountains and the sea. She had best keep her mind on her mission. With that reprimand, Jill slipped under the freshly ironed sheets of the carved walnut bed and fell instantly asleep.

When she awoke a few hours later, the illuminated dial on her travel clock read 2:58 a.m. She'd been roused by a disturbing dream, and lay for a moment trying to shake off the feeling of panic that remained. Then, with a sigh, she got up.

The Spanish tiles were cold under her feet as she walked to the bathroom. She splashed her face, listening to the ancient faucet creak as she tried to wash away the dream. Snatches of scenes kept floating through her mind.

Returning to bed, Jill curled up tight and burrowed into the pillow, but the sexy nightgown slithering on her body didn't bring on romantic images. The recollection of her strange dream kept her from falling back to sleep.

She was swimming in the ocean at Jones Beach. The sand was covered with people jostling each other and shouting—she could hear the clamor of voices even in the water. A doll floated past her, its pink organdy skirt acting as a sail.

Suddenly, a shark jumped out of the waves. It flew through the air toward her, its open mouth revealing all its wicked teeth. Just as it was about to swallow her up, something gently tugged at her, pulling her under the water where it was warm and safe.

She swam to the surface. When her head broke through the water, she looked up to find Frank in the distance, grinning at her. As the image faded, his hair turned blond and he grew a golden beard.

A huge wave rolled in, lifting her up and carrying her toward this stranger. She floated down onto a surfboard and lay basking in the hot sun, covered with sea foam, wearing nothing but a pink bonnet and a Moche nosepiece. The tiny golden disks lining its edge fluttered as she breathed.

Her surfboard rode the waves, up to the crest and down in the trough. At first it was a lovely caressing motion, but then it began to move faster and faster, racing over the choppy water. She clung to it in a panic as the waves rose higher and higher…

Jill shivered at the vivid memory. She recognized what the dream disguised. The threatening shark echoed her terror at the airport. But the last part, the surfboard pounding the waves until it woke her with this terrible anxiety—could the dream have been sexual?

Damn, but she was frustrated. Recalling the gently rocking surfboard earlier, she let her fingertips slide slowly down her body. Too soon she remembered she needed to be awake in two hours. That bleak thought snapped her out of the mood.

Straightening the sheets on the huge Spanish bed, Jill stretched out and tried the special breathing she had learned in yoga class. Eyes closed, she concentrated on a spot between her eyebrows. Her breathing became slower, deeper. Soon the spot began to glow faintly with a blue light. She heard nothing, felt nothing but her breath going slowly in and out. Prahna…the life force. Her calm returned, and she drifted off to sleep.

****

Dex slammed shut the door of his hotel room, still annoyed at the waste of his precious time and nettled by the woman's attitude.

Who did she think he was, a delivery boy? And what was she? Just some smartass New York City editor, used to ordering people around. Maybe it wasn't so surprising that old Frank fell into the arms of those compliant females.

As he began to undress, however, the vision of Jill as he had first seen her through the glass at Gate Two rose up before him. Her long legs, that sexy walk he was sure she was unaware of. Those lips, a Cupid's bow on top and a luscious bottom one he'd like to nibble on. He could feel his jeans tightening and hastily undid the zipper.

Jill was a puzzle, an enigma. Her green eyes invited, while her cool voice turned him down. It had been a while since his last summer romance with a grad student at a dig. A woman closer to his own age would surely be more experienced. That thought offered challenging possibilities.

Naked, Dex got under the bed sheet, his imagination fired up with suggestive scenarios. He stretched his long, lean body and put his hands behind his head. Finding Frank's wife so attractive had been a surprise. Perhaps he judged her too hastily. She must be tired from the flight and upset about her husband being missing. But how could she have stayed married to a guy like Flanders for years? Didn't she know? The gossip grapevine at the dig had the couple separated but, if it were true, why was she here?

Too much to think about. The drive had been long, and he was so tired. Turning over on his side, Dex murmured, "Jill...what a lovely name." His sleepy brain pronounced the J with a soft French sound. "A lovely liquid name..." He was still rolling it over and tasting it on his tongue when he fell asleep.

His wrist alarm sounded just before five a.m. Dex rose and hurriedly dressed in worn jeans, a faded denim shirt, and his comfortable old scuffed boots. He patted the silver and turquoise buckle on his belt for luck, finger-combed his shaggy hair. It had grown long and curled into the silky beard he always grew while away on a dig.

Backpack over his shoulders, he left the room. Lacking the patience to wait for the ancient elevator, he ran down three flights of stairs to the hotel kitchen and picked up the picnic basket he had ordered the night before. He hastened to Jill's room, knocked once, waited, and knocked again.

Her sleepy voice came through the heavy Spanish door, but he couldn't make out the words. Setting down the basket, he drummed his fingers on the doorknob. After a few minutes the door partially opened, and he could see Jill outlined in the rosy glow of dawn. Her hair, like polished mahogany, fell around her shoulders, and her feet were bare. She had thrown on a robe, but the blue silk of her gown peeked through at the neck. Without makeup she appeared younger, more innocent.

Dex gulped. "You're not ready?" *Damn, that was stupid.*

"I overslept," she apologized. "Give me ten minutes. I'll meet you in the coffee shop."

He gazed at her until she pulled her robe tighter and shut the door.

He was on his second cup of coffee when she appeared. This time, the dart of pleasure he felt at seeing her was mixed with exasperation. She wore high-heeled sandals and a backless blue sundress with big white dots. A matching jacket hung over one shoulder. Her hair, pulled back in a ponytail, was clipped with a pearl barrette that gleamed against the dark fall. Staring, he ran his tongue along his lips.

From the corner of his eye, Dex could see two men at the counter eyeing the smooth skin of her back and smirking. "You'd better go back up and change," he growled.

She slid into the other side of the booth, coloring as she bumped into his knees. "Why? It's my first opportunity to enjoy summertime in December. I decided to take advantage of it." She looked around. "What's wrong with this outfit? The other people here seem to like it."

"I wouldn't count too much on their approval." Dex flicked his head at the ogling men. "You might not care for what they're thinking, Ms. Flanders." Her face grew even redder. "Besides, I can see you're not accustomed to a tropical desert sun. It's summer here. You need long sleeves, long pants, a hat with a brim, and shoes that will protect you from spiders and scorpions."

Bristling, she drew in her breath. "I don't like your patronizing tone…spiders? Scorpions?"

He nodded. "This is dry, relentless terrain we're heading into. A primitive land."

"Are you deliberately trying to frighten me?" Her eyes narrowed. "Well, it's too late for me to change now. The porter's already brought down my suitcase. You'll just have to protect me."

He wanted to argue, for Peru was dangerous, and not only from the wildlife. But time was running out. "It's your problem," he said, though he knew it wouldn't be. It was up to him to watch out for trouble— another damn responsibility Harry had laid on him. "I'd like to leave in ten minutes."

"Don't worry." Her voice dripped with honey. "I'll just finish my coffee, Mr. Conroy."

"It's Dr. Conroy," he snarled. "Ian Dexter Conroy, PhD., at your service, *Ms*. Flanders."

His smile had turned feral.

Eyes widening, Jill's tone changed. "Doctor?"

"Yes. I have a doctorate in ceramic ethnoarchaeology from Berkeley. Do you want to see my diploma?"

Stung, she slid out of the booth and got to her feet. "Not even your Phi Beta Kappa key, *Doctor*. We can leave now."

From her carryall she withdrew sunglasses and a rolled-up straw hat. "I even have sunscreen on my face." Her smile mocked his. "At least I'm

29

appropriately dressed from the neck up." She unrolled her hat, and something black crawled out.

Jill jumped, stifling a scream.

Dex looked down, raised his eyebrows, then stepped on the hairy spider. He said nothing, watched her turn pale. Dropping some bills on the table, he took her arm, felt its slight tremble when they left the booth.

As he hustled Jill through the door, he was uncomfortably aware of gazes drilling into his back, following them out.

Chapter 3

The porter waited with their luggage beside the red pickup truck. Dex examined the vehicle thoroughly, muttering all the while about crime.

"Were you robbed?" Jill asked.

He turned toward her. "On my last visit to Lima, thieves slit the glass from a window, unlocked the door, and stole a package I'd left on the back seat—all while the truck was parked under a streetlight."

"My goodness. Where were the police?"

"What police? The crooks outnumber them."

As Dex checked the tires, Jill climbed into the cab. Surreptitiously, she removed a pair of running shoes from her carryall and shook them hard. *Spiders and scorpions...* She shuddered. Nothing fell out, so she slipped them on. Had he noticed? Jill searched his eyes for the telltale twinkle that had so upset her yesterday, but Dex was concentrating on the truck. Relieved, she leaned over and tied the laces.

They drove through the noisy traffic of Lima. Work started early downtown. Jill had never seen so many banged-up autos in her life. Drivers darted in and out of traffic with slippery skill—headlights dragging, hoods missing, bumpers dangling, fenders smashed. The streets resembled an automobile graveyard in motion.

Reaching a more affluent area, Dex pointed out the ornately carved wooden balconies on older Spanish buildings. "The *señoritas* used to sit up there with their *dueñas*," he told her. "Spanish gentlemen courted from the street below."

Was he was hinting that women still needed chaperones? She scowled, but he went blithely on with his sightseeing lecture, pointing out the presidential palace, Pizarro's statue in the town square, and the mountainside known as the *barriadas,* where the poor lived in corrugated tin-roofed shacks.

"There's no running water," Dex said, his tone bitter. "Trucks come twice a week and siphon water into barrels left outside the houses. They're firetraps."

"Why were they built?"

"Good question. First the Indians came down from the mountains, hoping for a better life, but there were no jobs for them in the city, no other places to live. The next wave came to escape the terrorists, who burned down their villages." His tone grew even more scathing.

Jill was appalled. Her annoyance with his macho attitude toward her faded as she realized how much he cared for this country and its people. "Can't the government do something?" she asked.

"The guerrillas slaughter the very peasants they're supposedly helping. Meanwhile, the government helps, all right—it helps the rich get richer." Dex shook his head in disgust. "Well, that's the end of my lecture. From now on you're only going to hear about the wonders of Peru. It's a fabulous country."

They left the local streets and picked up the Pan American Highway, driving north on a two-lane blacktop concealed in sections by drifting sand.

Treeless mountains—red, brown, and ocher—rose to meet deserted beaches lining a cobalt blue sea. Huge sand dunes on her right led to more bleak, stony mountains. She was surrounded by stark beauty in a sunlit landscape so bright it hurt her eyes.

For mile after mile Jill rode in silence, only too aware of Dex's presence beside her. She watched the desert roll by, ignoring the heat darting through her as his thigh touched hers whenever they hit a bump in the road. Every now and then she spotted an occasional patch of green where a river ran down from the mountains and irrigated a small field. Cotton grew in these oases, sugar cane in a few and, to her surprise, cherry trees.

They met no other cars. Occasionally, a beat-up truck going south passed like a mirage, shimmering in the waves of heat that rose from the tarmac.

By noon Jill was hungry, her throat parched and her eyes dry. The tepid water in the canteen tasted of chemicals, so she'd left it alone. If Dex showed no signs of discomfort, she would tough it out, too.

She was relieved when they finally pulled off the highway at the ruined fortress of Paramonga. The pyramid itself was huge and forbidding. Broken foundation stones lay scattered along its slope. No other life shared their landscape as far as her eyes could see.

The silence was eerie. Despite the brilliant sunshine, the loneliness of the spot made her shiver. She put on the jacket to her sundress.

"Good idea," Dex said. "You'll need protection from the sun." As they walked around the pyramid, he pointed out bones and potshards that littered the sand, grabbing her arm from time to time to avoid stepping into holes in the ground.

Jill forced herself to concentrate on his words, but her skin sizzled wherever his strong fingers landed, distracting her.

"The holes are shafts dug by grave robbers," he told her. "You'll see them at every ruin. There's a lot of loot still buried."

"Ah, the Incas."

"They're the most well-known, but there were earlier tribes. Many did stunning work in gold and silver, but no one beats the Moche." His eyes lit as he pronounced the two syllables. "Their necklaces and ear spools are in the museums—the Moche did marvelous metal work. But their pots are truly a revelation."

As he broached the subject, his face glowed. "The sculptures are extraordinary, but the paintings on the pots are my real challenge. Scenes are overlaid. It's hard to separate a drawing from the one behind it and figure out what it represents—kind of like cracking a code. But with each picture deciphered, a culture that died more than a thousand years ago comes back to life."

A lively, thriving civilization…Jill's thoughts jumped to the airport poster. "Some cultural practices aren't so hard to understand," she responded, her tone dry, her cheeks flushed.

Peering into her eyes, Dex grinned. "Ah, you've seen some of the erotic pots. My specialty, along with the paintings. In some respects, human nature hasn't changed at all."

"Aren't we the lucky ones."

"Sure are!" He ignored her irony. "Otherwise, we wouldn't be around…to say nothing of the fun we'd miss." He stopped teasing, picked up a potshard and handed it to Jill.

She turned it over and over in her hand. "Why, that raised part looks almost like a little figure. He's playing—what do you call them—the panpipes?"

"Right, the panpipes are ancient. And see how the bottom of the piece is curved? It's part of a lid, perhaps, broken off a pot. The little guy could be the handle."

Jill rubbed her thumb over the shard, thrilled at her connection to the past. "How old is it?"

"Hard to tell just from a fragment. From the feel of the clay…maybe eight hundred years."

"Wow!" She smiled radiantly at Dex, and he grinned back. "Better watch out, you'll catch the pot-hunting fever."

Oh no. Frank used this fascination to hook her. She couldn't let herself be sucked in again. Her head throbbed. Manhattan…books…publishing…the bright lights of Broadway. That was her world, not this blistering sun. Scrunching her eyes tight behind the sunglasses, Jill tried to force the headache back into darkness. Her fingers still clung to the shard. As they returned to the truck for the picnic basket and a blanket, she slipped the little piece of baked clay into her pocket.

Dex spread the blanket on the sand by the east wall of the fortress where a shadow was just beginning to form. "In a little while we'll be out of the sun."

"Good. So much bright light hurts my eyes. These sunglasses aren't much help. Besides, I'm terribly thirsty."

Dropping down onto the blanket, Jill winced. "That truck of yours could use better springs." She grabbed a bottle of Coke from the basket. "Warm but wet, thank goodness. I can use a sweet taste." She tried to twist off the top, but it was the old-fashioned kind. "Where's the opener?"

"Uh-oh. I forgot to ask for one."

Jill watched in amazement as Dex walked back to the truck and wedged the necks of the bottles into the crack between the door and the chassis. The caps popped off.

Her head was still pounding. "No Boy Scout knife with gadgets? A little forgetful, aren't you?"

He shrugged. "My bad. It's back at the dig. Your arrival was unexpected."

Making a face, she drank the warm soda. "Some cold water would be much more thirst quenching."

"The water here isn't safe for you to drink," Dex warned.

"I'm not a child," she snapped. "I knew cold water was just a fantasy. What's there to eat?" she added, her face heating as he grinned. She'd have to watch her mouth. This man saw double meanings everywhere.

He reached into the basket and brought out several bundles wrapped in waxed brown paper. A whole roasted chicken was in one, two rolls in another, shredded lettuce with chopped tomatoes in a third, and ripe mangoes in the last.

Except for a packet of salad dressing, there was nothing else. Holding out his empty hands, Dex apologized. "I guess they forgot the utensils."

Jill stared at him. "No knives, no forks, no napkins?"

"*Nada.*"

"Well really," she said, her irritation growing.

"Why didn't you check at the hotel? How are we supposed to eat this?"

"Like the ancient Peruvians did." He gestured toward the pyramid. "Improvise. Pretend you're a Moche priestess and dig in." His crooked smile held a challenge.

Jill's heart lurched at his look, but she refused to succumb to his charm. "You should have thought to check," she scolded.

"Picky, picky." He ripped off a chicken leg and held it out to her.

With a frown she reached forward and took it. He twisted off the other, then broke the rest of the bird into pieces and laid them back on the wrapping paper.

Cautiously, she took a bite. The chicken was succulent. Cumin and other spices made her mouth water. She hadn't realized how hungry she was. Already, food was taking the edge off her headache.

As she finished the leg and picked up a wing, Jill glanced at Dex. He had ripped open the packet of dressing with his teeth and was using his index finger to mix it into the shredded lettuce and tomatoes. He licked his finger, and she closed her eyes. A vision of sucking it clean for him flashed through her mind.

At the inappropriate thought, she laughed. The dry desert air turned the sound into wind chimes. She'd been bitchy. This man stirred a response in her she didn't want to acknowledge. But she couldn't help herself.

Their eyes met, and he, too, snickered. Jill's mouth was greasy, her hands sticky, and she'd rubbed at a smudge of brown spice on the middle of her cheek.

Pointing at each other, they laughed harder and

harder till they fell back on the blanket, too shaken to eat. The fit of giggles finally stopped. They sat up and returned to their picnic, their amazement reflected in two guilty grins. She hadn't laughed so uninhibitedly in years, and was willing to bet Dex hadn't either. For a while there, he became unglued. *Good to know.*

Jill chose a ripe mango and peeled it with her long nails. When she bit into the slippery fruit, the juice dribbled down her chin and onto her chest, sliding between her breasts into the deep vee of her blue dotted sundress.

As his gaze, darkening with desire, followed the trickle of juice, a delicious sensation pulled at her insides. She let out a tiny gasp. Perhaps her feelings weren't one-sided, after all.

Averting her eyes, Jill hastily finished the mango and dropped the big pit into the basket. Her fingers dripped with the sweet juice. "I've g-got to wipe them," she stuttered, watching him follow her hands as he licked his lips.

"I can suck them clean for you."

"Uh, no thanks. It's tempting, but…"

"Well, then, use my shirttail." Dex swiped a quick lick at his own fingers and unbuttoned his shirt. He pulled it from his pants, exposing a bronzed chest. Silky golden hair curled between the nipples. He leaned forward, offering the shirt to Jill. As their sticky fingers touched, clinging together, lightning crackled, ran up her arm, then scooted all the way down her body.

She snatched her hand away, breaking the connection. "Th-thanks," she mumbled, "but you don't want a messy shirt. I'll use the tissues in my carryall." Licking her thumb and forefinger, she opened the catch and gingerly drew out a small packet of Kleenex. "There's enough for both of us."

She reached out to offer the tissues, but he took her sticky hand into his big tanned one and pulled her toward him instead. "I should clean up that juice," he murmured. "Be a shame to waste it on such a thirsty day."

For a moment she stiffened. Then, with a sigh, she closed her eyes as he kissed her, tasting, through the mango juice on his lips, the sweetness of the man underneath.

"Ambrosia," Dex purred as he slowly released her mouth. "Food for the gods." He licked her lips, lapped at the juice on her chin. His tongue slid down her neck onto her chest.

"That's far enough." With an effort, she pushed his face away just as he reached the deep vee. "Tasted more like chicken," she teased, trying to break the spell this man had cast upon her.

"Are you accusing me of 'fowl' breath? That's f-o-w-l, of course."

Jill choked with laughter. "A punster, too. You're a man of many talents."

"I'd like to demonstrate some others…"

Biting her lip to hold back a giggle, she shoved Dex. He fell back on the blanket. As he looked up, a movement caught his eye. At the top of the pyramid, a shadow shifted.

"Shit." Throwing his body on Jill's, Dex rolled them away just as a huge rock came hurtling down. It lay buried inches into the ground.

"My God," Jill gasped. "We were sitting there a moment ago. What happened?"

"I don't know." He stood and pulled her farther away from the wall. His face had grown hard. "Ruins can be dangerous."

"But that seemed deliberate. Do you see anyone up there?"

Shading his eyes, Dex peered at the craggy top. "I thought I saw a shadow move, but no one's there."

She could hear the "now" at the end of his sentence, as if it had been spoken aloud. Shivering, Jill hugged her elbows, pressed her arms into her stomach. "Does this sort of thing happen often at ruins?"

His pause was a long one, as if he were deciding how much to say. "I've never heard of anything quite like this."

"It's so deserted here, so quiet. Surely, we would have heard a car."

"Yeah," he agreed, not bothering to mention how far the Indians could walk without tiring. Inca messengers were famed for their long-distance running.

She still looked troubled. "If that rock were deliberately pushed, I wonder who the person was after—you...or me? I arrived only last night, yet I've already been involved in two dangerous incidents."

"I'm sure it was a natural phenomenon. A sudden gust of wind, or a burrowing animal." He tried to reassure her. "Whatever, let's get out of here. We've a long drive ahead."

She opened her mouth, shut it again. She didn't like coincidences, but there would be a better time to question him further.

Quickly, Dex worked with Jill to collect their garbage. "Glad you're not a litterbug, but where would we archaeologists be if the ancient ones took such scrupulous care of their trash?"

She flashed him a quick smile. "That's a scientist's point of view."

He grabbed the end of the blanket, swearing as it ripped when he tugged it from beneath the fallen boulder. Shaking it free of sand, he folded it and hung it serape style over his shoulder. Jill picked up the basket.

As they headed back to the truck, Dex wrapped his arm around her waist, steadying her as they navigated the potholes. Jill couldn't suppress the frisson that rippled through her at his touch, comparing it to her fright when the rock fell. It was so different. She could still feel his tongue lapping at the mango juice trickling down her neck...deliciously unnerving.

Yes, so much better to concentrate on that. From somewhere deep inside her brain, Jill's conscience nagged her to stick to the purpose of her visit. But matters were no longer so simple. Somehow, a falling rock had changed the game.

Jill told her conscience to shut up.

Chapter 4

On the way north once more, Jill zoned in on the fascinating landscape for all of five minutes. She began to fidget, disturbed by Dex, by this itch of awareness she couldn't shake. She wanted to learn more about him.

"What made you choose ancient ceramics for your field?" Her fingers brushed his thigh, and she felt a muscle contract. She bit her lip to cover her pleased reaction. "Precious gems are thrilling, and finding buried art is exciting. Even skeletons have a ghoulish fascination, but pots sound so humdrum."

"You're wrong, Jill." The car swerved as Dex took his gaze off the road. "Pots and jars are endlessly tantalizing."

She moved farther back in her seat. "Please, watch your driving."

Grinning at her nervousness, Dex turned back to the dark ribbon stretching far ahead. He drove without effort, left hand on the wheel, right one placed deliberately on her thigh. The hot spot he created warred for her attention.

"Don't laugh, but I chose ceramics because of my mother. I don't usually tell people this."

"I'm a good listener…and I don't gossip."

When she didn't remove his hand from her thigh,

he continued. "Mom was a fine potter—she won lots of awards. When I was a kid, she let me throw clay on the wheel, and I grew quite skilled at making pots." He laughed, sounding almost shy. "I dreamed of attending art school and becoming a professional, but my dad wanted me in the family business. After high school he sent me off to Harvard, hoping I'd work toward an MBA."

"And?" She prodded as he grew silent.

"I hated it. Changed my major to archaeology in my junior year and focused on the history of ceramics in grad school. You can guess the uproar that resulted. Dad compares my work to ditch digging."

"I'll bet that doesn't sit well."

"No." His mouth grew tight. "Since my mother died, I don't go home much. I'll work right through Christmas and New Year's."

"That's sad."

"Not for me. There's a great celebration here on the thirty-first. Fireworks leaping and hissing into the ocean. Couples dancing on the beach. Kids running about, dueling with light sabers. I'll take that over freezing voices singing *Auld Lang Syne* in Times Square."

She laughed. "I used to watch the ball drop on TV, wondered if the people got frostbite."

"Want to be my New Year's Eve date, this year?"

A date with Dex on the beach at New Year's Eve...*oh, yeah*. Jill's heart jumped. "If I'm still in Peru, my answer's yes."

"I'll count on it." With a smile, he switched back to pots. "You can tell a lot about people from the ordinary things touching their lives. Gold jewelry and precious gems may belong to the nobles, but cooking pots are handled by everyone—men, women and children."

His enthusiasm was infectious. What a high it must be to solve a riddle no one else had been able to decipher. Touching the little clay shard in her pocket, Jill imagined the thrill. She'd never felt this buzz from Frank. His quest wasn't for knowledge.

As she compared the two men, Jill grew disturbed by the strange connection she felt to Dex. She hardly knew him. "Are you married?" she blurted.

He grinned. "I like to watch old movies. Do you?"

"Yes, but what does…"

"Remember *My Fair Lady*? There's a song in it, 'With a little bit o' luck you won't get hooked.'"

"That's your motto?"

"Mmm. *Mas o menos*. More or less. I never found the right person, and it's too late now."

"You're not exactly ancient!"

"Hey, I've hit that magic number, thirty-five. I'm set in my ways."

Jill wanted to argue. If Dex really thought it was too late for new beginnings, where did that leave her? She ignored his statement, listened only to his voice, so full of passion. Pots and ancient cultures. Could anything else bring on that spark?

She breathed him in, conscious of his hand on her thigh, raising her temperature till her dress stuck to her flesh. She liked the smell of his sweat—so different from Frank's. So much more…arousing. She wanted to lean over and lick his neck, see if he tasted as good as he smelled. He'd had his chance at the picnic, now it was her turn.

The clear air, the hot sun, the blue sky lighter than

his eyes—all were hypnotizing her.

Dex broke into her reverie. "Is it true that you and Frank are separated?"

So they were gossiping at the dig. "Yes, it's true." She should have left Frank years ago. She'd been so young, so romantic. So naively eager to believe this charmer had chosen her. How could she have known the "Cisco Kid" needed a slew of women to feed his ego?

Dex drove silently, leaving Jill to her thoughts.

Frank had convinced her that she was repressed, like her Anglo father and Anglicized mother. Oh, he had all the answers. It didn't take long for their sex life to become so perfunctory, she didn't miss it when he took off. She'd substituted school for sex, finished college at night and found a much better job. But ten years of settling for less were finally over. She deserved a chance at real happiness.

All Jill said aloud, though, was, "We weren't right for each other." She turned toward Dex. "Do you know Frank well?"

He hesitated. "No, I don't. We never became real friends."

"Why not?"

"Frank's good at identifying objects, but he couldn't care less about what we dig up in the middens—you know, the garbage heaps—that tell us about earlier civilizations. He's enthusiastic only when we find gold."

"I know what you mean. Frank expects to discover an unlooted tomb, skeletons dripping with jeweled necklaces, the grave littered with golden goblets. Then he'll become rich and famous."

"Yeah, I get the picture. Like Schliemann uncovering the treasure of Troy."

"Mm hmm, just like that. He promised to deck me out like Schliemann's wife—tiaras, pendants, earrings and bracelets up the wazoo." She giggled. "It's a wonderful fairy tale, and he tells it with great relish. It was his fervor that attracted me to him in the first place." She sighed, remembering how handsome he was ten years ago. All flashing black eyes and thick, wavy, movie idol hair. How he hated losing that.

"Talk of treasure still attracts unscrupulous people," Dex said, his tone unusually flat.

Jill sat up straighter, frowned. Before she could ask for specifics, he turned the conversation. "You're an editor?"

"Yes, bilingual. I work on both English and Spanish manuscripts."

"How did you get into that field? Was it by choice?"

"It's a long story."

"No problem. We still have a long drive ahead."

"Okay. Short version. My mother's parents left Argentina when Peron turned nasty. They raised their only daughter to be more American than Betsy Ross, and Mom followed their example with me. She wasn't so harsh when my brother came along twelve years later, but she still refuses to allow us to speak Spanish at home. She's Mrs. USA to the bone."

"What about your father?"

"Dad's from an old Boston family, so the only time I heard Spanish spoken was when my grandparents visited. They came often, and I gobbled up the language, as little kids do. Kept it a secret. It felt good to have something that was mine alone."

"I know what you mean." Dex squeezed her thigh, and she jumped. He said nothing, but his smile grew broader.

"I talked to my dolls," Jill chuckled, "so I didn't forget. Spanish was an easy subject in school, but when my teachers spoke, their accents were so different from my *abuelos,* I barely understood them."

He choked on a laugh. "Did you sass them?"

"Are you kidding? Only in my dreams. But I did rebel in my teens by choosing all Latina girlfriends. Truthfully, I never felt I belonged to any of the cliques in high school."

"Well, that's all in the past. Sounds like you have a great job now."

"*Mas o menos*, to use your phrase." She shook her head. "I shouldn't say it that way, I really love my work. I get to deal with writers from all over Latin America. It's a challenge to edit in two languages. Yet here I am in Peru, silly enough to be looking for my vanished husband."

"Why?"

She paused for so long, Dex started to pull over to the side of the road, but Jill waved him on. "Frank's a rat," she said, "but a familiar one. It's hard to turn off worrying when it's been your pattern. Part of me feels I owe him, though I'm not sure for what. And since I speak Spanish, I thought I could help with the search. Are any of you archaeologists fluent?"

With a rueful smile he shook his head. "Just enough to order supplies and read a menu."

"That's what I thought. What's been done to find him, Dex? I can't believe an experienced archaeologist like Frank could simply disappear. Why did Harry wait so long to send me the fax?"

He flicked a glance at her. "Better ask him yourself." A drift of sand had blown across the road, and Dex slowed.

Why didn't he give her a direct answer? Something funny was going on here. Jill's eyes narrowed, but she let the topic drop. It was only her second day.

The sun began to dip behind the western mountains, casting a golden path across the sea. The rich red and purple of the rocks faded as shadows fell. It was dark when Dex pulled into the small oasis town of Chimbote on the Pacific. "There's an inn on the beach," he told Jill. "The food's good, and there's a bar."

"I could use a drink." She got stiffly out of the truck when they parked and slapped a *rat-a-tat tat* on her ass. "Got to get the circulation going again," she mumbled.

"I could do that for you—it'd be my pleasure."

This time she clearly saw the twinkle in his eye. *"Muchos gracias, señor*, but I'll spank myself."

Grinning, he led her inside. "Well, if you ever change your mind… I'll meet you in the bar in twenty minutes."

Her room was clean but austere—a single bed, small table with a lamp, and a bench for her suitcase. She showered next door under the hose attached to the bathtub, changed into denim jeans and a red sweatshirt with white lettering reading, "Chess players know all the right moves." Loosening her hair, she brushed it around her shoulders, added a touch of lipstick and headed for the bar.

His eyes lit at the sight of her. "I've ordered you a

Pisco Sour, the national drink of Peru. Are you game?"

"Sure, what's in it?"

"Lemon juice, sugar, bitters, and a special Peruvian brandy."

She sipped the drink, finding it too sweet at first, but the taste grew on her. "Is the stuff strong?"

"Well, I wouldn't drink too many of them. But we need to relax after a day of bouncing around in that truck."

"And missed being a target for a falling rock, don't forget."

"I haven't forgotten. We were lucky."

"It wasn't just luck." Jill gazed at him. "You saved my life."

He shrugged. "Part of the service, ma'am. Drink up. You must be starving."

Damn, there's that ma'am again... "Okay, but remind me later to thank you properly."

"I'll remember." The look he gave her matched the heat in her Pisco Sour. The drink did a happy dance in her belly.

They entered the dining room and feasted on *Papas a los Ariquipeños*—boiled potatoes covered with a peppery avocado sauce, followed by *Chupa des Pescados*—a delicious fish, rice and egg soup, redolent of garlic. The main course, called a *tortilla,* turned out to be a potato and sausage omelet. The satisfying meal ended with mango sorbet and dark Spanish coffee.

Jill patted her stomach. "Everything was strange but delicious. I was so hungry."

"All the fresh air, not to mention the Pisco, gives one an appetite. How do you stay so slim if you eat like this?" he teased.

"It's yoga and my metabolism," she answered with a discreet burp. She felt so relaxed and comfortable with this man. Even when he was annoyed with her, his quiet strength was evident.

"Let's take a walk on the beach. It will help you digest your first Peruvian dinner." He glanced at her sweatshirt as they left the inn. "So you're a chess player."

"Mmm. It's my second favorite game."

Dex laughed. "I won't fall for that line—at least, not tonight."

She only smiled. They strolled under rustling palm trees, the full moon casting a silvery path on the water. "I love the wind in the palms, the crash of the breakers," she murmured. "The sounds, the rhythm, fill me with content."

He squeezed her hand, sharing the moment.

Offshore, a fleet of anchovy fishing boats were lit by the moonlight. "They're in mothballs this season," he told Jill. "The Japanese current drifted too far for these small boats to navigate. Unfortunately, the families will suffer."

"How sad. A town full of people at the mercy of something as uncontrollable as an ocean current."

"We're all susceptible to things we can't control."

She suspected there was more than one meaning behind his words, but he seemed reluctant to explain. She didn't ask, not wanting to break the mood. He put his arm around her waist, and she covered his hand with hers as they strolled on. The caressing breeze soon carried away the sadness. In its place came unexpected longings.

Jill glowed under his touch. She was sure it was the

Pisco Sours that made her feel so wanton, but was determined not to let things go too far. She wasn't ready for a fling. Everything was happening so fast, she told herself. Her second day, and she was intoxicated. The night was too beautiful, however, the Pisco high too satisfying, to worry her for long.

Anticipation tingled in her blood, but left her disappointed. No response to the red sweatshirt, to the silky hair brushing against him. No moonlight madness to serve as an excuse. When they returned to the inn, Dex pulled her into his arms for a sweet goodnight kiss—but it was no more than a brush of his lips, without the passion he'd showed at their picnic.

Jill's emotions ricocheted between relief and longing. She should have known. That delicious sexy kiss at the picnic was a freak thing—just a crazy, sticky-fingered moment. Her head drooped as she turned away.

Hands on her shoulders, Dex spun her around. "You've got to get your beauty sleep, or I'd have other ideas in mind." The gleam in his eyes left no doubt. "Tomorrow we have another day of hard driving, and you need to be sharp when you meet Harry. He's a chess player, too."

Jill stared at him, problems of the present returning in an instant. "Why?" she snapped. "It was Harry who sent me the fax about Frank being missing."

"Yes, but he never expected you to show up. Harry just wanted reassurance Frank hadn't hightailed it home with a bag of swag."

"You're joking. Frank wouldn't…"

"Probably not," he said cautiously, "but a little strategy won't hurt. Things haven't been going well at the dig, and not only because of Frank's disappearance. Harry's worried. I know he isn't happy about an outsider disrupting things even more."

"What makes you so sure I'll disrupt things?" Jill's dander was up.

"Well, you're disrupting me, and how sweet it is," he murmured, stroking her hair. "But that's not what's bothering Harry."

"What else is wrong?"

"You'll find out soon enough. I don't want to prejudice you before you speak to him. Believe me, Harry will try to discourage you, convince you to return to New York."

"Like hell he will!" Her eyes filled with suspicion. "Something is going on here, and I'm being kept out of the loop."

He didn't respond. She pulled his hands from her shoulders but clutched them, aware of his long, strong fingers sliding slowly over her palm. Frustrated, suspended between anger and desire, she forced herself to let go and enter her room.

"I'm not so easy to get rid of." Jill punched the pillow. "You pompous archaeologists can just get used to the idea. Until Frank shows up, I'll be haunting the site."

****

The cabin was not much more than a shack. Hidden among the dunes, battered by winds and high tides, it leaned like a listing ship. Inside, however, both the striped canvas sofa and rusting iron bed appeared sturdy. A snowy white alpaca throw covered the bed, waiting, perhaps, for a human caress. Water ran sluggishly in the sink, and an antique stove functioned beside the woodpile. The thatched roof had been repaired and kept the room dry. A flimsy outhouse, partly buried in sand, could be seen out back.

Manuel stood in front of the balding man lounging on the sofa. His hands held a wad of *soles,* and he looked pleased.

"Keep looking for more, Manuel," the man said, and he nodded. They spoke a rapid patois, part Spanish, part Indian, part gutter. "I will keep digging, *señor.* Are you sure you no want coca? I have friend at refining factory back there." He waved toward the jungle behind the dunes. "Very fine quality, *muy bueno.*"

"No. I don't want to tangle with that bunch— smuggling the gold and silver you dig up is making us both a nice profit."

"Si si," Manuel looked down at the payoff in his hands.

"And you did well selling the pot to the bearded man?"

"Si, he pay ver' good." Manuel stuffed the *soles* into a bag slung around his waist. "I make happy sale." He rubbed his fingers together. "But where I find it, the man ask and ask. He reach to take back *soles* when I not tell him…but in end he want jar more."

"He's getting suspicious, but he's greedy, too. That pot was a rare find, Manuel, but we can't rely on the ambition of my old colleague. Bring anything else you dig up in the cave to me. I'll give you a few *soles* even for a basketful of shards. I know someone who'll want them."

"Si, bueno."

"Watch out the man with the curly beard doesn't follow you. If he gets too nosy, you know what to do. I need a little more time for the big haul, and then I'm out of here."

Manuel's head bobbed up and down.

"Have you tried getting rid of him?"

"*Si, señor,* but luck not with me. I follow him to Paramonga, throw large stone down from top of pyramid. He have peekneek with lady, but he see my shadow and move *muy rapido.*"

"A woman you say? One from the dig?"

"I never see this one before."

The balding man stood up. "I don't like it. Do you have a cell phone with a camera?"

"No, *señor. Mucho dinero.* Most times, cells not work here in desert."

"True." He moved over to the bed, knelt, and removed a square box from beneath it. "Have you ever used a camera, Manuel?"

"*Si,* sometimes I borrow the one of *mi hermano.* He snap peektures, sell to *turistas.* Now he is tour guide to ruins."

"Is the camera a Polaroid?"

Manuel nodded. "Old but still work."

"This is an old Polaroid, too." The man handed over the camera. "Bring me a picture of the woman. I may have a rival collector, and that won't do. I must know who she is."

Manuel fondled the camera. "Okay." He grinned his toothless grin. "I meet you *Domingo,* after mass. Maybe find *otra tumba, mas oro.*"

"Adios." The man watched from the door until Manuel was out of sight. Then he shut out the blazing sun and groped behind the bed for the small pillows he kept from fading. They had been woven in brilliant hues of red and green and black, converting the dingy room briefly into a cheerful meeting place.

His expression smug, the balding man threw one onto the sofa, the others atop the soft alpaca fur that covered the bed. His woman was getting restless. It was time to take her out of hiding.

Chapter 5

Jill barely made it into bed before the exhausting day caught up with her. She awoke at dawn, still tired, chagrined at her overwrought response to Dex's failure to kiss her in the moonlight. Her eyelashes felt glued together, and the thin blanket had slid to the floor. Dreams filled with disturbing images, of a child's fear of being unwanted, had kept her body restless, even in sleep.

What had gone wrong last night? She'd been so relaxed at dinner. The Pisco Sour had quite a kick. Her fantasy of a passionate kiss under a palm tree, the breeze ruffling her hair while waves foamed on the nearby shore, had taken root. What romantic trash. Yet, even though that had fallen through, she'd still expected to fight Dex off when they returned to her room. It piqued her that she wasn't the one to say, "Stop."

But would she have stopped? Maybe not. Every rub of his thigh sliding along hers as they walked along the beach sent little shivers through her. Dex was not one of the timid, anxious authors she could gently manipulate. He wasn't a man who'd let her call the shots and, to her surprise, she found his quiet confidence and masculine certainty alluring.

He cared about others, too. She recalled his angry words as they passed through the Lima slums, his melancholy as they stood by the moored anchovy boats. She could fall in love with a man like that, if she didn't watch out.

That was the problem. She was beginning to feel that she didn't want to watch out. Though she'd only known Dex for two days, they'd been alone together the entire time. More quality time, perhaps, than in a dozen ordinary dates. And she couldn't forget that he had saved her life.

She'd been too busy to indulge in an affair during her unhappy marriage, never seriously considered breaking her vows. That was Frank's shtick. But soon she'd be free to look deeper into her own desires. Perhaps it was time?

Last night Dex could have…not that she would have…

They had been so close during their promenade on the beach. Or was that only in *her* mind?

She didn't believe his excuse about Harry for one minute. But what if he were telling the truth?

So many doubts. The confusion was giving her a headache. She had to keep her wits about her. Too bad that wasn't all she wanted to keep about her… A vision filled her mind of a tall, suntanned body. She could see herself unlacing the cords on his cotton shirt, feel her fingers dance on his golden skin, sense his hands on her hips, pulling her into him… God, she sounded like a sex-starved teenager. Pathetic.

Early morning sunlight spilled into the room. The air was still cool, and Jill donned a pair of tailored slacks and a lightweight safari jacket. Executive camouflage. If she appeared formidable to Harry Lang, she might get some answers.

Once they arrived at the *huaca* today, she and Dex would no longer be alone. Since he viewed her as the wife—well, semi-wife—of a colleague, she had to erase all thoughts of a relationship developing…for now.

Damn! She still vacillated between longing for a liaison with an appealing guy and trying to protect herself from getting hurt again. She dreamed of an affair with Dex when he hadn't even asked her. And, dammit, without the divorce papers signed, she was still married. This behavior was bad karma.

In New York she dealt with important people, made high-powered decisions daily. It was time she made this "complication" fit into *her* plans. Grabbing her bag, Jill strode out to meet Dex for breakfast.

On the road again, she thrust aside the tingling memory of his picnic kiss, the inviting taste of mango on his lips, and concentrated on the landscape's stark beauty.

Dex, too, was quiet. He seemed to have things on his mind, although he darted frequent glances at Jill with that same hot glint in his eyes.

The sun was high in the sky when they passed a small cemetery, the first sign of man's footprint since they had left Chimbote. Jill stared at the sad little patch of graves in the midst of nowhere. Weathered crosses and faded paper flowers battled the drifting sands.

As they slowed for a closer look, a car engine suddenly revved. A mud-covered vehicle roared onto the highway, sideswiping their truck.

Jill screamed as a white-faced Dex pulled them out of the spin.

"My God! What happened? Was that deliberate?"

His mouth tightened. "Hard to believe it was mere

58

chance. There's not another car for miles around. It must have been parked behind one of the dunes bordering the cemetery."

"Some drunk sleeping it off and waking up grieving for his lost love buried here?"

"Bravo for giving the incident a romantic twist, but I don't like it." Dex growled. "First the falling rock and now this."

Jill clutched his arm. "You're right. Two 'almost fatal' accidents. But who? Why?"

"Damned if I know. Guerrillas…looters…kids out to make trouble."

"Why are they aiming for us? Is this related to the trouble at the dig?"

Dex shrugged. "I haven't any answers. Let's forget it for now. No one's hurt, and one more dent in the truck will hardly show."

"True. We shouldn't let it spoil our day," she said, recovering her spirits. "Are we getting close to the site?"

"Look ahead to your right—pretty soon you'll see the pyramids. Did you ever go on a dig with Frank?"

"No. I wanted to. The thought of buried treasure and exotic countries fascinated me, but there was never a good time." Jill sighed. "I married young. Frank was in grad school, and I couldn't afford to leave my job."

She was talking too much, and Dex was too good a listener. Biting her lip, Jill stopped herself before she revealed more. But, oh, she wanted to tell him how much she resented all those hours of dull work to pay for Frank's tuition. She'd barely had time to eat before evening classes started, and weekends were spent on study. Then Frank began to go away on digs.

Deep in thought, Jill forgot to watch the scenery flashing by. "Look, there it is!" Dex suddenly called out. Off to the right three pyramids loomed, stark and forbidding in the sun's glare.

"They look close," he said, "but they're a mile apart. "The biggest one is *Huaca del Sol,* it covers an area as large as Egypt's Great Pyramid at Giza. The middle one is *Huaca de la Luna*, and the one that's farthest is ours—*Huaca de las Estrellas.* Didn't I tell you I'd give you the sun, the moon, and the stars?" He winked.

Turning off the highway, Dex drove along a rutted dirt road. Not a blade of grass was visible, only mound after mound of crumbling mud bricks and long vistas of sand. Dark gray mountains rose in the background. He drove carefully to avoid the looters' holes pockmarking the area. A few were immense craters—she could have been an astronaut on the moon.

As they neared a sprawling adobe building, he slowed. "You wouldn't believe it, but forty years ago this dilapidated box was a fine hotel. This area had lots of tourists then, before the *banditos* scared them away. Now it's our home and headquarters."

A shudder ran through her. What was Jillianne Adams Flanders, female executive, city born and bred, doing in the midst of adobe huts, mounds of debris, and pits in the ground? She glanced at Dex beside her in the truck, and for a moment his face looked unfamiliar.

It was hot. Despite the dryness, the long drive without air-conditioning had left her wet and sticky. Her power outfit had wilted. Even her hair was damp, and the careful braid had loosened tendrils that blew in her face, tickling her cheeks.

Where would she sleep—here in this crumbling hotel? It must be years since it boasted of running water. Were there even spare beds? She didn't think her body would accommodate a sleeping bag. That kind of toughness wasn't a requirement in high-rise Manhattan.

And how would she go about locating Frank? Should she speak to the police? Would they assist her if they found out she was getting divorced?

What about Harry? Could she count on him to help? She had acted rashly when the fax came, responded without taking the practicalities under consideration. Now she was here in the Peruvian desert, far from civilization, with too many unanswered questions.

Before the pickup had rolled to a full stop the headquarters door opened, and Harry Lang came rushing out. Dex gave her hand a reassuring squeeze. "You'll be okay," he said.

His touch sent a shiver down her spine again. Jill forced herself to turn away. Regardless of the grim conditions, she would find a way to stay for as long as it took to find Frank. When he had signed the papers and she was free, she would explore her relationship with Dex. No matter what, she would follow through. She'd made up her mind, and no Adams was a quitter.

Harry barely noticed her as Jill stepped down from the truck. "Dex," he shouted, "We've had trouble while you were gone. Bad trouble!" He mopped his forehead with a red bandanna.

"What the hell happened?"

"Looters again, that's what!" Harry was practically screaming. "They broke into the storage shed last night, tunneled through."

"Where was José? Wasn't he on guard?"

"He fell asleep. Luckily, I went to check on him about midnight. Scared those bastards off before they could get away with anything."

"The pot I was working on—is it safe?"

"Yes, yes. But they knocked over the skeleton Sam Stern was studying, and we're going to have to reassemble all those bones."

Fidgeting, Jill watched both men absorbed in their problem. She could have been invisible.

"Relax, Harry." Dex put his arm around the older man's shoulder. "We'll get it done. At least nothing of value was taken."

"I'm already shorthanded with two people missing."

"But you say Sam Stern's here?"

"Yeah. He flew into Trujillo yesterday and rented a car."

"He'll put the body back together, never fear. Sam's the best."

Jill cleared her throat loudly, and Dex turned to her at last. "Chief, this is Frank's wife, Jill Flanders." Flinching at the title, Jill bit her tongue.

Harry looked her over and nodded. "We've met. I tried to reach you after I got your fax, Ms. Flanders, but you had already left. You should have given me a chance to reply before you made the trip. There's nothing you can do here."

He glared at her, but Jill stood her ground. She had thought him a dreamer, but he could be intimidating when aroused. He was shorter than Dex's six feet two and wore his graying hair long and wild. A salt-and-pepper beard had sprouted all over his cheeks and chin, but his mustache was carefully trimmed.

Harry had no right to treat her that way. Dex could call him Chief, but to her he was a pompous, disagreeable, rude old man. "It's my husband who's missing, Dr. Lang." She stepped closer, her tone imperious.

His faded blue eyes lost some of their anger as he held the door open for her. "Come inside. No need to stand in the sun. Dex, I put the pot in your room for safekeeping. Look it over." He waved him away.

It was surprisingly cool in the adobe building. Cracked blue-and-yellow tiles covered the entrance hall. A wooden reception desk held a haphazard pile of clay pots of all shapes and sizes. A corridor beyond opened to an inner courtyard, where an agave and a barrel cactus struggled to stay alive. A thin layer of sand covered everything.

Walking around the reception desk, Harry led Jill to his office. Clay figures of strange-looking people and even odder vegetables were stacked in a corner. Scanning them, Jill wondered if any of the erotic figures she'd seen in the airport photos were in the pile, but Harry gave her no time to examine them. Motioning her to a canvas camp chair, he sat down at a cluttered desk. An onyx chessboard covered one end, the pieces set up for a game.

"What do you think you can do here?" he grumbled. "I sent you the fax only because there was a chance you might have heard from Frank."

"Well I haven't," she retorted.

"Your coming to Peru only adds to my problems. We're shorthanded, and Dex lost over three days' work going down to Lima to meet your plane. Now I have to worry about you—this isn't a safe place."

She was getting dumped on, Jill was sure, but she'd had plenty of practice handling disgruntled authors. "Frank has been missing for a week now, and your only concern is that you're stuck with extra work," she declared. "I'm his wife, Harry, and I intend to find out what happened to him—with or without your permission."

Looking away, Harry started to tidy up the mess of papers on his desk. He didn't reply.

So, handling an angry archaeologist wasn't any different. Jill's confidence grew. "I'm used to dealing with tough problems, Harry. I won't be any trouble. What do the police have to say?"

Pushing back his chair, Harry started to cough. "I haven't informed them," he said.

Jill stared at him. "For heaven's sake, why not? Frank could have been captured by bandits. Or fallen down a hole somewhere and be hurt! You said this is a dangerous place."

"Well, uh…I don't think anything like that has happened to him." Harry's face turned a mottled red. "We've had some break-ins by petty looters, but that's all. We're not political, or rich enough to interest *El Rio Flujo*. That's not the problem."

"So, what is?" She watched him struggle to find the right words.

"Someone else is missing, too. A young woman…" He plucked the black queen from the chessboard and began turning it over and over in his sweaty palm.

It was Jill's turn to flush. "So what? Are you implying that they ran off together?"

Avoiding her eyes, Harry mumbled. "That's what

we all figured. Poppy has been very...friendly...with Frank."

He was embarrassed, but she had stopped caring about the philandering swine years ago. "You may be right, Harry," she said, "but they've been gone a week without a word. Isn't it time we reported it to the police?"

"I'll think about it." Her scowl returned, and he hastily added, "Right away. Now, wouldn't you like to see where you're going to sleep? I've given you Poppy's room—it's the only one in the women's quarters that's empty."

"Women's quarters? Isn't that a bit medieval?"

"Not in this country."

For now, she had nothing more to add. "Yes, I'd like to unpack and wash up." Automatically, Jill smoothed her hair, tucking back a curly lock that had come undone from the twist.

"The women sleep in an annex down the road," Harry added. "It used to be the maids' quarters when the hotel was flourishing. There's a hut for showers nearby. The accommodations are primitive, but they're the best you'll find here."

The brilliant sunlight hurt Jill's eyes the minute they stepped out of the cool dark room. She squinted, bumping into a figure moving toward her. He was a short, heavyset man in his late sixties, smoking a pipe and wearing a safari hat that matched her jacket. As both of them started to apologize, Dex hurried over, a big grin on his face.

"So you two have met, sort of. Sam, I heard you were here. It's good to see you." He threw an arm around Sam in a bear hug, his chest barely missing the hot pipe.

"Jill, this is Dr. Sam Stern, an authority on old bones. I took a forensic anthropology class with him a dozen years ago, after I switched my major. What a revelation that class was—he's why I became an archaeologist. Sam, this is Flanders' wife."

Jill offered her hand, and Sam took it in both of his. He looked her over with an approving smile. "I'm pleased to meet you, Jill, but right now I have to see a man about a skeleton." Dropping her hand, he turned to Harry. "I'll need your help, old man, sorting those bones."

"Come in. Shut the door before the heat gets in." Harry mopped his face again. "I'll work with you, Sam, but let's sit down and relax. Dex, can you join us for a few minutes? Then you can take Ms. Flanders to Poppy's room."

"Sure." Dex walked Jill to a nearby table and bench under an awning. "Are you okay to wait here? I'll be back as soon as I can."

She smiled. "No worries. I'll be cool in the shade."

Giving her hand a quick squeeze, he hurried back to Harry's office.

Jill leaned against the table and shut her eyes, trying once again to shake off the tingling spell his touch cast upon her. It was going to be an uphill job.

****

"Good-looking woman." Sam settled in the canvas chair while Dex propped himself up on the corner of the desk opposite the chessboard. "Seems like a smart cookie—I'll bet not much gets by her."

"I hadn't noticed." Harry's curt response didn't match his pained expression.

"Sure, sure, we've known each other too long for me to believe that. What's wrong? She giving you a hard time?"

"This whole thing with Flanders is more of a headache than I need right now, Sam." Harry replaced the black queen on his chessboard. "Keeping one step ahead of the tomb robbers is enough."

"They sure did a number on my skeleton."

"It's those bones and the new stirrup pot I want to concentrate on. Tell him about it, Dex."

The excited gleam was back in Dex's eyes. "We've got a female skeleton with two deliberately broken arms buried in a tomb. Beside her is a painted pot depicting a priestess holding a goblet in each hand, blood overflowing from them and dripping down. Maybe the key to the mystery is in the pot? Can it tell us why the arms of the priestess were broken…perhaps a bloodletting rite we don't know about? It was found in the same grave. There must be a connection."

"Intriguing idea. Are you working on it?"

"Yes. Trying to decipher all the symbols in the painting…"

"When he can find the time!" Harry interrupted. Leaning back, he took a bottle of whiskey and paper cups from a bottom drawer. He poured them each a drink. "I tell you, Sam, with all that's going on, a disappearing middle-aged Lothario I don't need. And now the wife shows up. Everything distracts me from what's important."

"You're still calling her his wife. Didn't I hear that they were separated?"

Dex leaned forward, intent upon the reply.

"Frank's been close-mouthed about it. He uses his

marriage as protection, keeps his other involvements short and sweet. But one maudlin Friday night he blurted out that he no longer heads home when the season ends."

"Well, I guess the marriage is still legal, or the woman wouldn't be here." Sam's pipe had almost gone out. "You really believe Flanders ran off with this Poppy?" He puffed away to rekindle it.

"I did at first, but now I'm not so sure. There are some gorgeous beaches near Trujillo, great for a spot of hanky-panky. But it's been a week. Poppy couldn't hold Flanders' interest that long, even with that cheerleader body—hell, she's only about eighteen, and a bubblehead at that. Maybe something's happened to them."

"What's your guess, Dex?"

"It's a possibility, but there are others. I'm not sure that's the answer." Moving away from the desk, he started pacing.

"The girl's disappearance has fouled me up, too," Harry went on. "She was working on the records, feeding data into the computer, and now everything is all messed up. We're falling way behind, and I'm worried about getting the grant renewed. We need another season here."

"Careless of you, Harry." Sam chided his colleague. "Too much excitement, old man. We'll have to think of a way to get you out of this predicament."

"We'd better think fast. Frank's wife wants me to call in the police, and you know the red tape that will cause."

"Hmmm. Not only that. Once the workers see *guardia* roaming around, you're apt to lose some men."

"That's all I need. We'll have to close shop."

"Pour us another shot of that firewater, Harry, and let's review everything that's happened over a game. It'll clear our minds." Sam moved his chair nearer to the white pieces on the chessboard. "Dex, you can head out and take care of Ms. Flanders while Harry and I go over the situation step by step, see if there are any clues we may have missed. I'm confident we'll come up with a workable plan."

"You're the Man, prof." Dex slapped Sam on the back and hurried out the door.

Chapter 6

Dex carried Jill's suitcase as they headed for the women's annex. "How'd it go with Harry?" he asked.

"Not bad, though I sense there's more to his resentment than my unexpected appearance. Did Frank and Harry rub each other the wrong way?"

Switching the suitcase to his other hand, Dex paused. "They're both difficult men, but Frank had other friends here."

"Is that your attempt at diplomacy?" Jill lowered her voice. "Your Big Chief told me about Poppy, so you don't have to protect me. That part of my marriage to Frank was over long ago."

His tense look relaxed, turned surprisingly cheerful.

"Is anything else going on here that I should know about?"

"Nothing you haven't already heard. Items have been disappearing from the storeroom. That's our biggest worry."

"And you've no idea who's responsible?"

"There's no evidence. If Frank is involved, he's been clever about hiding it."

Jill heard the anger behind his words. "Tell me about Poppy, then," she persisted. "If we talk about it, maybe we'll come up with a clue to their

70

disappearance."

They had reached a lean-to where a canvas awning shaded a shard-covered table and bench. The day was growing hotter. Glancing guiltily at the heavy suitcase Dex still carried for her, Jill suggested they rest. As he slid along the bench beside her, their thighs touched. Jill jumped. She looked at Dex, but he made no attempt to move away.

"Poppy's a bright kid. Has a BFA from Bennington."

"Is she, uh, pretty?"

"Yeah, if flighty blondes are your thing. Poppy's into anything New Age. Claims to believe in Pyramid Power. Talked about this site being the Perfect Place. Did you catch all those popping P's? That's typically Poppy. She said she could see Frank's aura—all because of a World War I poem about Flanders Field her mother liked to recite. As if the kid could relate to such 'ancient' history."

"That sad little poem," Jill sighed. "'In Flanders Field the poppies grow, between the crosses, row on row.' I had to memorize it, too. The old-fashioned schools used it to teach patriotism."

"Well, you'll soon be out of Flanders 'field.'" Dex grinned. Leaning forward, he brushed his lips across hers.

Jill's heart raced. Her fingers moved to reach for him, but she stopped herself. "Did Poppy d-drop any hint that she was going off with Frank?" she stammered. His lips were still dangerously close.

"None that I know of, but I get lost in my work. Don't pay much attention to the gossip."

"Assuming they did take off together, an entire

71

week has passed without a word. That's not like Frank. He's been excited about this excavation since the tomb was found. You don't suppose he could be checking out some artifact on his own? A turquoise mask or a golden necklace…?"

"Doubtful. Anything he found would be confiscated."

"If he were caught. Frank's never before disappeared from a site. At least, not longer than a weekend's dalliance. I don't believe he cares for women nearly as much as the thrill of the chase. Once they've been ensnared," her tone was bitter, "he loses interest mighty fast. He wouldn't burn his bridges over a female."

"You're certainly candid." Dex searched her expression. His fingers caressed her cheek. "Brave woman."

"Just stupid for sticking so long." Jill put her hand over his, sending a tiny tattoo of sharp nails along his knuckles.

"Bull." He bent toward her. Lips parted, Jill closed her eyes and surrendered to her wildly beating heart. His tongue brushed across her teeth and slid into her mouth, claiming her.

For a heartbeat, she melted into him. But before Jill's arms could tighten around his neck, they heard footsteps coming down the path. Stifling a groan, Dex pulled away. He slid off the bench and reached for her suitcase.

"You have no idea how good you taste, Jill, but there's no privacy here. I keep forgetting that we've *got* to find Frank first."

Breathing deeply, Jill straightened her jacket. Dex

would make her stick to her priorities. Why couldn't life be simpler? "It has been a stressful few days," she murmured.

"I'll say! One day soon," he whispered so softly she barely heard him, "I'll take that stress away."

As they walked along, Jill became aware of a rumbling noise. It grew louder as they approached.

"That's our generator." Dex pointed to a nearby shack. "We turn it off at nine every night to save fuel, and make do with the kerosene lamps."

"Sure is noisy."

"When it stops, the quiet blows your mind. You can hear the sand sliding down the dunes." He paused, looking off at the horizon. Shadows were beginning to inch across the distant mountains.

"Tell me about the middens." Jill wanted to hear the warmth in his voice a bit longer.

"Archaeology has been called the science of rubbish," Dex said, enthusiasm spilling from his words. "That's because we spend so much time looking through primitive people's garbage dumps. It's hard to describe the rush you get when you make an important find."

His eyes lit at some private memory. Once again, his intensity excited Jill. Did she dare trust her heart again to a man whose work was so important he could forget everyone else?

"When we found that untouched tomb, you could have heard our shouts back in New York. Its occupant is a female, with both arms intentionally fractured. The skeleton is a unique find, that's why Sam's here. And we think it's her portrait on the pot we found lying beside her."

Jill listened raptly, knowing she was responding less to his words than to the passion in his voice. She wanted to hold his hands and feel his excitement radiate through her fingers. The late afternoon sun shining on his sandy hair, curly beard and tanned skin turned Dex into a golden god. She couldn't remember feeling this fascinated by a man before.

It was so different from her first encounter with Frank. He'd been movie star gorgeous, she a teenage groupie, so willing to be convinced of hidden depths beneath his handsome, shallow surface. She'd thought she won the prince. How crushed she had been to watch him turn into the frog.

Two young men and a woman in wide-brimmed hats and camp shorts headed in their direction carrying trowels, picks and brushes. Dex waved a greeting. "This is Jill Flanders. You'll meet her properly at dinner."

She smiled as they passed, conscious of how young everyone looked. "Are all the workers college students?"

"Grad students, most of them, though we do get some help from the locals. Siesta's over. Now everyone will work until it's too dark to see."

They continued down the path, stopping at last in front of a small, shabby adobe structure.

"This is where the women bed down." Dex opened the door, dropping off her suitcase in the second of the three rooms leading off the familiar chipped tile corridor. He waved his arm at the furnishings. "We call this Peruvian Archi-Deco." He winked. "It's a lot better than you'll find at most sites, believe me."

Wincing, Jill took in the dark little room. "It'll be

fine."

Dex stroked her cheek. "I'm glad you've come." His deep voice carried a caress. "Don't worry about Harry, he'll calm down after a while."

Jill could see his reluctance to leave. It made her happy, even though she knew it shouldn't. With an impish smile she shoved him toward the door. "You've got work to do, and I have to unpack."

A last quick peck on her forehead, where the blue light materialized when she meditated, and Dex left. Now the spot flared hot and red.

Jill glanced around her temporary home. On the cracked tiles stood a cot and a small table with a kerosene lamp. Beside it, left over from a bridge set discard, stood a rusting metal chair. Across the room, a worn chest of drawers leaned crookedly against the wall. Folded at the end of the bed were linens, a pillow and a blanket.

The room's one window was small, and the light bulb hanging from a cord couldn't have been more than twenty-five watts. More light was needed for her to get anything done. Taking the matches she saw on the table, Jill lit the kerosene lamp. A basin and a filled water jug had also been left. She could freshen up in the room, wash off the road's grime. There was a lipstick, a comb, and a copy of the magazine, *Astrology Today*, on top of the dresser. Poppy must have been anxious to depart.

As she reached out to pick up the magazine, Jill suddenly sensed someone watching her. Her hand stopped in mid air. She turned quickly, eyes widening, and gulped.

Staring at her from a corner of the room, its china

blue eyes glittering in the lamplight, was a baby-sized doll. Like the ones on the plane. Like the one in her dream. With the same pink organdy dress and bonnet.

Her hand shook, but the panic lasted for only a moment. With a giddy laugh, Jill pulled herself together. Maybe Frank had bought it for Poppy. It would be like him to give his latest conquest a doll— that's how he treated his women.

She forced herself to pick up the doll and drop it onto the bed, taking off a bootee since the other was missing. Lying on her pillow under the weak electric light, the doll looked much less threatening than it had sitting in the corner, staring glassy-eyed in the kerosene lamp's wavering flame. She would turn it to face the wall when the generator went off.

All at once the room seemed terribly confining. Jill felt a tremendous urge to step outside and breathe fresh air. The sun was lower now, casting shadows down the sides of the *huaca* and across the sand. Breathing deeply, she stretched out her arms and made slow widening circles. She could hear her yoga teacher coaxing, "Squeeze the dime between your shoulder blades."

The air was still. Perched atop a sand dune, a seagull fluffed its feathers as the setting sun washed over it in brilliant orange. The bird's saucy pose reminded Jill of her best friend, Jo, who wore a bright orange blouse over a flirty brown skirt at her birthday dinner two years ago. She'd turned thirty that day and was counting on a lavish meal at Angelo's, the trendy Italian bistro, to stop her from obsessing on that number. Where had those fabulous twenties gone? Even Angelo's homemade pasta smothered in the chef's rich marinara sauce didn't work. Next to her flamboyant friend, Jill's drooping shoulders made her chic black suit look drab.

"Cut it out!" Josefina had scolded over a glass of *pinot grigio*. "You're still young and attractive. Sexy, too, if you'd only let it show."

Jill pouted. "Thirty is on the way to maturity. I've missed out on the fun years."

"Nonsense." Jo sighed. "Frank really did a number on you, Jill. At the office people admire you for your skills, your competence. In fact, you're pretty young for all the responsibility you carry there. Why are you reacting like this?"

"I know I'm doing a damn good job at work. But once I leave the office, I find my life is drifting away…"

Josefina leaned forward, pulling Jill's hand off the wine glass. "You sound like a scared teenager. Life after work can be quite stimulating for a sophisticated woman. I'll show you when you finally get around to divorcing that philandering husband of yours. The right makeup and a little attitude will make all the difference."

Jill gulped the rest of her wine. She wanted to blurt out that she'd decided to proceed with the divorce, but knew what would happen if she did—forced to face Jo's rejects. She didn't want to turn into her best friend's next romantic project. And who knew how long the proceedings would take? She had to find Frank and get his agreement first.

Jill kept her thoughts to herself. She didn't want to hurt her friend's feelings. As she picked up the menu, Jo batted it away.

"Don't hide behind that," she scolded. "I can see your eyes. They reveal everything. Remember when you were promoted? Your eyes sparkled then. And when you allow yourself to be angry, they turn as dark as green tourmaline, and darts shoot out. Strong emotion there. But it's been too long since your eyes reflected...let's call it your feminine awareness."

"Oh, come on!"

"I mean it, Jill. There's a certain...open invitation look. Not exactly teasing, just...sensual. Knowing something special could happen between you and this sexy male if you'd give it a try. He feels it and you feel it. The possibilities. Deep down you've experienced what I mean. You've just forgotten."

Josefina was right. Her eyes did feel different. They didn't glow the way they had before she married Frank. She'd poured the last of the *pinot grigio* and forced a smile. "Wrong topic for my birthday. Let's talk about something else."

"Well, I hope my pep talk has given you an appetite," Jo teased. "I hear the calamari are bathed in a divine sauce—*muy picante.* And that's just for starters."

Starters... Jo's words had stayed with her. They'd opened her to new possibilities, given her the will to drop everything and take this trip to Peru. They'd freed her to acknowledge her desire for Dex, not deny it. She could care for a man once again, make herself vulnerable to love. Frightening thought—but she felt so alive.

And her eyes felt different.

As the purple shadows crept across the mountains, Jill's spirits rose. She could manage, no matter what surprises lay in store. Self-confidence, that's all it took.

And attitude!

Whistling, she went inside to unpack.

****

Under the faded brown awning, Dex sat at the picnic table with pencil, notebook, magnifying glass, tape measure and the Moche pot. He copied the complicated pictures to study them, layer by layer. The intermingled drawings challenged him.

Gently, he turned the pot around, leaving the enigmatic priestess behind to examine the curved lines of a reed boat, like the ones still used by the local fishermen. He measured the boat's length, then dropped his pencil with a sigh.

Running his fingers through his hair, Dex gazed unseeing at the dunes. How was Jill making out in Poppy's room? She had looked so tired, he'd wanted to take her in his arms and kiss away the lines of strain around her eyes. If she stayed for long, he was going to ache from keeping his hands off her. And not just his hands...

Jill was the first woman in ages to take his mind off his work. Once he got beyond her businesslike exterior on that long ride from Chimbote, she'd seemed so vulnerable. And so desirable. He'd had to fight the urge to pull over to the side of the road and make love to her—right there in broad daylight.

But she was still married. He had to restrain himself from moving too quickly with this unsettling woman. Back in his university days, he and Sharon had been a couple. When she'd moved on, he'd seen his father's warning come true. Hadn't Sharon left because she saw no rich future with an archaeologist?

After her treachery, his career took over. Brief

affairs were fine, but emotional entanglements were taboo. Being passionate over pots instead of people became a great breakup ploy. A man madly in love with a two-handled jug—the visual was irresistible. It ended the romance with giggles instead of tears.

Now Jill was forcing him to re-examine his lifestyle. Might there be a more satisfying way? Being indecisive made him uncomfortable, so he focused his anger on Frank. The bastard belonged behind bars. If he got the chance, he'd make sure Frank saw the inside of a Peruvian jail for a long stretch.

But Jill was something else. He was hypnotized by her radiant smile. So much thrilled her. Shards or scenery, the smell of the sea or the wind in her hair—all brought on that delighted look. It was an incredible turn on. Even her frown when he provoked her stirred something within him.

How could Frank have let this slip away? Jill had a rare beauty that comes from magnificent bones. And he was an authority on bones. Next to her, the younger women at the site were unmolded clay.

"Dex…hey!" Sam walked toward him. "How's it going? Figured out the Mystery of the Moche Pot yet? Great book title."

"Hi, Sam. Have a seat. I can use an interruption."

Sam lowered his 220 pounds onto the other side of the bench and lit his pipe. "What's the matter? Are you missing insights into the Moche mind?"

"You jest, but I'm coming to believe the Moche conducted savage rites. They may have created sophisticated pots and gorgeous jewelry, but some drawings indicate bloody rituals, even human sacrifice."

Sam puffed at his pipe. "I've been reaching those conclusions, too. The woman's broken arms don't seem explicable in any other way. And those chalices, overflowing with blood! But why do you need me to distract you from your work? Are things at the dig not all they should be?"

"No, as I'm sure Harry told you, but my mind keeps wandering. Jill..." His voice trailed away.

"Ah, the ravishing Ms. Flanders. She seems a lot more interesting than her husband."

"You worked with him at Pachacamac. What did you think of him?"

"Not easy to get along with. Flanders knew his stuff, but he didn't mix with the rest of us. He preferred a little romantic dialogue to talk of pots and bones. The ladies ate it up."

"He's been spreading his charm here, too. I don't know how Jill put up with him all these years. She's not one of those career women without heart..." He stopped, suddenly embarrassed.

"You've learned a great deal about her in a very short time," Sam teased. "Don't forget, she's still married to Flanders."

"It's over between them," Dex insisted.

Sam looked at him, concerned. "You seem smitten. I hope you're right."

"Don't worry, old friend, I'm sure I'm right. We've just got to find the bastard and let *him* know."

****

Jill stuffed her belongings into the dresser drawers, then upended her suitcase to use as a bedside table. She stripped off her sticky clothes and tried a few naked yoga stretches. More relaxed now, she poured water from the pitcher into the bowl, dug into her purse for the tiny bar of soap she'd taken from the hotel, and washed all over.

It felt good to be clean again. Putting on a white satin bra and lacy, high-cut panties, Jill lay down beside the doll. It was foolish, but she turned it to face the wall before closing her eyes. A short nap would help.

Instead, her thoughts returned to the day Harry's fax had interrupted her busy schedule. An insidious voice in her head had whispered, *"How much simpler things will be if Frank disappears permanently."* Her pulse had skipped a beat. No! She didn't mean it. She refused to let "Francisco" lay another guilt trip on her. She didn't even want to see him in jail, especially a jail in Peru. She had heard nasty things… All she desired was Frank out of her life.

That night, she'd opened her jewelry box and lifted the false bottom where she'd put her wedding band the day she'd applied for her divorce. If she planned to keep secrets, she would have to wear it again. Her finger had twitched as she slid the ring down, shrinking from its touch.

Now, her ring finger twitched again, as if commiserating with that earlier moment. Sometimes, her body had a mind of its own.

What had she done next? Packed, of course. Had Frank taken his belongings when he disappeared? Harry hadn't mentioned any missing clothes. Maybe she could find a clue to his disappearance among the objects he'd left behind.

All thoughts of a nap gone, Jill hopped off the bed, threw on jeans and a tank top, and hurried off to locate Frank's room.

****

The balding man squinted at the photograph Manuel handed him. "So, she's here," he muttered. "Why? What mischief is she up to?"

"You know her, *señor*?"

"Oh, yes." He was quiet for a moment. Manuel waited.

Pulling on his earlobe, the man spat. "It's time for me to round up this adventure and get out of Dodge." He spoke sharply, ignoring Manuel's puzzled look. "Remember, you told me your brother had located the place the bandits hid their loot? You promised to take me there."

Manuel nodded, but his eyes shifted away.

"*Hombre,* you'd better not have changed your mind." The threat was clear.

Glancing around fearfully, he nodded again.

The man's voice grew deadly quiet. "One more haul is all I need. Then I'll disappear from this fucking country. The bandits are so busy with the coca harvest, no one will notice a few missing artifacts."

The mestizo turned sullen. "But…you promise, *mucho dinero.*"

"Yes, yes. I have the *soles* ready. You'll be paid as soon as you get me safely back to this cabin. But we must be certain the woman doesn't interfere. See to it, Manuel. Rough her up if you have to, she could use a lesson. Try not to kill her…unless it is absolutely necessary. *¿Comprende?*"

"*Si, Señor.* And *el profesor?*"

"Whatever…I leave that up to you. Just make sure the woman doesn't poke her nose in where it doesn't belong. She has a nasty habit…"

After Manuel left, Frank paced the room. Jill was here. Why the hell had she come? They were divorced now—she had no hold on him. It was what the woman wanted. She certainly wouldn't have bothered to fly all the way to Peru over her precious laptop. It made no fucking sense. He'd signed the divorce papers, returned them to the lawyers, so what more did the bitch want?

Frank paused in his pacing. Drank some beer. He had mailed them, hadn't he? A sudden vision of his last visit home flashed through his mind. He saw his mother's furious face, castigating him for considering a divorce. He saw himself handing her the fat brown envelope for the lawyers, caught her glancing at the address. Then the vision of the cut glass bowl on the foyer table where all the junk mail lay crossed his mind. Had Mama tossed the envelope in there just as he walked out?

Frank began to laugh. All these months. If he'd guessed right, and Mama had defied his order to mail the packet, Jill must be desperate. Ironic that he was having the last laugh.

But hey! Mama had messed with him again. Decided she knew better…at his fucking age! Frank smashed his fist into the wall. He had to get rid of Jill before she discovered what he was up to. It would be like Miss Prissy to call the cops.

Gulping down the last of the beer, he threw the bottle out the door. Manuel would take care of the matter. The mestizo knew good and well where his stack of *soles* was coming from.

Chapter 7

In Harry's office, a young woman frowned at the computer, muttering. Her stringy brown hair framed a freckled face with a pimple on its chin. She swiveled when Jill entered.

"Hi. I'm Frank Flanders' wife."

"I'm Karen, one of the volunteers. Didja hear me talking to myself? Sorry you caught me in such a bad mood. I'm terrible at this cataloguing. It's my friend Poppy's job…" Her voice trailed off, and color rose in Karen's sallow cheeks.

"Isn't that the girl my husband supposedly ran off with?" she asked.

"Oh, you've heard?" Karen studied Jill's face. "Well, ya know, everybody says so, but I don't think Poppy did that."

Startled, Jill stared at her. "Harry believes it."

"Yeah, well, Poppy's my best friend, we came to Peru together. She wouldn't have gone off with Frank without telling me." Pausing, Karen looked down. "Poppy didn't hit on Frank for, ya know, sex, though she let people think so. She kinda looked up to him."

"Have you mentioned this to Harry Lang?"

"Well, sort of, but he didn't pay attention. I don't think he believed me."

Jill wondered about Harry. It was one thing to

assume Frank had gone off with Poppy when they first disappeared, but by now he should be worried. Why did he disregard what Karen told him? Was Harry covering up something? Did it have to do with the missing artifacts?

Or, my God, could he and Frank be in this together?

Jill's suspicions grew, but she didn't want to take her bad mood out on this child. Confronting Harry would come later. "Thanks for leveling with me, Karen."

The girl blushed again. "Well...sure...ya know...glad to help." She turned back to the computer. "I'm trying to fill in for Poppy, but it's not my thing. These records are all mixed up."

Jill glanced at the monitor. "I know that program. Maybe I can give you a few pointers."

Karen's face lit up. "Wow, do you think you could? That would be great!"

"We'll see what Harry says. Right now I want to look through Frank's things. Which room is his?"

Jumping up, Karen walked Jill to the door. "It's the second room on the right." She pointed down the hall.

"Is it locked?"

"There aren't any keys here, except for the padlock on the storage room. To keep the artifacts safe, ya know."

"Okay, thanks." Jill smiled and left. She tried knocking first, just in case, but no one answered. It was Frank's room, all right. Pants and shirts were hanging neatly on pegs. Surprising that so many things had been left behind. Poppy's clothes had been cleaned out.

Peering at the dresser top, she saw no family

pictures. Really, she had to get rid of these last guilty remnants about the divorce. She wasn't in Frank's thoughts. His duffel bag, looking good despite a sprinkle of sand, lay in a corner. Not too many archaeologists owned a Louis Vuitton duffel.

Jill searched the room, but the matching attaché case was gone. Made sense if Frank were off for a weekend—he could fit in his shaving gear and a clean shirt. But he certainly would have taken his duffel for a longer trip. She'd seen him carry the duffel when it wasn't needed—just to show off.

On top of the dresser, a silver traveling mirror lay face down, part of a comb and brush set Frank was proud of. The other pieces were missing. Why would he leave the mirror behind?

Picking it up, Jill held it close to her face as she had so many times in the past. She half expected Frank to appear behind her, his dark head only a few inches above hers. She could almost see his taunting eyes and suggestive smile, those lying lips that had seduced her into overlooking the many disappointments in their marriage.

She sat down on the neatly made bed, lost in a jumble of memories. Frank on their brief honeymoon, so sweet at the start. His devotion didn't last long. He was off on a dig when she'd lost the baby. How she had missed his support then!

Dex would have been there. An image of Dex holding their baby, his bare arms covered with pale blond hairs that matched the baby's fuzz, popped into her thoughts. She imagined him playing with the tot's tiny fingers, while the warmth of his tender smile encompassed them both.

Annoyed at the path her thoughts were taking, Jill moved toward the window. Why couldn't she concentrate? Maybe she should lift a line from Poppy's book. Blame her distraction on the Pull of the Pyramids. Hah.

Shaking off the mood, Jill looked at the duffel again. Frank had dipped into their joint account when his article on Peru's trophy head cult was accepted by *Current Anthropology.* He'd come home gloating.

"Quite a payoff," she'd said, her voice laced with exasperation. "Do you really need such fancy cases for a dig in the desert?"

"Expensive luggage makes a statement, my dear Jillianne. You can afford it, now that you're an executive editor."

The bile in his voice made her cower. He was jealous, but she couldn't face another row. Instead, she'd walked out. She never knew what to say when he mocked her for her competence—and for her lack of femininity. "A woman in the corporate world is just a man's shadow in skirts," he'd jeered.

She should have answered back, but it was impossible to reason with him, and useless to show anger. He would only take advantage of it. Anyway, she'd seen herself in Frank's eyes, assumed he was right. Who knew women better than her husband? They flocked to his side. There had been other Poppys, she knew, even if it took her years to admit it.

Mulling over the painful recollection, Jill had a sudden flash of insight. This pilgrimage to Peru had more than one purpose. It wasn't only because she was worried about Frank. She had needed some distance from her familiar routine to see her life in perspective.

The half-life she'd been living—her professional life flourishing while her emotional life withered away—was not what she wanted for the rest of her days.

She deserved better. Frank would never change. As soon as he showed up, she'd get him to sign the papers. The torment of indecision would finally be over. She didn't know if her relationship with Dex would develop, but whatever happened would be *her* choice. She felt lighter, happier, as her doubts disappeared.

Buoyed by this decision, she picked up the duffel and dumped its contents onto the bed. A few pieces of dirty laundry lay on top. Underneath, neatly folded, was his favorite *guayabera* shirt, the black satin one trimmed with white embroidery. It masked the small paunch he was growing. Surely, he wouldn't go off without that shirt, not when he wanted to impress a young woman.

For the first time since she had received the fax, she shivered with a premonition that he was really in danger. The Cisco Kid hadn't just galloped off into the sunset. He'd expected to return. Had he found a clue and set out on his own to search for buried treasure? Was he lying hurt somewhere in one of the unexcavated ruins?

Stop it! Refusing to give in to sinister imaginings, Jill returned his clothes to the duffel. As she packed the *guayabera* shirt, something pink fell out of a pocket.

She looked at the tiny object, and her eyes narrowed. A knitted pink bootee—just like the one missing from Poppy's doll. As she had suspected, Frank must have given the doll to Poppy. But why did she leave it behind, especially if it were a gift from him? Things just didn't add up.

Jill's head began to throb, and her eyes burned. Slipping the bootee into her jeans pocket, she wondered where Dex was. The intensity of her feelings for him after so short an acquaintance distressed her. And why was she thinking of this now? Right after she had begun to feel more secure, more in command of her fate, delving into Frank's belongings had undermined her resolve.

Voices in the hall. A door slamming. Jill looked out the window, saw people crossing the patio to enter the chow hall. Spotting Dex across the courtyard, she called to him, but he was moving quickly, unable to see her peering out the shadowed window. It was irrational, but she was disappointed.

"I don't feel sociable," she told the mirror. "I want to take a shower and crawl into bed." But she had to see Harry and Dex, tell them of her findings in Frank's room—the pink bootee, the silver mirror, the expensive duffel—all left behind. Besides, she was hungry. Her mother always said problems were easier to solve on a full stomach.

Jill straightened her clothes and smoothed her hair. One more look in Frank's mirror—she would do. Closing the door quietly, she took three calming breaths, then waved to Karen and walked out the door. The spicy aroma of sausage and salsa wafted to her nostrils.

As Jill entered the hall, mugs of iced tea were being passed around. Dex saw her at once and pointed to the empty chair beside him. "Hey, gang," he called out. "This is Jill Flanders. Stop jawing for a minute while I make the introductions."

The room quieted, and he nodded to a small man

with a high forehead. Wire-rimmed glasses shielded sad black eyes, and a cigar wrapper banded his dark hair in a skinny ponytail. "This handsome dude is Luis Gomez," Dex said, "our Peruvian specialist in Moche archaeology."

Smiling, Luis started to rise. Jill waved her hand. "Please, don't bother to get up."

"On his left," Dex nodded again, "we have Maria Topol, Lima museum authority on textiles. She's examining our pieces of mummy cloth."

A heavy woman acknowledged Jill with more scowl than smile. Her glossy black hair was wound into a tight bun, emphasizing the high Mayan cheekbones in her long face.

Hostile, isn't she? Wonder what's eating her.

"Next are Don and Hank, student archaeologists from my school, U Penn. Across from them are Karen from Bennington and Marge from UA."

"That's Arizona for you ignorant Easterners," Marge called out. "Home of the Wildcats, yeah!" Mock groans filled the room, and Jill laughed.

"I stopped at the women's dorm," Dex said as he held her seat, "but you weren't there." He raised his eyebrows, but Jill didn't want to explain twice. She ladled some rice, topped it with beans, then skewered a sausage as Dex filled her glass with iced tea.

"A step down from *Chupa des Pescadoes*," he whispered in her ear.

His warm breath tickled, and she tried to squelch the thrill sliding down her body. "I'm famished. This hits the spot." She popped the sausage into her mouth, watching his lips curve as she chewed. Was he reading a double meaning in her words again?

Putting down his fork, Dex turned to join Harry and Sam as they conversed about excavation sites. "Chancay, Chimu, Chan-Chan, Pachacamac," were all she could make out. The odd names sounded alien and left her uneasy.

As she listened to snatches of conversation, her discomfort increased. She couldn't relate. Her sense of being an outsider grew. Frank may have felt at home in this environment, but she belonged to the noise and hustle of Manhattan, a world where she could control her life. What could she accomplish here in Peru? Wouldn't it be better to leave everything to the authorities?

Momentarily defeated, Jill turned away and wrapped a tortilla around black beans. As she raised it to her mouth, she caught Harry staring at her. His disgruntled look triggered her resentment. She was sick of feeling in the way. The "Chief" had to answer to her, not the other way around.

"I just searched Frank's room."

Harry's fork stopped midway between his mouth and plate. Jill stared back in challenge. The table grew quiet.

"His attaché case is missing," she rushed on, "but his duffel bag and most of his clothes are still there. Frank would never have gone away for this long without taking them."

"See here, Ms. Flanders, we looked in his room when Frank first disappeared. All was normal." Harry glanced at the others for confirmation before continuing. "Poppy left with him, that's obvious."

"I'm not so sure about that. All Poppy's clothes are gone, not just a weekend's worth. The girl is your responsibility, Harry. She's still a teenager."

Crestfallen, Harry's stern expression slipped.

"Too much time has passed," Jill continued. "These absences should be reported to the police."

At last Harry gave in. "Very well, Ms. Flanders. Have it your way."

Dex, who had been watching Jill take on Harry, gave her a thumbs up. "I'll go," he volunteered.

The Chief, however, dismissed the idea. "You've already missed too much work. You, too, Sam," he added as the older man opened his mouth. "And I've got to keep up with the damned records."

"I'll go," Jill offered.

"No, it's too dangerous."

"Lonely road…bandits…"

"Maybe we could send Hank?"

"We don't know for sure Flanders won't come waltzing back," Harry said. He looked around, caught the dirty looks. "Okay, okay, someone should tell the cops about those looters, too. We can kill two birds…"

As the men argued among themselves about who would report to the police, Jill glowered. They wouldn't be doing this if she were a man. "I said *I'll* go," she interrupted. "I'm quite capable of handling the matter by myself. And I can communicate in Spanish," she added, a triumphant gleam in her eyes.

"Don't be ridiculous," Harry snapped. "Drive all that way alone? And face the police? Forget it. The Latin male won't believe a woman, no matter what language you speak."

"Look, Harry, I'm not that naive. I know it's dangerous, so I'll keep the car doors locked all the way to the station. And I can handle a policeman. It can't be any harder than some of the authors I've worked with. Someone has to go, and the rest of you are busy. I may as well be of use while I'm here."

"It's definitely not a good idea." Concern and dissent threaded through Dex's voice, but Jill ignored it.

"Just tell me how to get there," she commanded, "and whose car I can borrow."

The men gaped at her. Sam broke the impasse. "You could take the Beetle I drove down from Trujillo. It's a stick shift. Can you drive that?"

"I learned on one, and it's only a two-hour drive."

"I don't like it." Dex growled, shaking his head, but Harry reluctantly agreed. "I don't like it either, but we can't spare anyone else. We haven't much time left before we return to the university. Just go to the police station, Jill. I'll give you a note for the chief of police."

From the corner of her eye, Jill could see Dex's mouth thin in anger. She refused to look at him. Did they think she was an incompetent child? Or was sexism rearing its ugly head again? She had a snide remark ready, but restrained herself. Winning the argument was enough for today.

"Trujillo's a lovely city," Karen called out as Jill resumed eating. "You must take the time to see it before you leave Peru. Don't miss the *Huaca del Dragon*. It's only a small fortress, but there are unbelievable dragons carved on the walls."

"Thanks, I'll keep it in mind."

After dinner, Dex walked Jill back along the sandy path to her room. The full moon and bright glow from thousands of stars bathed the pyramid in silvery light. It was a warm evening, and Jill felt at peace with herself. She had made some decisions and taken action. It was good not to feel so helpless.

Dex's arm felt strong and comforting, even if she was annoyed at the way he had treated her at dinner. But she had gotten her way, so she would forgive and forget.

At her door, he peered into her eyes for a long moment—a strange, compelling look—then brushed her lips lightly and left. What was he not saying?

Standing in the doorway, she watched him head back to the main building. For a big man, Dex walked with the lithe grace of a panther on the prowl. She felt only a twinge of disappointment that he hadn't really kissed her. There would be other times. Tonight she was drained, unable to focus on anything but her visit to the police.

Grabbing her soap, a towel, and her terrycloth robe, Jill walked along the path to the shower shack. As she approached, she heard voices above the running water. One belonged to Poppy's friend, Karen, the other to the blonde who'd been sitting next to her at dinner.

"Did you see Jill stand up to Harry?" the blonde said. "She's a classy lady. I hope I'm like that when I'm her age."

She stopped short. Just how old did they think she was?

"Jill's nice," Karen responded. "Harry is giving her a hard time about her husband."

"Yeah," the blonde went on. "The Chief doesn't like Frank. He's probably secretly pleased the man's gone, even if it does mean extra work for the rest of us."

"Well, I'm glad she's going to the police, Marge. I'm really worried about Poppy."

Marge scoffed. "I'll bet they're having a high time at some hotel in Lima. Or maybe they've taken off for someplace wild, like Machu Picchu. That's the most gorgeous spot on earth when the full moon shines on those fabulous ruins."

"How do you know?"

"I stayed overnight once. The funny little train had left, taking away all the tourists. I shared the ruin with the alpacas grazing on the slopes. It was so peaceful, like living in a dream."

"I'd pick the Amazon for romance, even if it is steamy," Karen said. "Gliding silently in a canoe after dark, hunting for wildlife by flashlight." She sighed. "Great memories."

"Yeah," Marge sighed too. "Speaking of memories, I almost got turned on by Frank last summer." She giggled. "He's kinda sexy, with those roving eyes! I go for the sophisticated older type."

With a grind and a thump, the running water stopped. Not wanting to be caught eavesdropping, Jill started to walk away. She paused when she heard Karen say, "Dex Conroy's the guy Poppy was really into. Sure, she flirted with Frank, but if she was gonna go off with anyone, it would have been Dex."

"Isn't he a hottie?" Marge drawled. "Deep…and a great body. I tried hard, but Poppy's the one who made it with him, so I heard."

A fist to her mouth to stop her gasp, Jill turned and ran—all the way back to her room.

Dex and Poppy—she should have known. He was no different from all the other macho studs. She'd be one more notch in his belt, and she almost fell for it. Stupid, stupid!

Picking up the doll, Jill threw it against the wall.

****

Shirt off but still in his pants, Dex sat propped up on his bed, the pot between his knees. One hand aimed a powerful flashlight on the painted goddess. With a magnifying glass in his other, he leaned close to examine the worn pectoral etched on her chest, turning it to get the room's shadows to highlight the carving. Could it be? Excitedly, he dropped the magnifier and reached for a pad and pencil. Repositioning the flashlight, Dex began to sketch.

Yes! Filling in the blanks where the clay had worn away, he could just make out the jaguar god—he felt it in his gut.

This put the find in a new light. Apparently, the god's fangs spread as far as this isolated settlement on the central coast. Spilling blood was part of the jaguar cult. The broken arms of the priestess had to be a sacrifice. He was lucky they had buried her. She could have been tossed into the flames, or thrown over the cliffs into the sea.

All fired up, Dex wanted to tell Jill. She would be fascinated by the legend of the jaguar god. What was she doing now? Was she asleep in that narrow little bed? Dreaming of him?

He was still angry with her for being so stubbornly blind to the danger she was courting. The hell with Harry. He would go along and protect her tomorrow.

Letting his fantasies take over, he imagined Jill here with him, her gleaming mahogany hair cascading down her back. She'd be wearing the silky blue gown he had glimpsed back at the hotel. He would slide it down to her waist and nibble at her breasts, see the nipples firm, hear her quickened breaths. When they were both flushed and panting, he would carry her to the bed, settle between her smooth thighs, and let those long legs wrap around him...

Cursing, Dex put the pot down. Wrong time for a woodie. He blew out the lantern, undressed and got under the sheet, groaning as it tented over his cock. He tuned out thoughts of the priestess pot, the jaguar cult, the boost to his career. Only the picture of Jill in his bed, dark hair flowing over the pillow, sheet sliding off the soft mounds of her breasts, remained. As he drifted off to sleep, his last image was of moss-green eyes dreamily closing, long black lashes resting on satin skin, and a smile of satisfaction parting kiss-stung lips.

Chapter 8

The sun had not yet risen above the mountains when Jill awoke, and the room was chilly. She snuggled under the blanket, wishing she were wrapped around Dex's hot body.

Then she remembered. He was involved with Poppy. The bimbo blonde of her imagination was real after all, only attached to the wrong man. She might have known there was a reason he treated her in such a brotherly fashion. A moment of madness at the picnic, quickly forgotten. A friendly flirtation here and there. How foolish of her to think it meant more. And yet, a small voice deep inside continued to whisper—what she and Dex had felt together was real.

Throwing off the covers, Jill looked into the small mirror. She examined her face in the day's early light, saw her neck firm and smooth. Those tiny lines at the corners of her eyes only made her more intriguing, a woman of experience. She tilted the mirror and caught a flash of light from the wicked gleam in the doll's glass eyes as it lay tossed into the corner.

It was unnerving. "Good thing I'm not superstitious. Otherwise, I'd think Poppy is giving me the evil eye—using the doll to spook her rival!"

With an edgy giggle, Jill turned the doll around to face the wall. "I'm not Poppy's rival. I don't need Dex, or any man. Back home I handle much more sophisticated men than Ian Dexter Conroy!"

The pep talk helped. She was more than ever determined to find Frank, get him to sign the divorce papers, and return to the safe, familiar world of computers and page proofs, touchy authors and tough publishers.

Conjuring the office in her mind, Jill concentrated on her sleek glass-topped pedestal desk, her amethyst geode paperweight, her raku planter trailing dark green philodendron leaves all the way across the back of the desk to twine around her clear Lucite telephone. She pictured the brightly plumed birds of her Mexican bark paintings, and the memory bolstered her confidence.

She'd been trained to handle obstacles, but even in violent New York City she'd never dealt with the police. For only a moment, Jill doubted she could cope. Perhaps she had bitten off more than she could chew by coming to Peru. She might be able to speak the language, but she didn't know the customs of the country. When it came down to the nitty-gritty, could she hold her own?

Her thoughts darted back and forth between desert and city, the comfort of the familiar, the attraction of the strange. Then she straightened. Stood tall. She was intelligent, she could improvise, and damned if she wasn't determined. Jillianne Adams Flanders would not let anyone down.

Pouring water from the pitcher into the little basin, Jill washed all over, splashing the cold water till it brought color to her cheeks. It was time to put her people savvy to a new test. She'd made the decision to come to Peru. There was no turning back.

Shafts of morning light picked out the red highlights in her dark hair as she fastened it into the French twist. Once more she wore her safari jacket with tailored slacks. A man might get away with a T-shirt and wrinkled jeans, but not a woman who wanted to be taken seriously. One last glance in the tiny mirror and she left the room, narrowly missing Maria Topol, the textile expert, in the dim hallway. Didn't the woman ever smile?

In the dining room, Jill lit the flame under the coffee urn and helped herself to cornflakes and canned milk. A bowl of fresh cherries had been left on the counter, and she dipped into the local product with pleasure.

As she was eating, Sam came in and took a seat beside her. He wore khaki shorts this morning, spindly legs descending from his heavy frame. His unlit pipe was already in his mouth.

"Morning, Jill. Nice day." Sam chewed on the pipe stem.

"Mmm, lovely. How are things going with your skeleton?"

"The old lady is almost put together again. Actually, she isn't that old—about thirty, *mas o menos.*"

Jill gulped. *Thirty, old? Don't go there.* "You archaeologists love that Spanish expression, don't you?"

"'More or less' covers a lot of territory. Often it's about as accurate as we can get. And it sounds better in Spanish." He gave her a conspiratorial smile. "Hasn't Frank let you in on that little secret?"

"My husband never talked about his work to me,

except to complain. I learned more from Dex in two days than from Frank in years."

"You don't say? I was trying to hold an archaeological conversation with Dex yesterday, but all he wanted to discuss was you." Sam grinned. "You're a most attractive distraction."

Jill's laugh was bitter. "Thanks, but you're imagining things, Sam. His intentions are elsewhere."

"What makes you think that?"

"Well," she swallowed, "there's a lot of talk about Dex and Poppy."

Sam shrugged off her remark. "If you'll pardon my saying so, I'm surprised to find you so insecure, Jill. I understand you have a prestigious job in New York as a bilingual editor."

Jill looked away. "It's owing to my bi-cultural heritage. At times I don't feel I fit in anywhere."

"I've developed a theory in my studies of anthropology." Sam lit his pipe and took a few puffs. "The first generation of immigrants come to a new country wanting to belong, but are secretly afraid to adapt and lose their own culture. Their children, the next generation, have been born here and are eager to assimilate, to be accepted. They fight against the old ways. Of course, there's a reaction when the third generation rolls around. These kids are caught between the comfort of their grandparents' culture and their parents' insistence on the new ways, along with the hard work entailed to achieve it."

"How do they handle it?"

"It differs with each person. Some choose going back to their grandparents' old ways, but face all confrontations with a chip on their shoulder, making arbitration difficult. Others stick to the new, but there's a chip on their shoulders, too, for being forced to make the effort. Still others learn to compromise and accept."

"Is number three the most mature way…or the most cowardly?"

"I make no judgments. But no solution comes without occasional hurting and being hurt. That's part of being alive."

"No gain without the pain?"

Sam chuckled. "In a nutshell."

They were silent for a moment, sipping coffee companionably. "You know, Sam," Jill reflected, "I was an only child for a long time, and pretty much intimidated by my scholarly parents. They were so all-American, even though Mom's folks came from Argentina. I rebelled in my teens by choosing a Puerto Rican girl for my best friend. Never felt inferior in her circle, but I still felt different. Then, when I began dating, my gang assured me Latinos were better lovers. It seemed safer never to challenge the statement. That's how I met Frank—he was called Francisco back then."

"Ahhh." Sam sucked on his pipe. "I can see why you're unsure of yourself around Dex, but you're too smart to let it bother you for long. People grow all through their lives, Jill. I'm a firm believer in that."

Impulsively, Jill leaned over and kissed his cheek. "Thanks, prof. You've given me a lot to think about. Say, does your offer of the car still hold?"

"You're really planning to go?"

"Oh, yes!"

He gave her the keys, patting her hand as he did so. "Remember, Jill, get back before dark. Take a canteen of boiled water with you, and throw in a sandwich, in case you're delayed. I don't know where the police station is, but any officer can tell you."

Sam's concern was so genuine, Jill didn't mind his fatherly advice. "Will do," she told him. "It's only a two-hour drive to Trujillo. I should easily be back by dinnertime." Squeezing his hand, she went into the kitchen to fix her lunch.

With a cheese sandwich in her large canvas carryall and a canteen over her shoulder, Jill headed for Sam's car. Lots of dents in the sky-blue Volkswagen, but the tires seemed okay. The headlights looked out of line, but she would be back before dark.

A quick swipe at the dust on the windshield, and she was on her way. For several miles, Jill drove carefully along the rutted dirt road. The car's springs had long ago given way to hard driving. She cursed as her spine hit the worn upholstery with every bounce.

At last, the Pan American Highway appeared. The VW turned north toward Trujillo, its exhaust emitting a plume of dirty smoke that left particles of soot spreading like a rash across the pale sand. High in the sky, the sun flattened the mountains into a two-dimensional backdrop. A wave of heat, rising from the tarmac, curled in upon itself.

Jill chugged along, catching bright glimpses of the sea beyond the dunes. She was relaxed, confident, pleased to handle the problem all by herself.

She hummed the tune from *My Fair Lady* Dex had mentioned. The old musical had stuck in her mind after he'd offered his motto, "With a little bit o' luck you won't get hooked." Now a different song took over. She struggled to bring the lyrics into her consciousness without success. The words would come when she least expected them.

Suddenly, Jill heard a thud, followed by a hiss. *Oh no!* Something else she wasn't expecting. Rolling down the window, she craned to look at the flat tire still oozing air. *Damn!* She pulled out her cell phone. No reception—she should have realized. Was there a spare tire? She'd better check the trunk, although she wasn't sure she could change a tire if she found one.

Stepping out, Jill gazed at the puncture, hands on her hips, foot tapping. Her lips puffed in and out. What was that sticking out below the hubcap? Had she somehow picked up a nail out here in nowhere? As she knelt down to look closer, something whizzed by her ear.

Omigod! Jumping up, Jill ran to the door, threw herself into the car and pushed the lock buttons. She heard another whirring sound, ducked, then reached up blindly to roll the window shut. Trembling, she lay across the seat, too frightened to think.

Minutes passed. Her heartbeat slowed, and she took a deep breath. She heard nothing but the soughing of the wind. Cautiously, Jill raised her eyes to the window. All she viewed was sand and more sand, hillocks undulating into the distance.

Sprawled out across the two front seats, she tried to figure out what to do. The sun beat down, and her breathing grew ragged. She would suffocate in the car if someone didn't come along. *Don't panic. Don't panic. Don't panic.*

Off in the distance, she caught the rumble of a truck. Sound carried far in the desert, and she prayed it wasn't too far away.

The sound grew louder. Minutes passed. Gathering

courage, she raised her head and peered out the back. The tortilla delivery truck was heading her way, slowing down. The driver must have spotted the car.

Jill hit the horn hard, continued to hold it until the truck came to a stop behind her. The driver got out, walked over to her front window, and peered inside. *"¿Señora, esta bien? ¿Qué paso?"*

She opened the window and pointed, too overcome to remember the Spanish words for flat tire. The man squinted, then walked back to the tire, bent down, and pulled out a six-inch dart. His head shot around as he surveyed the landscape. Nothing to see but rolling dunes.

By now Jill had settled down enough to remember her Spanish. "What is it?" she asked.

"A dart from a blow gun," the driver said, turning it in his hand. "The Indian tribes near the Amazon used them. Today, they are blown for tourists."

"But…there's no one out there…"

"El hombre, he hides behind a dune, then runs away. The darts can be blown quite far and with much force, *señora."*

Jill began to tremble again. "C-can I ride with you into Trujillo? You can drop me off at the first garage. I'll get a couple of men to drive out here and pick up the car."

"Si. That is best. I have more deliveries to make."

Unsteadily, Jill grabbed her canteen and carryall. Leaning on the driver, she climbed into the truck. The engine coughed and started to roll. When they picked up speed, her breathing finally slowed to normal.

On the outskirts of the city, the tortilla truck stopped at a filling station. The driver helped Jill arrange for the VW to be picked up, and the tire repaired. Money changed hands. They took off again, and soon reached the heart of the colonial city. Thanking him for the drive, Jill climbed out at the central plaza. She ignored its picturesque bandstand and splashing fountain, headed straight for a traffic policeman in a dazzling white uniform who directed her to the police station.

Across the square, near the imposing cathedral with one bell in its twin towers, stood an ornate Spanish building. Carved balconies hung over its stucco walls. Inside, a bored police sergeant at the front desk told her to wait. She sat down on a hard wooden bench, one hand inside her carryall as she clasped and unclasped the metal fastener of the purse tucked inside.

The minutes ticked by. An hour passed before she was led into a grimy room with wrought iron grillwork over the windows. From behind a cluttered desk, a handsome man with wavy black hair and a narrow mustache rose to greet her. He was no taller than Jill, but solidly built.

She steeled herself for the inevitable mental undressing as his gaze raked her body. What was it about Latin men?

"*Señora* Flanders, I am Lieutenant Raul Castillo. How can I help you?" He spoke in English, and Jill did the same.

"I want to report the disappearance of my, er, husband, Frank Flanders. He's an archaeologist, digging at the Pyramid of the Stars. Do you know the site?" Nervously, she twisted the gold band on her finger.

"*Si*...yes. It is the smallest of the three pyramids

near here with heavenly names." The lieutenant came out from behind the desk, his dark green uniform appearing just pressed. The knife-edge creases in pants a half-inch too short revealed black socks above his highly polished shoes.

"*Por favor,* sit down and tell me what is wrong. How long has your husband been gone?" His hand brushed the back of her neck as he held the chair for Jill.

Such Spanish courtesy… Aloud, she said, "Frank has been missing for eight days now."

"More than a week? Why have you waited this long to report it?"

"I've just arrived in Peru. I was under the impression that it had been reported."

"Ah." Gazing intently at her, he steepled his fingers.

"Lieutenant, there's something I must tell you. A volunteer at the dig—a young woman—is also missing. Harry Lang, the director, assumes the two went off together, that's why he didn't report this sooner. However, I strongly suspect this is not the case."

Castillo stroked his mustache. "Explain, *señora, por favor.*" His eyes, whiskey brown under arching black brows, hung on her every word in a manner Jill found flattering but unnerving. It was as if he were studying her under a microscope: species, human—gender, female.

"My husband's belongings are still in his room." Jill hoped he took her seriously. "Poppy's clothes are gone."

"Poppy? Is she the *muchacha* your husband ran away with?"

"She's the girl who's missing. Lieutenant Castillo, if my husband intended to leave with her, surely he would have taken his clothes and suitcase. His favorite *guayabera* shirt is still here…" She was getting rattled, talking too much.

"I see." He reached for a notebook. "Describe your husband to me."

She dictated slowly as Castillo jotted down the description. "He's thirty-seven, five feet ten, about 180 pounds, with licorice-brown eyes and thinning black hair. There's a bald spot on top, but he lets it grow long in back." Jill paused. "I'm sorry I can't describe the girl, for I never met her, but I know she's a blonde, about eighteen years old."

"No matter, *gracias*." Putting down his pencil, the lieutenant held her gaze once more with that soulful Spanish look. "Has there been any trouble at the *huaca* with *banditos*…looters?"

"I heard that some men broke into the storage shed recently, but they were discovered before they had a chance to make off with anything. That's all I know."

"Ah, one moment, *señora*." He pushed a button on his desk, and another sharply pressed police officer entered. *"Perdón."* Castillo smiled, flashing shiny white teeth.

As he talked rapidly to his assistant, Jill concentrated on keeping her features expressionless. She was glad she had given no indication that she understood Spanish. The speed at which he spoke slowed down her comprehension, but she did catch the key words.

"…missing   scientist…tomb   robbers…inside job…*muchacha   insignificanté…¿El   Rio*

Flujo?…mucho oro…" The conversation ended with swift orders from the lieutenant and a hasty retreat by the policeman.

Castillo turned to her with his high wattage smile. "I beg your pardon, *señora*. Urgent business."

"I understand," she said sweetly, going along with the game. "What will you do to find Frank?"

A moment passed as they looked steadily at each other, the lieutenant emitting almost tangible waves of masculine authority and sexuality.

"All that is in our power, be assured." He came over and took Jill's hand. "A beautiful woman like you should not worry. It is probably only a little—how you say—fling, the *señorita* and your husband."

She started to protest, but he kept patting her palm. "I will look into the matter, personally," he promised. His hand moved to the small of her back, rubbing lightly as he escorted her to the door.

What did this policeman take her for, an idiot? Just because she had breasts. How humiliating! Aware of the policeman's magnetism, but fuming inwardly nevertheless, Jill allowed herself to be led from the room.

She hastened back to the plaza. The police were alarmed about missing gold and nearby gangsters. Frank could be caught up in something criminal. It could involve those terrorists, The Flowing River. His life might be in danger, but would they tell a woman anything? No. Not even his soon-to-be ex-wife!

And Castillo had said the "girl" was insignificant. Even if it turned out that Poppy wasn't involved, he had no right to decide that beforehand. She'd like to show them all just how insignificant *they* were.

All of a sudden, the words to the song she had been humming earlier came to Jill. They had applied to Dex then, but would do for the handsome lieutenant as well. "Just an ordinary man…who desires nothing more than just an ordinary chance…to live exactly as he likes and do precisely what he wants…"

Damn, damn, damn—it's a man's world!

The lieutenant was so condescending. He must see her as an empty-headed American woman, jealous because her husband ran off with a young girl. If he were to be convinced this matter was serious, she would need help. Infuriating, but she had to concede that a woman alone would be kept out of the loop. And if they found out she was soon to be divorced, the silence would be deafening.

Unbidden, her thoughts turned to Dex, to his strength and imposing presence. Perhaps she could lean on him, just a little. Strictly as a friend.

A taxi emptied across the plaza. Jill hurried over and directed it to the garage. Once there, she sat on a bench in the hot sun, fanning herself. A mechanic brought her a bottle of Inka Cola, and she thanked him. Finally, she spotted her car driving in. She was warned the spare tire wouldn't hold out for many more miles, but Jill didn't listen. Her day was ruined. She couldn't bear to go back to the dig and face the men with her defeat. Not yet.

It was early enough to look for the site Karen had mentioned, the Dragon Pyramid. The girl had said it was not to be missed. She had the address, so it shouldn't be hard to find.

Sliding in behind the wheel, Jill turned on the ignition. Her safari outfit was wilting, but it would be cooler inside the fortress. Dragons sounded exciting. Today, she had been shot at by a blowgun, patronized by a policeman, and roasted in the sun. Enough. It was her turn to see what attracted the tourists to this little bit of civilization along the barren coast of Peru.

Chapter 9

Dex couldn't sleep. He lay awake, tossing and turning at the thought of Jill driving alone to Trujillo. Dozing off toward dawn, he awoke late. With a silent curse, he threw on his clothes and headed for the chow hall. He would tell Jill about the jaguar god he'd discovered on his pot, enthrall her with its eerie legend, then talk her out of going to the police alone.

He looked around, but Jill wasn't there. Cornering Harry, Dex yanked his arm. "Has Jill come in yet?"

"Been and gone. Sam loaned her his car."

"Damn." Dex glanced at his watch. "I might have known she'd do it. Was it the Dragon Fortress Marge told her to visit after seeing the police?"

Harry nodded. "Hey, where are you off to?"

"I'm going after her. I'd no intention of letting her drive there alone. Should have told her last night, but her guard was up at dinner, thanks to you. I thought she'd be more open to reason in the morning."

"Now see here, Dex, you're needed at the dig. You've only just returned from three days away."

"Don't be an ass, Harry. You know she's not safe going to Trujillo alone. Haven't you enough on your conscience with Poppy missing?" Grabbing a swallow of coffee, he dumped the rest and hurried out.

****

Jill gunned the motor so hard the VW stalled. Swearing, she restarted the engine and tried to follow the traffic cop's directions to the *Huaca del Dragon.* Some streets didn't have signs, others indicated one-way traffic in the wrong direction. Baffled, she stopped and asked for help three times, losing an hour before the route led her to a shabby suburb of Trujillo.

Rickety shacks, paint peeling in long shreds like party streamers, surrounded a sandy field the size of a football stadium. At the far end stood the Dragon Fortress.

Stopping at the gatehouse, Jill paid the guard ten *soles* and walked over to the walls still standing. She fanned herself with the admission ticket—the sun was so hot! By the time she reached the structure, the traffic noise had faded. All she heard was the humming of insects. It certainly wasn't a well-known tourist attraction. Looking back at the neighborhood, she could guess why.

Turning once more, Jill spied the frieze of dragons clumping along the thick adobe walls. The lines were so sharp, they could have been carved yesterday. In between the six-foot, long-tailed dragons, smaller fish and pelicans had been cut into the mud brick with splendid detail. She had never seen anything like it.

Delighted to have found this magical place, she forgot the morning's scare, the heat, and the handsome but patronizing Lieutenant Castillo. Taking her digital camera from her carryall, she began to snap pictures of the fortress. She walked all around the perimeter, not wanting to miss a single photo op. Sweat gathered at her hairline and trickled under her arms. She ignored it, eager to frame the dragons in dramatic shots she would pass around the office.

When she finished admiring the outside walls, Jill entered a maze of passageways. They were a respite from the sun, but the deep shade inside the fortress created a gloomy atmosphere. She had to use her flash to shoot the fabulous carvings.

The minutes flew by, turned into an hour. She was halfway through the maze of corridors when she became conscious of footsteps behind her. She turned quickly. A dark, hulking man in a shabby black suit stared at her, then faded away into a side passage.

Frightened, Jill began to hurry. Why hadn't she packed her pepper spray? As she turned a corner, she glanced back. The creepy man was following her again.

Her heart began to pound. She'd been warned, but had she listened? Speeding up her walk, she tried to find a way out of the tangle of passageways. In minutes she passed through an unfamiliar opening. There was no exit!

Cornered. Oh God. Women were insignificant in this country. She'd overheard the lieutenant and had listened to Dex's tales of looting, thievery, or worse! Jill looked wildly around for a weapon to defend herself, even a stone, but the corridor had been swept clean. Gripping her large carryall to use as a club, she turned to face the looming menace. She would not be robbed or raped without a fight!

The man stopped a few feet from her, and her throat constricted. She smelled garlic on his breath, sweat on his body. She fixated on his coarse, bushy eyebrows hanging over eyes that could kill.

As the man's huge hand went to his jacket pocket, Jill knew he was going for a knife. She raised the carryall, ready to strike, but his hand came out—holding a batch of photos! He waved them in her face.

"Antiquities, *señora?* I have colored peektures."

Her heart thudded. She stared in disbelief as he thrust the Polaroid snaps into her hand. Her fingers trembled as she shuffled through the photos. A black clay stirrup pot with a man's face engraved, a small burial cloth embroidered with blue fish, and an Inca stone mace with its six sharp metal spikes. Her rage mounted as relief set in. The look in his eyes had been not murder, but guile.

"You're nothing but a thief, a grave robber!" she shouted. "You're selling your heritage. I shall report you to the police."

The man's eyes widened. "No, no, *señora.* No *policia, por favor.*" Grabbing the photos from her hand, he scuttled back down the passage, shrinking as he moved farther away.

Jill followed slowly, knees too weak to hurry after him. She soon lost the scurrying figure in the confusing maze. Her heartbeat speeded up. She had no idea how to get out of the *huaca.* The thick walls ensured that no one would hear her if she yelled.

She began to run, panting as she raced along the passageways. At last, on the point of hyperventilating, she stumbled into the light. Blinded by the bright sunshine, Jill began to sway. As she keeled over, strong hands grabbed her.

Jill tried to scream, but couldn't. Choking, her heart leaping into her throat, she breathed in big panicked gasps. A familiar scent penetrated the haze. Her eyelids flew up to face the man holding her.

With a weak grin, Jill closed her eyes and let her

body sag against him. Until her breathing settled back to normal, she would revel in Dex's strength.

****

"What are you telling me, *hombre*? You failed again?"

"I puncture the tire of the VW, *señor*. I borrow the blowgun of my brother, the one he trade with Amazon Indians to show *los turistas*. The tire go flat—ftttt. I hear it hiss in the wind. But I not practice blowing through pole to hit target. The *señora*, she move too fast." Manuel's tone was abject, but his eyes revealed his fury.

The balding man paced back and forth in the small room. "I can't wait any longer. You must take me to the cave your brother found, Manuel."

"But the bandits? They will torture us. My brother will kill me!"

"If they don't, I will. You can blindfold me, Manuel, and you can lead me. I will see nothing. I will not remember where the cave is located. We'll pick a safe time, and I'll take only a few pieces. The bandits won't notice anything missing, I swear…and we'll both be set for life."

"I…I am afraid, *señor*. I drink too much tequila when I tell you about cave."

"It was a brilliant idea, even if you were drunk. I must have one big splash, one spectacular success before I return to the States." The man's eyes blazed. "I will *not* let you off the hook, Manuel. If you back out now, your brother will learn everything. He'll tell his bandit friends, you can be sure of that. And then…" The *Americano* slashed a hand across his throat.

Manuel   wet   his   pants.

Chapter 10

Jill's ragged breathing finally eased. She looked up at Dex. "You can put me down now."

With a sigh, he slid her body inch by inch down the length of his.

She trembled. His hard muscled torso rubbing against hers, combined with the adrenaline still in her system, left her shaky. "I c-can't believe it's you. What are you doing here, Dex?"

"Looking for one stubborn female." He glared at her. "Did you think I was going to let you go to the police by yourself? You were so hell-bent on being macho last night, I held off arguing with you until you'd had some sleep. But when I got to the chow hall this morning, you had already left. I almost socked Sam for giving you his car."

"How can a woman be macho?" She snickered.

"Hell, you tell me!" He locked his fingers with hers and began to drag her across the sandy field. "Let's get out of here."

"Hey! Not so fast. I haven't fully caught my breath yet."

Scowling, Dex slowed. "What happened in there, Jill? You gave me quite a scare—not that I don't appreciate your collapsing in my arms…"

"I did?" She widened her eyes. "Oh my, I guess I

did."

The red truck was parked next to Sam's VW. He helped her into the car, then sat down beside her. "You aren't hurt, are you?"

"No," she patted his hand. "Just scared. A silly misunderstanding, and then I couldn't find my way out."

"Misunderstanding? You look like you've seen a ghost."

She squirmed. "A man followed me, a big, creepy looking guy. I thought he was a mugger. I've heard how wallets and passports get stolen down here, and I didn't like the look in his eyes when he got closer." She bit her lip. "He seemed sinister, so it was only natural that I grew frightened."

"Did he grab you?" Dex growled. His hands tightened into fists.

"No, no. Holster the six guns, Dex. Turned out he only wanted to sell me some antiquities. He had a pocketful of Polaroid 'peektures,' guaranteed authentic. The rest was all in my imagination," she added in disgust.

"Unfortunately, digging up artifacts and selling them to tourists is fairly common."

"But it shouldn't be!"

"Not in the best of all possible worlds—a world where half the population isn't starving."

Jill grew silent, disturbed by his words.

With a grimace he changed the subject. "How did you make out with the police?"

"You know I've already been there?" She eyed him suspiciously.

"They recalled you quite easily." His eyebrows

rose as he looked her up and down, imitating the officer's leer. She covered her mouth to muffle a giggle. "It's lucky I remembered Karen told you to visit the *Huaca del Dragon,* or God knows what would have happened to you."

"I would have pulled myself together and made it back. I wasn't helpless."

"No? Then it was just your delight in seeing me that made you fall into my arms?"

"Well, that too," Jill muttered, burrowing into his chest as she recalled her harrowing flight through the passageways.

With a sigh, he rubbed the tension spot between her shoulder blades. "Suppose you begin at the beginning."

Taking a deep breath, Jill told him about her hour's wait for Lieutenant Castillo, his supercilious attitude, and the directions he'd given his assistant when he thought she couldn't understand.

"Don't say you weren't warned," Dex pointed out.

"Real men don't rub it in!"

"Sure about that, are you?"

She smacked his hand. *Count on Dex not to miss a trick...*

"I didn't feel like coming right back, not with my tail between my legs, so to speak."

"What a visual!" He choked out a laugh.

"So I drove over to the Dragon Fortress." Jill hurried on, deciding not to mention the blow dart in her tire. The day had been bad enough without being yelled at again. "The carvings are magnificent. I had a grand time photographing the friezes until I heard footsteps and realized I was being followed."

He stiffened. "The tomb robber?"

"Yes. I planned to hit him over the head with my carryall, but it wasn't necessary. He showed me his photos. When I threatened to call the police, he hurried away. I was a little stressed out by then," she admitted. "Tried to follow him, but he was moving too fast, and I lost my way. That's when I got a touch of panic. Thought I was stuck in that gloom forever."

"Just a *touch* of panic, hmm."

"Yes," she insisted. "Just a touch, but I'm glad you found me."

Jill smiled, watching Dex relax as he drank in her disheveled state. She must be a mess, but he didn't seem to mind. She leaned into him, and he kissed her hard, pressing her close and running his tongue along her lips before he set her back and slid out of the car. "Follow me back to the police station. I'll see if I can get any more information, *mano o mano*."

Recovering her composure after that sudden devastating kiss, she stuck out her tongue and razzed him.

Jill waited in the car while Dex talked to the police. The dry heat surrounded her like a soft blanket, and her eyelids drifted closed. In a short while, he returned and slid in beside her. "The cops are definitely worried about the looters," he said. "Lima's been after the gang, too. They're not sure if the guerrillas are behind the looting—they don't have the right overseas connections. More likely, it's a rival gang of thieves using *El Rio Flujo* as a front. The true revolutionaries are into bigger, rougher stuff."

"Bigger?"

"Mm hmm—bank robberies, drugs, and murder."

Jill shivered. "Sounds like a lot of killing."

"Thirty thousand corpses in one year, according to the news reports. A lot of innocents got in their way."

"My God! The truth is worse than the stories I've read."

Her lips trembled, and Dex returned to what he had learned from Lieutenant Castillo. "The police think Frank's description is a lead to the looters. Who knows? They may be right that he's involved."

"It wouldn't surprise me, despite the damage to his career. Knowing Frank's lust for gold…" She left her sentence unfinished.

Dex took her hand. "Castillo hinted that you might be in danger."

"Me? Why?"

"Isn't it obvious? You're poking into criminal activities. Opening areas of investigation that had been carefully covered up. I don't know why, bribes perhaps, but whatever their reason, the police want you to discontinue any investigating. No sticking your pretty nose into dangerous places."

"Well, of course. I won't go out of my way to get into trouble. But what if this 'inconsequential female' accidentally discovers something? I came here to find Frank, Dex. The police don't care about his disappearance. They only want him to lead them to the looters."

"Following clues isn't safe, Jill. These bandits don't value human life. Whether they claim it's being done for a cause or admit they're in it for power and riches, they're still murderers."

She shook off a chill of fear. "I won't take any foolish chances. I'm an intelligent woman, not one of those movie heroines who climbs up alone to investigate the noises in the attic."

"I'm not so sure about that. Promise me you won't do anything without telling me first."

Jill grew silent. She considered hunting for Frank on her own, but she'd need the police to follow up any clues. They wouldn't listen to a woman. Besides, Dex wanted to protect her, and she rather liked the idea.

"Okay. We're partners, right?"

"Holmes and Watson." He patted her hand. "But mostly we'll leave it to the police. Right? I can't help worrying, though. You draw trouble like a magnet."

"What do you mean?"

"Shall I count the ways? A riot at the airport, a poisonous spider in your hat, a falling rock just missing us at our picnic, a car sideswiping us, and now the robber in the fortress. Five incidents in as many days."

She bit her lip, hesitated. "There, er, was something else…"

He turned sharply. "What?"

"Someone shot out my tire on the way into Trujillo. With a blow gun dart."

"Good God, what did you do?" His fingers rolled into fists as he ground his teeth.

"Stayed in my car till the tortilla truck drove by. I hitched a ride with the driver, then got some garage mechanics to pick up the car and fix it."

"That settles it. We can't blame a blow dart on coincidence. Did you keep the dart?"

Nodding, she took it from her carryall and handed it to him.

"So we have proof. I wish you had told me earlier, Jill. The lieutenant was just leaving when I showed up.

It's too late to catch him now. Until we can get back to town, I'm attaching you to me like a Siamese twin."

"Hmm. That has possibilities." Torn between relief and a thrill of pleasure, she asked, "When do you think we'll hear from the police about Frank?"

"Give them time to set their traps. This little adventure may keep you here longer than you'd planned."

She looked up, saw the mischief in his eyes. Her pulse raced. *This has got to stop!* She couldn't go on reacting to this man like an adolescent with a crush.

Jill sidestepped. "Do we have time for something to drink before we head back? No one is going to attack me in front of the police station, and I'm parched."

"Haven't you been carrying water?"

"I took a canteen, but in all the excitement I forgot about it."

"We've got to hydrate you right away. There's a café on the corner of the plaza that squeezes fresh fruit juices."

"Sounds like heaven."

"There's a price to pay if you order mango juice," he told her as they walked over. "I get to lick up any dribbles."

Jill gazed at him. The memory of his tongue lapping at her chin, then sliding down her neck to follow the trickling mango juice, sent a delicious wave of heat through her.

They sat at a small umbrella table and ordered frosted glasses of pineapple and papaya juice. Relaxing now, Dex switched to travel guide mode. "You've got to see Chan Chan while you're here. It's an entire city in ruins, with pelicans, fish and dragons still carved on its damaged walls."

"I'll fit it in. Sounds fascinating."

"I'd also like to take you flying over the Nazca lines before you leave Peru."

"The runways of an alien landing field in the middle of the desert?"

"That's nonsense, of course. People believe the darnedest things. But besides the lines, there are huge animal and insect drawings you'll see when you fly over in a small plane. There's a gigantic spider, and an enormous monkey with a curled-up tail. They'll take your breath away. The pilot dips his wings left and right, so the passengers can get a good view. Feels a bit like a roller coaster ride."

"My stomach is roiling at the thought of that plane dipping. But I'd love to see those animals and the strange lines. Imagine them still being visible after so many centuries."

"I'll take you there someday." For moments they sat sipping their drinks, smiling at each other.

"Tell me about your childhood," Dex suggested, his thumb sliding caressingly over her palm. "I want to know all about you."

Forcing her attention away from the sexy tingle between her fingers, Jill looked into the distance. "I'm almost embarrassed to tell you." She pulled her hand away to fan herself. "I find it hard to admit it was a very ordinary one."

"So?"

She turned to him. "Dozens of manuscripts cross my desk every week. I read and read. Every important character rises out of a miserable childhood, overcoming alcoholic parents, drug pushers, poverty, cruelty, foster homes, crippling accidents...I could go on and on." She took a deep breath.

"These people conquer every physical and emotional block to become the heroes and heroines. The rest of us, those who grew up with caring parents and food on the table, end up dull and boring."

"Hey, you don't really believe that makes you dull?"

"I think it's why I stayed in a bad marriage for so long," Jill told him. "I never learned how to be tough."

"You're wrong. Sticking it out takes strength. When I think of you, Jill, dullness is the farthest thing from my mind. You're a fascinating woman."

"Is that so?"

"Sure is. If I were a poet, I would count the ways you make me sizzle."

She laughed. "Do you get far with that line?"

He chuckled. "This time, I'm sincere. You intrigue me even more now that you've shown me this other side of you. I can't believe you'd put yourself down like that. Did you ever rebel?"

"Sam asked me the same thing. It's my mixed heritage. Makes me insecure, but I got to know the best curses in two languages!" She smirked.

"Useful."

"And how! My friends convinced me, too, that Latinos were the best lovers. I never tried to dispute it."

"Wow. That's a challenge!" His answering smile was pure dare. Her pulse speeded up again.

"Stop teasing me. What about you? Was your childhood full of obstacles?"

"I already told you the basics. I enjoyed squishing clay in my mom's studio." Dex smiled. "Mom praised my first piece of sculpture, a car, but Dad called it a lumpy apple with four stems."

He laughed, but Jill looked thoughtful. "Funny that you still remember it."

He shrugged.

"Did your father object to his wife being famous?"

"Just the opposite, her reputation added to his prestige. But when I started to think about a career in art or science instead of business, we almost came to blows. Dad can be a pompous bastard, but I was stubborn, too."

Jill reached out, covered his hand with hers. "Did the two of you finally come to terms?"

"We reached an 'accommodation' when I got my degree and became an ethnoarchaeologist. I think he liked the sound of the big word. We still avoid each other whenever possible, though."

"That's sad. So you left squishing clay behind?"

"Pretty much. I'd enjoy squishing some moldable parts of you," he murmured, his voice growing husky. Taking her hand, Dex placed a kiss between each finger, sucking her pinky into his mouth before letting go.

Watching him, she drew her wet pinky into her own mouth. As her tongue swirled around it, she caught him staring. His eyes grew dark. *Down, boy,* she heard him murmur, and grinned.

A shadow crept across their table. "We'd better get cracking," he said. "It'll be dark before we're back at the dig. I wish you didn't have to drive, Jill, but Sam needs the car. Just stick close behind me."

By the time they reached their vehicles, the sun was slipping behind the mountains. Palm trees whispered in the evening breeze. Ancient buildings faded into dusky silhouettes. As Jill followed Dex's truck out of town, the last sliver of golden ball melted into the sea. Stars popped out, one by one, shining in the unfamiliar southern sky. *Night arrives so quickly in the tropics,* she thought. *There's almost no twilight.*

With a sigh, Jill switched on the car's headlights. The left one glowed brightly. The right headlight remained dark. "I don't believe it!" She banged her fist on the steering wheel. "Can anything else go wrong today?"

Chapter 11

Fingers gripping the wheel, Jill stuck close to the red truck. It would be easy to slide off the road into a ditch or a looter's pothole. At least the darkness kept her safe from blow darts. Blinking away her tears of frustration, she flashed back to Dex's truck being sideswiped on their way to the dig. Her pulse raced. *Calm down,* she scolded herself. *Concentrate on the road.*

Two tension-filled hours passed before she saw lights streaming from the headquarters building. As she parked behind Dex's truck and pried her stiff fingers from the steering wheel, her door flew open. Harry and Sam stood there.

"Where have you been?"

"Are you all right?"

"You had us all on edge," Harry chastised. "Haven't enough people disappeared without you scaring us so?"

"Hey, it's okay. Dex found me. Good thing, as only one headlight works." Jill pointed.

As one, the two men turned, but didn't bother to check the headlight when they spied Dex walking toward them. "Conroy, did you talk to the police? Did they know about the looting? Have other sites been raided?"

"Yes, yes, I spoke to them. Easy, guys, everything's under control."

Jill watched their attention focus solely on Dex. For all of a minute they were anxious about her. In the next, she could have been another hole in the ground to bypass. Interrupting, she tapped Dex's arm. "You can explain everything. I'm off to bed."

Jill left them still asking questions. Dragging her weary body to the room, she turned on the light and caught the doll glaring at her. Poppy's doll. *Dex and Poppy*... The memory punched her in the gut.

She was overreacting again, but couldn't stop her exhausted self. The day's frights had finally caught up with her. Falling onto the bed, Jill burst into tears. She sobbed into the pillow, never pausing to wonder who had turned the doll around.

Minutes passed before Jill realized someone was knocking on the door. Sniffling, she called out, "Go away!"

"Jill, what's wrong? Please let me in."

"Leave me alone."

"I won't go." Dex's sharp tone carried through the wood. "We have to talk. I'll stay here all night if I have to."

"Be my guest."

He continued pounding on her door until Jill's resistance gave way. She dragged herself off the bed and washed her face in the basin, glaring at the haggard image in the little mirror above. She picked up her comb with shaking hands, found it impossible to unravel the knots in her hair. Well, if Dex couldn't stand the sight of her like this, she might as well find out now. Flinging the comb away, she walked to the door.

In the dim hall, she barely made out the anxious look in his eyes. "I was up half the night thinking of you," Dex told her, pushing into the room. "Then when I discovered you had left, I was furious. But I thought we'd made up this afternoon. Our long talk…" He reached for her hand.

Seeing the doll out of the corner of her eye, Jill started to pull away, but his spicy scent surrounded her. The crying jag had worn her out, and she surrendered to his touch. The ghastly day, her fears for Frank, her doubts about Dex—all were forgotten in her overwhelming need.

He wrapped his arms around her, rubbing her back as she clung to him. He murmured her name over and over until the catches in her breath subsided. "I wasn't really crying," she said, rubbing her nose to disguise the sniffle. She looked up at him but didn't move away.

"Of course not."

"I never cry."

"No. Red noses are the fashion."

"Don't look!" She glared.

He shut his eyes but held on to her.

"I was going to manage all by myself."

"Independence is good, but you never came to say goodbye, Jill, or to hear my warnings. I had a lot of 'thou shalt nots' to lay on you before you left. It upset me to find you gone."

"I had my reasons," she mumbled as he maneuvered her to the bed and sat beside her.

Holding her close, Dex stroked her tousled hair, his strong hands fondling her as gently as his precious pot. "What a shocking welcome to Peru you've had. It's such a beautiful country. I want a chance to show it to you in the right way."

She thrilled to hear the tenderness in his voice. Fighting to subdue the electric charge that coursed through her body each time he touched her, Jill decided to ask Dex about Poppy.

But before she could speak, his mouth was on hers, softly at first, then insistently. As he deepened the kiss, a whirlpool of sensations spun inside her, pulling her under. She forgot where she was, or why. Memories faded into mist. Her body dissolved in his earthy male scent, in the lapis blue of his eyes.

The day's ominous events had driven away her control. Gone were the doubts, the suspicions of Poppy, the years of unfulfilled longings. There was only Dex, the touch of his hands caressing her, exploring her. The heat of his body ignited her blood. She had never responded like this before, never wanted so much to lose herself in a man, to crush him so close they flowed into each other. Jill could hear nothing but the wild beating of her heart!

Until the generator stopped.

In the devastating silence, his fingers grew still. He lifted Jill's hand from his chest. "My God," he whispered. "What am I doing?"

From under heavy lids, she saw his sandy hair fall over glazed eyes. His shirt was open, and the curly hairs she had been pulling on his chest glistened with sweat. His belt was undone, his zipper halfway down, his pants bulging.

How can he stop at a moment like this? Her body throbbed. She wanted to scream, to beg him to continue, but she clamped her mouth shut.

It was this room. It was cursed.

Slowly, she began to pull away. Dex was holding back because of Poppy. They must have made love here on this very bed. When the light dimmed to no more than the sputtering lantern, he had remembered.

Turning away, Jill hooked her bra and buttoned her blouse. She willed herself to hide the hurt. But Dex cupped her chin and swung her around to face him. "This isn't the right time," he said hoarsely. "After what you've been through today, you're too vulnerable. And there's still Frank. I can't take advantage..." His glance darted to her wedding ring.

Before she could unscramble her thoughts to speak, he planted a last long kiss on her bruised lips. "I'm sorry," he whispered. "Forgive me." Throwing the blanket over her, he tucked her in and strode from the room.

Alone on the cot, Jill lay trembling. Her body writhed with thwarted anticipation. She threw off the blanket. How could Dex leave her in a fever of desire? Was this how Anglo lovers behaved? What kind of monster was he?

And yet...his touch was so sweet, his lips so tender. Nowhere could she feel his actions false, his words a lie.

Did he really believe he was taking advantage of her? Ridiculous. She had fully cooperated.

Were they to live with this frustration until Frank showed up? Dex's code of honor was not only old-fashioned, it was obsolete. And what would happen if Poppy returned?

Would there ever be a right time?

Shivering as her sweat evaporated in the cool night

air, Jill curled up tight, her arms crossed over her chest in a forlorn hug. Gradually, exhaustion crept over her once more. Her eyelids slid shut, wet lashes sticking together. As she drifted off into a frazzled sleep, she kept hearing the yearning in Dex's voice, kept responding to the urgency of his embrace.

****

"You've got that rag tied too tight, Manuel."

"No, *señor, por favor*. You must not remove it." The guide slapped at the balding man's hand. *"Mi hermano,* he keel me. We are almost there. *Cinque minutos mas."*

"I will kill you if anything goes wrong," the man grumbled, subsiding as the boat began to rock with his movements.

The mestizo didn't reply. Shortly, the slap of waves against land could be heard. Jumping out, Manuel beached the canoe. The boat rocked, and the startled man opened his mouth to shout. *"Silencio,"* Manuel whispered hoarsely. "I will lead you to cave now, then remove blindfold."

Manuel helped the impatient *jefe* clamber out of the boat, pulled him quickly across a sandy spit of land and up a small incline. The man reached again for the blindfold, and this time he wasn't stopped—they were inside the black hole.

Turning on a pencil flashlight, the guide sent a thin beam up the winding slope of the cave. The men climbed until they reached an opening in the passage. Ahead, nature had carved a huge room out of the rock. Stepping aside, Manuel let his *patrón* enter first. On the floor, burlap sacks surrounded the larger artifacts—vases, sculptures, and masks. A pile of naked dolls had been tossed into a corner, their pink dresses lying in a heap beside them. The visitor's eyes opened wide as the light passed over a breastplate of gold and turquoise links lying on top of the stack. His breaths quickened.

"We must hurry!" Manuel whispered as the balding man continued to stare. With an avaricious grin, *el jefe* stooped and untied the nearest burlap bag. Digging his hand in deep, he came up with a magnificent cloak pin of gold and crystal. He reached again for a silver ceremonial knife, the chunk of turquoise in the handle carved into a jaguar's head.

"We go now!" Manuel whispered urgently. "I hear sound of oars."

One last greedy thrust, and the man's hand came up, clutching a pair of royal ear spools. A row of golden beads encircled a central design of bright feathers.

"Out!" Manuel tugged at the man's arm. There was no time to argue. Sticking the knife in his belt beneath his shirt and the pin in a pants pocket, the man scooped up a pink bootee from the heap of doll clothes on the floor. As they raced back down the corridor, he stuck the earrings into the bootee and stuffed them into his other pocket.

This time, when he felt the air change to the briny scent of the sea, *el patrón* did not object to the blindfold.

****

Jill awoke the next morning determined to put Dex out of her mind. She would concentrate on the problem that had brought her to Peru—finding her almost ex-husband.

Since she was forced to wait for the police to act, she offered to help sort the expedition's records. Harry was grudgingly pleased, and Karen overwhelmingly grateful.

After three hours at the computer, however, she had made little headway. It was maddening. Poppy certainly had an original way of handling statistics. Not quite everything fit into the shape of a pyramid.

In the outer room, a fax machine began to clatter. *Déjà vu.* Jumping up, Jill hurried to receive it. To her surprise, the fax was for her, not Harry. Her brother, Tim, "on their *abuela's* order," was flying down to Peru to make sure she was okay. He would be there before the week was out.

Goodbye to her private moments with Dex. But hadn't she decided to give those up? So why the disappointment?

Returning to the records, Jill grew dizzy from concentrating on the confusing entries. She stopped for an early lunch, passing the area where men and women were sifting soil, first into coarse sieves, then into a finer mesh. Nearby, Dex sat at a table gluing together shards of broken pottery. Jill stopped and watched him work on a pot. His long fingers caressed the round shape forming in his palm.

A stab of pleasure ran through her as she looked at those strong hands, recalling how they had caressed her the night before. The memory of his touch made her quiver, erasing the image of her despair when he'd left. For several moments she watched him, mesmerized by the flash of sun on his nails, the lights dancing off his sun-bleached hair.

Sensing her presence Dex turned, smiled in delight.

"I didn't m-mean to disturb you," she stammered.

He laughed. "You disturb me all the time, Madam

X. That's X for EXecutive. Have you straightened out the dig's files yet?"

"Hardly. What a mess. Poppy's mind couldn't have been on her work." She wanted to kick herself for mentioning Poppy.

His smile disappeared, but then he shrugged. "She probably expected 'Pyramid Power' to put everything in order while she slept."

"I had a similar thought."

"Ah, great minds... Want to see what I'm doing?"

"Yes." She edged closer, and he patted the bench beside him. "Have a seat."

Jill watched, fascinated. "It's like a 3-D jigsaw puzzle," he said. "You match color, shape, markings, and rough edges." He picked up a shard, brushed off the sand and held it out. "Some designs are painted, others etched onto the clay."

"Looks like fun. I loved doing puzzles when I was a kid."

"It can be mighty frustrating when you've hundreds of fragments and don't know how many pots they came from. This mess isn't so bad. Probably only three or four pots, with a few large chunks to serve as guides."

As Dex resumed working, she glanced over the pieces. Spotting two that looked the same shape and color, she reached for them, turning the shards this way and that until they locked together. She looked up, a question in her eyes.

"Seems like a good fit. We'll make a pot hunter out of you yet."

This time, her shudder was less vehement. "I'm starving," she said as she rose. "Let's go eat."

"Give me ten more minutes here—I've got the bowl going well. I'll meet you at the food table." As she returned the shards to the heap, Dex squeezed her hand. The pieces fell from her fingers.

Glancing back as she walked away, Jill saw him already concentrating on his work. Ten minutes, he'd promised.

A half hour later, Dex walked into the chow hall. "Sorry," he said, glancing up at the clock. He held out his hands, palms up. "I got carried away."

Just like Frank…. Jill cut off the thought. She had no right to put herself ahead of his work. She was still married, after all.

What would it be like if she were living with Dex? Refilling her coffee mug, Jill pictured an oasis in the desert. He'd be digging while she sat under an awning, holding a manuscript, sneaking peeks at him above the pages. He'd be shirtless, his back gleaming under the hot desert sun, muscles rippling as he moved. Soon he would join her under the awning and tell her about his finds. As she offered him a cool drink, his hand would touch her arm, his fingers sliding up…up…and the magic would unfurl inside her. They'd race back to their tent, the scorching sun forgotten in the sizzling heat of their passion.

Or maybe it would be spring. Dex would be fitting together pieces of his pottery puzzle at a dig in a meadow, where a riot of wildflowers perfumed the air…

"Why the secretive smile?" He interrupted her daydreams.

"A private fantasy."

"Too private to tell me?" he teased. "I'm into

fantasies."

I'll bet you are. "Maybe someday."

"I'll hold you to it." He laughed as he put together a sandwich, chatting about pots and shards, never once referring to the night before. Jill didn't know whether to be disappointed or relieved. "Gotta get back," he finally said. "See you later."

She watched him go with a longing she couldn't suppress.

****

Alone once again in his beach cabin, Frank Flanders stared at the stunning ear spools in his hands. He had stopped at his secret hiding place to drop the cloak pin and the jeweled knife onto his pile of stolen splendors, but he couldn't bring himself to part with the earrings so soon. Now he gazed at them by firelight, admiring the craftsmanship of the primitive jeweler. The intricacy of the gold work was astonishing, and the diminutive portrait of a warrior inlaid with feathers in the center made him blink in wonder. Too bad he couldn't keep the earrings on his person for long.

Where could he hide these little gems? The bootee he had used to carry them out of the cave lay on his bed, reminding him he had given a doll to that kid, Poppy, when he was angling to get into her pants. It gave him an idea.

Frank picked up the tiny map he had drawn from memory when his blindfold slipped. It would come in handy if he decided to return, and if it were found, no one would be able to interpret his sketchy symbols. Carefully, he folded the map around the ear spools and replaced them inside the bootee. One had fallen off Poppy's doll before, but the scatterbrain had never noticed. She'd be just as oblivious to its return.

His new lover would hide the earrings for him. Frank's lips twisted into a feral smile. She would do *anything* for her Francisco.

Chapter 12

"Excuse me."

Timothy Adams turned away from the airplane window to see a slim blonde standing in the aisle holding a backpack. She was a fox! Her lemon-drop hair hung straight down from a central part, while thick bangs nearly covered her eyes. A crystal pyramid the size of a peach pit hung from a fine gold chain, drawing his attention to her high round breasts under a neon green T-shirt. He noticed her jeans, too—held up by a macramé belt with tassels on the ends that bounced as she moved.

Tim sat up straighter, his knees at an awkward angle, since his feet rested on a large duffel protruding from the seat in front. The one beside him was still empty, and he pointed. "Yours?"

The girl nodded.

"Would you rather sit by the window?"

She gave him a delighted smile. "No thanks. The aisle seat will be fine, but could you help me with my backpack? It's a small one. I think there might be enough room to wedge it into the corner of this compartment overhead."

Tim swung his feet off the duffel and sidestepped to the aisle. The girl stood close as he forced the backpack into the narrow slot. He breathed in the scent of white lilacs.

"Thanks." Her smile dazzled him as he popped back into his seat. She glanced around the cabin and sat down, the tassels on her belt sliding with a faint swoosh between her legs. "I'm so glad you speak English. Nice that we get to sit together for such a long flight."

"It certainly is." Dragging his eyes from the tassels, Tim grinned at her.

"You on vacation?" she asked as she fastened her seat belt.

"Sort of. I'm in law school, but right now I'm chasing after my sister. How about you?"

"I'm supposed to be helping out on an archaeological dig, but I played hooky for a week. Had an urge to go skiing. My home's in Vermont."

"I've been there. Mom wanted the family to see the Grandma Moses museum one summer."

"You know her paintings? Parts of Vermont are still like that, covered bridges and all. Quaint." She wrinkled her nose. "I'm bored when I'm there, but when I go away I miss it, especially during ski season. Where are you from?"

Tim blinked. The way her hair swung about, just brushing his shoulder, rattled him. "Uh, Boston, right now."

"I'll bet it never gets boring there!"

He grinned. "Well, no, but sometimes it's nice to get away. I liked how green everything was in Vermont. It's a lot different from Peru, isn't it?"

"Sure is, the desert part. 'Course there's the jungle, too. It's so hot and muggy there you can wring out the air, yet it's different…exotic."

"I expect I'll find everything in Peru exotic."

"Is this your first trip to South America?"

"Mm hmm. What brings you to Lima? Is your dig near?"

"No, that's just where the plane lands. I've got to get back to the Moche Indian site, farther north."

"How come you're returning before Christmas? Won't your family miss you?"

"Mom and Dad are off on a cruise. Aunt Linda is down here somewhere on a hunt for handicrafts. She runs a boutique selling gifts from around the world."

"Sounds like a fascinating career."

"Oh, it is. She hires a small transport plane, just big enough for two people and the cargo. She and her pilot fly around to all the little villages looking for the handmade stuff."

"Wow!"

"Yeah. My family's always up and running. Last week, I had this terrific urge to shoot down a mountain, feel that icy wind on my face." She dimpled. "I have a reputation for being impetuous. I'm a Pisces, ya know, so it's expected. I get these vibrations from the pyramid crystal. Then I've gotta do something right away."

Tim couldn't take his gaze off her fingers playing with the sparkling pink ornament lying between the swell of her breasts. "Like Joseph Campbell said, 'Follow your bliss'?"

Her smile grew even wider, and his heart began to thump. "That's it, exactly. I feel I know you well already!"

"So you left the dig on a whim?"

"I had another reason, too. One of the older guys at the site started putting the moves on me." She scowled. "It was getting uncomfortable, so I decided to leave."

"That sucks."

"Yeah. Will you be staying in Lima?"

"Nope. I'm headed for a site near Trujillo. The Pyramid of the Stars."

She stared at him. "Hey, that's the same one I work at. *Huaca de las Estrellas.*"

"No kidding! Then I'll be seeing you again." They smiled warmly at each other. "How are you getting to the dig?" he asked.

"Bus, it's the cheapest. You, too?"

"I suppose so. Hadn't figured out that part. Perhaps we can travel together?"

"Great idea. It's a long bus ride, and it'll be nice to have someone to talk to."

"Then we should introduce ourselves. I'm Tim."

"Poppy. Is your sister at the dig?"

"Mm hmm. She's on some crazy mission to find her missing husband. Maybe you know him, Frank Flanders?"

"Uh-oh," Poppy mumbled. "The crystal strikes again."

"What did you say?"

"Nothing. Just thinking out loud."

"So why are you going back, if that guy gave you so much trouble?"

"Leaving wasn't fair. I'm their computer expert." She winked and grinned. "And he'll be over it by now. I gave him time to cool off."

"Well, that guy was no friend." Tim persisted. "What's his name? I'll watch out for him when you're around."

Poppy spoke the first name that came into her head. "Dex," she lied. Crossing her fingers, she turned their conversation to other topics.

Before Tim realized it, they were landing in Lima. He helped Poppy take down her backpack, watching the bright green shirt stretch tight across her breasts when she reached up. He breathed a little faster. Passengers crowded the aisle, and a heavy woman shoved her way into the line.

Poppy poked Tim. "Look," she said. "That woman is carrying a baby doll just like the one I left back at the dig."

He turned around. *"Feliz Navidad.* Wonder what they use for Christmas trees down here."

"Let's find out. You speak Spanish?"

"Yeah, my grandparents on Mom's side are from Argentina, so I kinda picked it up."

"I never was any good at foreign languages. It's a talent I'm missing." She pouted. "All those strange things your mouth has to do." Poppy made a little gargling sound, rolling an "r."

Tim stared at her pink lips as the husky sound emerged. This trip had the makings of a much better vacation than he'd expected. He reached out and adjusted the backpack straps on her shoulders, breathing in white lilacs again. "Is there time to snack on some real Peruvian food before we get on the bus?" he asked.

"Oh, yeah. A Quechua Indian sells ears of corn at the station. Wait till you see the size of the kernels, all slathered in butter. They're huge. I never saw corn like it back in the States."

Tim ran his tongue across his teeth. He could watch Poppy's mouth again, shining with melted butter as she bit into the cob. This trip kept getting better and better.

"Will you have to go back to work as soon as you get there?"

"'Fraid so. I'm behind in cataloguing the dig's finds. There's more than a week's data to download into the computer."

"Hope you'll have some time to show me around." He sounded anxious.

"Oh, I'm sure I can fit it in."

Tim gazed into her eyes and laughed. The message had been received.

****

Jill spent another frustrating session at the office computer. As she left, Karen handed her an envelope filled with correspondence sent on by her New York office to the site's weekly mailbag. "More junk mail," she muttered, and dumped it into her carryall. Dragging herself back to her room, she soaked a washcloth in cold water and lay down, placing the compress on her forehead. The doll lay on the pillow beside her. Absently, she ran her fingers through the fake yellow hair.

She would stay until Tim came—but then, what? Should she give up and head back to New York? Would she ever see Dex again? Would all the fascinating new emotions she was experiencing be forgotten by next year?

Annoyed at the direction her thoughts were taking, Jill twisted the doll's long hair around her wrist. She imagined Poppy beneath her frenzied fingers, and gave the toy a vigorous shake. As her anger subsided, she heard a rattling noise. Did the sound come from inside the doll?

Jill shook it again, even harder. Yes, there definitely was a rattle. Intrigued, she slipped her hand under the organdy dress and felt the doll's body. Her fingers touched a tiny slit in the back she hadn't noticed before, as if the doll required a windup key to start it walking. Removing the bonnet, she slid the little pink dress over its head. She stared at the inch-long crack above the doll's rounded rump, then tried inserting her fingernail.

At first nothing happened. Hoping her nail wouldn't break, Jill began to twist her finger. The crack grew longer. Excited now, she rose to get a nail file, then pressed the doll into the mattress and exerted pressure. Suddenly, the spot gave. A block of plastic skin covering the doll's back sprang out, revealing the cotton batting that filled the interior.

Eagerly, Jill dug her fingers into the stuffing. When she felt nothing, she shook the doll again. The rattle was still there, so she began pulling out wads of filling. Deep down in the little rump, her fingernail clicked on something firm. She turned her hand inside the cavity and touched a bumpy packet. Flipping the doll over, Jill spanked its bottom hard, dislodging a paper-wrapped bundle. One more vigorous shake, and it tumbled out.

Grabbing the little package, Jill unfolded the paper. She gasped, hardly able to believe what she was seeing. Resting inside was a pair of gold and turquoise ear spools over an inch in diameter. They were magnificent! Picking one up, she turned it round and round. In the center, brightly colored feathers had been woven into an intricate design of a warrior. He was surrounded by a ring of gold. A mosaic of turquoise chips formed an outer ring, and a wider band of golden balls encircled the entire piece. These earrings were fit for a princess.

Or, judging from their size—a prince.

For several moments Jill sat on the bed, staring at the jewels in her hand. The perfection of the workmanship held her in awe. The smooth gleam of gold, the exquisitely matched sky-blue turquoise, the brilliant red-and-yellow feathers. The ear spools were sensational!

At last she pulled herself together. Shoving the piece of wrapping paper into her pocket, she closed her fingers tightly around the spools and ran from the room. The naked doll was left facedown on the bed, surrounded by cotton batting. In the sunlight beaming through the open window, the gaping hole in its back cast a dark shadow.

As Jill raced along the path, face flushed and ponytail bouncing, she tripped over a large pebble. She staggered, her fists still tightly closed, and glanced back. Were there eyes peering out of her window, watching her? She squinted. No, it had to be a trick of the light.

Approaching the work area, she slowed. The place was humming with activity. A college boy with a Maori tattoo on his arm, that was Hank, shoveled earth into a coarse sieve. Another, must be Don without the tattoos, wet down the dirt and handed it to the girl from UA, Marge, who wore a silver snake twined around her right earlobe. She sifted the fragments through an even finer sieve, picked out pieces of clay, and laid them out to dry in the sun. At the long table Dex sat among his colleagues, writing in a notebook.

"Dex!" she called breathlessly.

Frowning, he turned and saw her. His scowl disappeared, but his look was still distant. "I'll be with you in a minute, Jill. Have to finish checking these figures."

She stood behind him, switching her weight from one foot to the other. He finally quit working, glanced at her feet and started to suggest a trip to the outhouse. His teasing stopped mid-sentence as his eyes rose to her face. "What's wrong?"

Furtively, Jill looked around, then slid onto the bench beside him. She slipped her fisted hands under the tabletop to shield them from view. "I found something," she whispered, opening her fingers one at a time so that only Dex could see what lay in her palms. At his quick intake of breath, she fisted her hands again.

He gripped her shoulder, lips barely moving. "Where did you find them?"

"Did you notice Poppy left a big doll in her room?"

"Mmm… Something pink?"

"Yes, the ear spools were hidden inside the doll. And, Dex, it's wearing two bootees, but when I arrived it had only one on. I found the other bootee in a pocket of Frank's best *guayabera* shirt and stuck it in my jeans pocket. It's still there, I checked. So how did it get back on the doll?"

"Odd…"

"There's something else. Remember when you met me at the airport? Several native women on the plane were carrying dolls almost identical to this one. They stuffed them in the overhead compartments. The scene was so macabre I even dreamed about it that night." She shivered.

Taking her arm, Dex moved them off the bench

and away from the table. "It looks like the looters are using the dolls to smuggle small items—jewelry like these earrings, or loose gems. The dogs can't sniff those." He grimaced. "It's time we informed Lieutenant Castillo. We still need to report the blowgun shot aimed at you, but this loot will grab his attention even sooner."

"Should we tell Harry first?"

"At the moment, let's keep it to ourselves. The fewer who know about your find, the better. I think Harry is hiding something. He's been stalling about bringing in the police."

"I noticed that too. Still, there could be other reasons for his behavior."

"I know. Part of me thinks it's impossible to link Harry with what's going on, but he does need more money for the dig. Funds are drying up, and our discoveries are vital to his reputation. If he sells just a few pieces to raise some cash…"

So Dex didn't even trust Harry. What a snake pit this was turning out to be. "Do you think our glorious leader could be in cahoots with Frank?"

"They weren't the best of friends… Still, the lust for gold makes strange bedfellows. I'd like to wring Frank's neck."

Jill winced. "What's the next step?" she asked.

"I want to reflect on this. Meanwhile, we've got to hide the artifacts safely until we can get them to the police."

"Should we put them back inside the doll?"

"No. Someone else knows they were there."

"Of course, I'm too excited to think straight."

"I'll bet that doesn't happen often, Madame X." He winked. "But enough whispering. People are giving us suspicious looks. Give me a few minutes to finish measuring these pots."

"I'll wait here. Don't want to return alone with these in my hands."

Dex grinned. "Need a strong arm to protect you?"

"You bet your bootees!"

Five minutes later, he closed his notebook. They left together, his hand covering one of her tightly closed fists.

As they reached the women's quarters, Jill admitted why she had shaken the doll so vigorously. Dex eyed her. "Jealous of Poppy?" he asked, his tone unsure.

Forgetting that he knew nothing about her eavesdropping in the shower shack, Jill defended herself. "Poppy's still a kid. If she's mixed up in this, she's doing some very dangerous things."

They came to her door, and Dex pushed it open. The doll was no longer lying on her bed. It had been flung into a corner of the room, the wrinkled dress and crushed bonnet fluttering on the floor beside it.

Jill gasped. "Someone's been in my room. The doll has been moved!"

"Whoever did it just left." He strode to the window and peered out. No one was in sight.

"Hang on a minute." He ran out.

Gnawing on a knuckle with worry, Jill watched from the window. She saw him round the corner of the building and race along the outside. In a few minutes he returned, disgusted. "No sign of anyone, and the sand is too scuffed for footprints."

She sighed. "What do we do now?"

"You'll be safer if you give the ear spools to me.

I'll hide them in my room. I doubt anyone would search for them there."

"Take them." She thrust the earrings at him. "I'm paranoid about having them around." Her mouth tightened. "I hate the thought of someone pawing through my things."

He took them from her, squeezed her hand. "When the office is empty this evening, I'll call Castillo and hint that he request an official visit from me tomorrow. Harry will have a fit, but I don't want these ear spools in my possession a minute longer than necessary."

"Then you're really not going to tell Harry?"

"It's too dangerous. Even if he's not involved, the news is bound to leak out. The fewer people who know about your find, the safer you'll be. When I talk to the lieutenant, I'll insist that he keep your name out of this affair entirely."

Her heart sank. Dex was planning to do this on his own. "Can't I go with you?" she appealed. "After all, I was the one who found the earrings."

"Well," he raised an eyebrow, "as long as I'm taking the day off, and you've given up on the computer, there's no reason why we can't include a picnic on the beach. Since you got here, Jill, you've been shot at, accosted, and had your room broken into. You deserve an afternoon's relaxation. First we'll face the police, then we'll catch some well-earned R&R."

Her smile was spellbinding. "I can hardly wait!"

****

Harry was furious.

Dex paused until the storm clouds blew over. "I'll work at night, Harry," he cajoled. "Make nice, now. It's almost Christmas."

"You know there's not enough light once the generator goes off."

"Then I'll transcribe my notes onto my laptop. The screen is bright."

"What about the deadline? You know we have a deadline!"

"Of course. You'll have my deductions about the paintings on the pot clearly documented before then. On my honor."

Rolling his eyes, Harry grumbled. "I'm gonna count on that."

"And I'll start work at the crack of dawn."

"Yeah, and you've got a bridge to sell me."

Dex grinned. He slapped Harry on the back. "Not to worry. This dig means a lot to me, too. My reputation is also on the line."

"Hmmph. Well, get back as soon as you can."

"Sure, sure."

****

At eight the next morning Jill met Dex, her hair swinging loosely on her shoulders. She wore her freshly washed blue and white dotted sundress, chosen to soften the lieutenant's attitude toward women. When Dex spied her, she could see the memory of their picnic kiss reflected in her own.

Ignoring the twinkle in his eyes, she stepped up into the cab of the truck. A familiar whistle came from behind her, and she bit her lip to keep from laughing.

"Did you bring a bathing suit?" he asked.

"It's in here," she pointed to her carryall, "along with my straw hat."

"Good. I like your hair swaying across that gorgeous neck. I've heard the Japanese find necks the sexiest part of a woman's body." Reaching over, he lifted her hair and blew on her nape, then pressed his lips to the spot.

She gulped as he twisted a strand of hair around his finger. "Weren't we talking about the Japanese?"

"Ah so. Velly nice."

Jill giggled. Dex was incorrigible. Reaching for his hand, she replaced it on the steering wheel. "I like your neck, too." She put an arm around his shoulders, letting the inside of her wrist slide back and forth beneath his sandy hair. "But the front seat of your truck is much too public a place."

"Who's teasing now?" Laughing, Dex started the engine. "The thought of *policía* will keep me in check for a while."

They drove along in silent pleasure, enjoying the anticipation of a special day. In the brilliant blue sky, cottony puffs of cloud floated above the mountaintops, wrapping the peaks in collars of ermine. Jill sighed with contentment.

After the first hour she dug into her carryall and brought out a bagful of fresh cherries. "Want some fruit?"

He glanced at her. "Feed me."

Jill popped a cherry into his mouth, feeling the softness of his lips as they wrapped around her finger. She closed her eyes. Dex murmured, "The pit," and they flashed open.

Leaning over, she held her hand under his chin. As he dropped the pit into her palm, his tongue wriggled across her sensitive flesh. A quiver ran through her.

"More," he demanded.

"Uh, m-maybe it's not such a good idea," she

stammered, "while you're driving."

He turned once more and grinned at her. "I can stand the torture if you can."

"Dex, please watch the road!"

He chuckled, straightened the wheels. "So feed me. I promise I won't look at you."

She popped another cherry into his mouth, sensing the promise of his lips, the softness of his beard as she held her hand for the pit. Once again she felt the tickle of his tongue on her palm. It *was* torture, delicious torture.

They drove on, Jill attempting to widen the distance between feeding him cherries, while Dex prompted her to continue. At last, the outskirts of Trujillo came in sight.

"What are you planning to say to the lieutenant?" she asked.

"You're not coming in with me?"

"I've had second thoughts. I think my presence will only make it harder for you...to get information," she added as his lips quirked.

"Well, boss, I'll show him the ear spools and tell him where you found them. Then I'll ask for info on the search for Frank and the looters. Will that satisfy you?"

She punched his arm. "Are the earrings in your knapsack?"

"Mm hmm."

"I'd like to look at them one last time before you turn them over."

"Okay." Dex parked near the police station and reached for his knapsack. He'd wrapped the ear spools in an old T-shirt and handed it to Jill.

She unwrapped his shirt, enjoying the masculine

scent wafting to her nose. A moment later, turquoise and gold gleamed, their reflections dancing on the windshield. Red-and-yellow feathers sparkled. Jill was awed. "These earrings are magnificent, but they'd be awfully uncomfortable on a woman."

"More likely they were made for a priest or a king. From what we've learned so far, many of these tribes liked discomfort. We found evidence that the ruling Mayan males pierced their penis with a rope of thorns."

"Good Lord. It hurts me just to hear the words."

"Think of what that visual does to me."

Jill gulped. "Omigod. Yes."

"The primitive still retains its ability to shock, doesn't it?"

"Mm hmm. Whatever we think man is capable of, he always surprises us."

"Alarms us, more like. Now, I've a request before I face my grueling ordeal." His crooked smile appeared. "One more cherry from your tender fingers, and a different way of getting rid of the pit."

She reached into her carryall, got out a cherry and popped it into his mouth.

"Delicious." Red cherry juice glinted at the corner of his lips. She reached up to wipe it, but he grabbed her hand. "Lick it off, and I'll give you the pit."

His mouth came down to hers. Her tongue slid out to catch the juice, and he pressed his lips to hers, rolling the pit down her tongue. Then his kiss deepened.

Jill clung to him, lost in the sweet taste of his cherry covered tongue. She moaned, forced herself to push him away. "This is another public place, and the wrong time too."

Lifting his head, his voice rough, Dex vowed, "A

right time and place is coming soon, I promise."

Jill's smile couldn't hide her yearning. Taking the cherry pit from between her teeth, she popped it into a pocket for a memento. "I'll meet you in the plaza," she pointed, "on that bench under the palm tree."

"Right." He finger-combed his hair. "As soon as I'm through we'll have lunch. I know a great restaurant with a patio on the beach."

"Sure you aren't too full of cherries?" she teased.

"Never." Grabbing his knapsack, he came around and helped her down from the truck. "Don't pick up any handsome Latinos while I'm gone," he admonished. "And keep the jacket on."

"Now, now, don't go getting possessive."

"Behave yourself." He grinned wickedly. "I remember the reaction you got the first time I saw you in that dress. I should be back before you get into too much trouble."

"But getting into trouble is okay with you, right?"

"Oh yeah. Right time, right place, right partner— trouble is good." His fingers danced up her arm, starting the tingle. And then he left.

Chapter 13

Relaxed now, Jill sat on the fancy wrought-iron bench beside the plaza and absorbed the busy scenes around her. Children playing tag. Women in embroidered dresses carrying baskets of fruit. A man selling roasted corn from a cart. Another, in a striped poncho, offering chunks of sugar cane. A photographer with camera on a tripod, waylaying tourists. Bouncy music from a teenager's boom box.

She gazed at the passersby, absently twisting her wedding band round and round her finger. Suddenly aware of what she was doing, Jill looked down, spotted the red stain under her nails from the cherry juice, and dug into the carryall for tissues to clean them. As she delved, her fingers touched the mail packet Karen had handed her yesterday. In the excitement of finding the ear spools, she had forgotten all about it. Licking her fingers, she cleaned them with the tissues and took out the correspondence.

Jill shuffled through the ads, discarding the pile. Reaching a thick brown envelope with her office return address, she opened it. A note from Francine, her secretary, was attached to a pile of papers. "These arrived from your lawyers," she had written, "with a memo attached informing you that Mrs. Flanders Sr. apparently forgot to mail them. The lawyers received them right after Thanksgiving, but as you'll see, the original date on the correspondence is mid-September. I thought you might be anxious for them." Francine had added a little smiley face to her signature.

Heart thumping, Jill unfolded the papers. She peered at them all, turning the pages slowly. The bottom of each carried the signature, "Francisco Esteban Lorenzo Flanders." A long sigh escaped. Frank had indeed signed the divorce papers. She'd been right when she said he, too, was eager to be free. Yet he had left them with his mother. She wondered if he knew how Mama would react. She wouldn't put it past him to have counted on it.

Once again, Jill glanced at the signatures. It was a good thing the family had changed their last name when they came to the U.S. Otherwise, it wouldn't have fit on the line. At last, she could joke about it.

She hugged the papers to her breast for a full minute before replacing them in the envelope. Then, with a decisive nod, she slid the ring from her finger, opened the purse she carried inside the carryall, and dropped it in. At the tiny clink it made when it hit her compact, she snapped the purse shut. Shoving the envelope back in, she took a deep breath. Her lips curled into a secretive, satisfied smile.

Still grinning as her stomach rumbled, Jill debated buying a stalk of sugar cane to munch on. Where was Dex? She looked across the street. As if she had conjured him, Dex was there, peering anxiously about. He spotted her sitting on the bench and hurried over.

"Sorry it took me so long, but I'm relieved to have those baubles off my hands." He sat down beside her.

"How did the police react?"

"Lieutenant Castillo was *muy* excited. This confirmed his suspicion that someone at the dig is involved with the looters. But he warned me again that these men are dangerous, Jill. Completely ruthless. The police have found more corpses than they've told the public." He looked closely at her. "Did anyone else see you with the ear spools?"

"I don't think so. I kept them hidden in my palms, with my fingers wrapped tightly around them. Remember? When we returned to my room, I gave them to you."

"But the doll on the floor made it clear an intruder had been there. I don't like it. Someone knows you found the jewelry."

"But I don't have the earrings any more. We don't know who put them there, so the burglar is safe."

"He can't be certain of that."

"The police said this was the work of professionals. It won't do them any good to come after me now. Don't worry so." She reached up to smooth the lines wrinkling his forehead. "I'm hungry. The restaurant you mentioned is calling my name."

Covering her hand, Dex moved it to his mouth and kissed her knuckles. His tongue gave a quick lick at a spot between two fingers, and she jumped.

"Okay. We've got better things to do," he said. "Let's forget our worries for today. Onward to *Los Mariscos*."

They walked arm in arm to his truck. As they drove north out of Trujillo, stretches of smooth, sandy beach came into sight. The restaurant nestled between palms near the tiny village of Huanchaco. Under red-and-white striped umbrellas flapping in the ocean breeze, tables were set on a patio overlooking the sea. A waiter hurried over to seat them. All around, guests were munching on pizza-like tortillas, spread with salsa and loaded with lobster, shrimp, and fish just hauled out of the sea. Red peppers, black olives, and goat cheese decorated the tops.

The aroma was delectable. Turning away from the wavelets skipping over one another in their rush to meet the shore, Jill smiled at Dex in pleasure. When their Pilsen Callao's arrived, she lifted her beer in a toast. "To my idea of heaven—lobster pizzas under a blue Pacific sky."

"Hear, hear." He raised his mug. "To us, and today's magic." He took a long swallow. "Your eyes are moss agate today." He scrutinized her face. "Deep, deep green, sparkling with golden rutiles."

"And yours," she examined him, "are that sliver of turquoise where the aqua dissolves into the sea's deep blue."

"Sounds like a poem," he teased.

"They're worth a verse. Roses are red/ Your eyes turquoise blue/ Mine are moss agate/ But will you be true?" Jill snickered as the meaning of her impromptu words hit her. What had she unexpectedly revealed?

"So that's what you want to know. Gotcha!"

"Wait, wait. I'll change that last line to, 'I think I should sue.'"

"Too late. Hasn't got the same ring to it."

"Well, I won't submit it for publication." They laughed and toasted again.

After lunch, Jill and Dex walked along the sea's edge carrying their shoes and the picnic blanket, leaving their footprints to be washed away by the tide.

The shorefront was dotted with huge boulders. Eventually, they passed the rocky area and the scattered sunbathers to venture into unexplored territory. Around them, nothing moved.

Dex led Jill up a sand dune. With each footstep, a tiny funnel of sand drifted down behind them. Whooping with laughter, they slid down the other side. He spread their blanket in a sheltered spot between two towering dunes. Jill raised her arms and spun, her sundress whirling around her thighs. "What an enchanted spot." The secluded site held only the warmth of the sun, the rumble of the waves. Above them, seabirds wheeled and glided, calling in sharp, high notes.

Dropping to the blanket, Dex reached up and took her hand. As he squeezed it, he raised an eyebrow, confused. "Jill, you're not wearing your wedding ring." He pulled her down beside him. "Did you lose it?"

Her eyes twinkled. "Not exactly."

"What does that mean?"

She laughed at his puzzled look. "I've got a surprise for you."

"Oh?" He sounded suspicious. "I'm not sure I like surprises."

"You'll like his one, I promise." She stroked his cheek. "When I quit work on the computer yesterday, Karen handed me a packet of mail from home. I put it in my carryall and soon after that took out my frustration on Poppy's doll. That's when I heard the rattle inside and found the ear spools. I got so excited by my discovery, I forgot all about the mail until I was waiting for you in the plaza. I opened it up—and guess what?"

He stared at her, still not comprehending. Taking the papers from her carryall, she handed them to him. "Voila! I'm officially divorced!"

Startled, Dex looked at the papers. After a minute's perusal, his eyes widened and a huge smile broke out. "You're a free woman!"

"Free as a bird." Jumping up, she twirled around. He rose and grabbed her, danced her around the dune. Happy laughter mingled with birdcalls until the laughter turned into sighs and the sighs into kisses. It wasn't until much later that Jill told him about the delay in receiving the divorce.

"Mama got even, at least for a while."

Dex pulled her even closer. "It's incredible not having to wait any longer." He kissed her again, his mouth devouring her. "Why did you wait so long before telling me?"

With a sigh, Jill snuggled into him. "Before I left New York I was told I'd be safer traveling as a married woman. Then, when I met you, I let you assume what you wanted."

"You knew it wasn't what I wanted!"

"I didn't know for sure. Are you going to punish me?" She looked up, batted her eyelashes.

"You bet! You'll feel it from the top of your head to the tips of your toes."

"Promises, promises."

His mouth brushed her hair. "You smell like moonlit lemon blossoms. Sweet and tangy." His hands moved down her body, exploring, while he swept his tongue in her ear. She shivered, grabbed at his shirt. The straps of her sundress slid down her arms, and he cupped her breasts, bent to lick a rosy nipple.

Fire radiated from his touch, and Jill melted into him. Her hands began to roam over his body as well, touching and squeezing until their heated foreplay speeded up, grew wild, and left them both shaking.

"I…ah…have some condoms in my carryall," Jill gasped.

Bursting with unexpected laughter, Dex hugged her tightly. "Madam Executive," he murmured in her ear, "how I love your efficiency."

She handed them over, and they fell back on the blanket, resuming their hot, frantic kisses. His hardness pressed into her as his hands crept beneath the sundress. Running the silk of her panties between his fingers, Dex slid them to her ankles. With a kiss to each foot, he lifted them off. Jill reached out and tugged at his zipper. A moment later, they were naked.

This first time, neither could slow down. His fingers caressed her moist opening, and Jill shuddered, arching into him. Her ragged moan streaked through his body like lightning. He ran his teeth across a nipple, sucked her breast into his mouth. As she gasped, he moved to the other, then dropped kisses all the way down her torso, his tongue swirling. She closed her eyes, her legs parting at his touch. He slid into her, deep inside, and she forgot to breathe. Together they rode the rising waves, until her scream of pleasure and his shout of joy plunged them into the churning whirlpool.

Locked in his arms, Jill panted until the ecstatic shivers slowed and finally stopped, leaving a delicious feeling of languor. She glided her fingers through his hair as Dex rested his head on her breast, lips moving in lazy, fluttery kisses.

Eventually, reluctantly, he withdrew. "Want a

swim?"

Shaking off the lovely, boneless feeling, she sat up and reached into her carryall for her bikini.

"No skinny dipping?" he teased.

"A boat could pass close by," she mumbled. Hand in hand, they ran down to the water. Jill clung to his arm, dipped in a toe, pulled back. "The water's a bit rough, today."

"Are you afraid?" he asked.

"A bit." She took a few more steps. "There seems to be an undertow."

"It'll be calmer beyond the breakers."

"I know, but I'm uneasy. Go ahead and swim, I'll play in the water. It feels lovely when the waves break over my body. Tell you a secret. I could gaze at the ocean for hours, but I'd rather swim in a pool."

"Ah-ha. So there is something that can scare you."

"Well, I'm human."

Dex gave her a quick hug. "I'm going to find out what's behind that fear, you know, but not now. You'll be okay if I take a short swim?"

"Honestly, I like splashing about in the waves. Brings back happy childhood memories. I won't miss you."

"Is that a challenge?"

She kissed his salty cheek and gave him a push. "Have fun."

Dex swam out beyond the cresting waves. Jill watched anxiously for a moment, but when she saw his sleek body moving effortlessly through the water, she returned to jumping the waves, giddy with laughter as she recalled her dream that first night in Peru. Somehow her subconscious had known they would share the sea. It was a mystery.

Feeling an unexpected shape between her legs, Jill leaped, but Dex was beside her, his hands stroking her beneath the waves. "All washed nice and clean?"

"Mm hmm."

Without warning, he picked her up and carried her out of the water. She leaned her head on his broad shoulder. "You've had your swimming fix?"

"In the ocean. I haven't done enough swimming in other pools of bliss." He ran his tongue slowly across her lips. "And this time I'm not in such a hurry."

Jill marveled at her body's instant, thrumming response. She stripped off her wet suit. Already naked, Dex stood legs apart, outlined by the sunlight. The wicked, sexy smile on his lips turned her on. Once again, she saw her golden god.

I'm falling in love with the man. Jill knew the truth in that instant. She had no desire to break her fall— short term or long, she was hooked.

Does a mortal always pay, the fleeting thought crossed her mind, *when she gives her heart to a god?*

Dex sat down beside her. "You're breathtaking, lying on the blanket with nothing but your tumbling hair to cover you. I'll dream of this moment, forever."

Your dreams will have company.

He bent over and lapped at her breast. His tongue circled the nipple, and as it peaked he began to nibble, first on one, then on the other. The delicious pleasure drove the thrills downward till she ached below. Jill had never felt this way with Frank. His touch had always been self-serving. She moaned as Dex's thumbnail flicked back and forth, and the fleeting memory of her ex faded away.

Trailing a series of tiny kisses all the way down to her navel and beyond, he reached for her foot. "Let's start from the bottom, this time."

"What do you mean?"

"Tell me how you like this." His fingernails drummed a tickling tattoo on the soles of her foot, and a tingling sensation radiated upward. He leaned down and took a toe in his mouth, biting gently.

She gasped.

"Feels good?" He slid his tongue along the base of her toes, then nibbled and sucked on each in turn. "Your scent is as fresh and foamy as the sea, *sirena*. You taste salty and tangy. The flavor is—shrimp cocktail."

She giggled. "With sand for the sauce?"

"No sand. Why do you think I carried you?" He nuzzled her instep as he spoke.

"My God," she breathed. "I could become a foot fetishist. It's an incredible delight, just as long as you don't stop there."

"This is just the appetizer!" He lightly massaged her heel, then nipped at the tender spot behind where it joined her leg. Jill was lost in a wave of sensation. Pressing a kiss onto her instep, he reached for her other foot. "Have to play fair."

Her mind completely blown, Jill reveled in the sensual feelings Dex evoked. His lips began to move up her calf, behind her knee, inside her thigh, kissing and caressing until he ran his fingers through the dark ringlets curled tight between her legs. He parted her heated folds, a finger pushing deeper as his lips nibbled on her most sensitive spot.

With a gasp Jill arched against him, pulling him

even closer. "I can't wait any longer," she moaned. "Come with me, Dex."

His eyes were glazed, his erection huge, as he slipped on the condom, slid up her body, and wrapped her legs around his waist. Drinking in her wanton whispers, he plunged into her. Pulling partway out, he thrust even harder. Jill felt as if she'd swallowed him completely, and it was glorious.

Together they rocked, side to side, in and out, harder, faster. The music of Jill's cries outdid the birdcalls. Wave after wave of pleasure surged until, in a huge flare of rainbow colors, they exploded.

Sated, limp with satisfaction, they lay motionless, letting the ocean breeze dry the sweat from their bodies. At last, Jill pushed Dex gently away.

"I think I've had about all the sun I can take."

"Good Lord. I hadn't thought of that." He sat up quickly. "Aren't you wearing sun screen?"

"On the parts of me that are usually exposed, yes. But the rest of my body isn't used to it. It's not used to a lot of the things that happened," she grinned at him, "but it wouldn't mind if they became a habit."

"That's a wrap." His smile was sly. "We'd better get you back to a warm shower and some good lotion." Handing Jill her clothes, Dex put on his jeans and shirt.

They walked back along the beach, swinging hands. She paused now and then to pick up pretty pebbles and unusual shells. Since the wind off the water kept blowing her hat off, she used it instead as a basket for her finds. The breeze flowed through her hair, heightening the day's sensual magic. It did a number on her full skirt too, catching it and lifting it as high as her hips. Jill laughed and let her skirt blow, in the mood to tease. From the look on his face, Dex was enjoying the view.

"That scrap of silk under your dress is sexier than a thong," he murmured, and she winked.

As they passed a huge boulder off shore, Jill pointed. "Isn't that dark shadow an opening in the rock, Dex? I don't recall seeing it before. The tide must be ebbing."

"Too bad it wasn't visible earlier. We could have found a private cave out of the sun."

"Today was perfect just as it was. And there's always next time…"

"That's my girl!" Eyes twinkling, he squeezed her butt, then ran a finger all the way down between the globes.

"Enough!" She'd never make it back if he kept her quivering. Jill moved his hand to her waist. "Soon Harry will have a posse out looking for us."

"Ready to rope me to the nearest palm and string me up," Dex added. "Or more likely, tie me to a prickly cactus. You win. It's back to work."

They returned to the inhabited area of the beach, passing the ancient reed boats still used for trapping crabs and lobsters. Tipped up to dry in the sun, curved prows buried in the sand, the boats resembled an octopus's waving arms. As Dex explained how the traps worked, they were interrupted by a loud noise.

Four motorcycles roared past. Their shadow crossed the couple on the beach, and then was gone.

"Wh-what on earth?" Jill stammered, turning to watch the men in dark gear and black helmets.

Dex scowled. He looked down at the tracks left on the sand, then turned back to the ancient boats.

"Incongruous, isn't it? Probably some teenagers out to make noise. Let's not allow it to spoil our day."

She returned her gaze to the reed boats. Behind them, the setting sun sparkled on the water. As the roar of the machines faded, she listened to the birds calling, breathed in the spicy scent of the sea. "This is the scene I'll always remember when I look back on our special day."

"There are other scenes I'll remember first."

She glanced up to catch him grinning. Her thoughts flew to the moment he had stood naked between the dunes, outlined in golden sunlight. "Mmm." She ran her tongue along her lips. "You may have something there…"

The last swirls of billowing sand subsided. On the beach near the reed boats, a ragged fisherman sat mending a net, legs out straight in front of him, one end of the cord attached to his big toe to hold the net taut. He didn't look up.

"Incredible," Jill muttered, not quite able to put the incident out of her mind. "The modern world encroaches."

"Sweeping aside everything in its path," Dex added. They gazed at the native. The grizzled man appeared so indifferent to the grating noise, so placidly accepting. "Even he won't escape for long. The tide of change is rolling in."

"Depressing thought. Let's get out of here. Race you to the truck!" Gathering her skirts, Jill started to run.

****

Quiet but comfortable on the ride back to the Pyramid of the Stars, Dex mulled over the day's contradictory events. Once past Trujillo, he drove with one hand. His other arm rested on the back of the seat, fingers touching Jill's shoulder. Every now and then she leaned back and twisted her head against his hand, her hair falling in a dark mass that tickled him. He tugged on a few strands in a tiny caress.

After a while he turned and looked at her. Her eyes were closed, her lips tilted. Was she dreaming of him with that contented, cat-in-the-cream look?

As if she sensed his glance, Jill wet her lips and rubbed her head against his hand once more. Dex smiled. He felt terrific. Warm and peaceful, yet turned on at the same time. Oddly possessive. He'd not felt that combination with any other woman. Shaking his head in wonder, he tabled his concerns. The potholes in the road needed all his attention.

****

So much has happened today, Jill thought drowsily. *How much is real?*

When Dex made love to her, he had given all of himself. She, in turn, had responded with an abandon she hadn't known she was capable of. Would it happen again? Could this wonderful sense of freedom, of living in the moment, last beyond her few days in Peru? *Carpe diem,* her father would say.

Did Dex live for the day, she wondered, with no thoughts of the future? Was this heightened emotion something they alone shared? Or had Poppy felt it, too?

She yearned for the electrifying sensations to go on and on—to last forever. But a thrilling affair, awakening her to her own sensuality, was no longer enough. Was she asking for too much, too soon?

In her reverie, Jill relived the moment she knew

she was in love with Dex. She could feel his hands, his lips, his tongue, his body within her. So damn good! Oh yes, she wanted more.

As her thoughts wandered, tracing her trip to Peru since the moment the fax arrived, she recalled her reaction to the airport poster. Did the people who posed for those erotic pots so many centuries ago feel the same urges, the same desires?

Chapter 14

"Have a nice day?"

Harry's snide tone made Dex grin. "It had its moments."

"What did the police say?"

"They know about all our finds, even what we've uncovered since Frank left. There's definitely an informer among the workers here. Castillo doesn't know who the traitor is, but he suggested vigilance and extra precautions."

"Fat lot of good that does. Does he think we've been inviting the scum in for tea?"

"He'd like more guards at night, patrols around the perimeter of the compound."

"So would I," Harry huffed, "but we can't afford to pay any more local men. They're not easy to vet for security, anyway. Does he have some cops wanting to moonlight?"

"I hadn't thought of that. It's a possibility."

"Not really." Gloom laced Harry's words. "There aren't any *soles* available. But I'll speak to the others. Maybe we can take turns doing a closer watch."

Won't do any good if the spy is one of us, Dex thought but kept it to himself. "Castillo said they've had problems up and down the coast. The looters must have a network of informers."

"Clever bastards. Did you learn anything about the man who broke into Jill Flanders' room?"

"No, not a clue."

"Damned if I can figure out why he singled her out to search. She's only been here a few days. It must have something to do with Frank."

More than you know. "Keep your eye on the others. I'll look out for Jill."

"I wonder where Ms. Flanders fits into all of this?" Harry oozed suspicion.

"What do you mean?"

"He's gone, but she's still here. And information is still leaking out."

"How the hell would she know anything?" Dex scowled.

"She has access to the computer now."

"Only old stuff in there. No one has caught up with the data since Poppy left."

"Well, what about Karen?"

"She hasn't figured out a thing. Poppy screwed up the statistics thoroughly."

"I wonder if Poppy…?"

Dex shook his head. "She's too scatterbrained to have organized any of this."

"Perhaps she had help? Do you think, Frank?"

"Hmmm." Dex paused, thinking. "Well, not much point in speculating. They're both gone. We'll have to hope the police find them."

****

Jill waited for Dex outside Harry's office, and they walked to her room. As they opened the door, a chill crept up her spine. "Someone's been in here again."

"Are you sure?" He stepped inside, looked around.

"No, but I feel uneasy. The room isn't quite the way I left it."

"What's different?"

"I can't put my finger on it, but my subconscious is picking up something…"

She sniffed. "There's a trace in the air, a wisp of cologne, maybe."

He took a deep breath. "I don't smell anything. Wish I could move in with you, keep you safe." He winked at her, and she relaxed.

"Sounds cozy. But we wouldn't get much sleep, two of us on that narrow cot."

"It's not the cot's size that would keep us awake."

"And here I've heard size doesn't matter." She fluttered her eyelashes. "It's all in the technique." He ran his hands lightly up and down her arms, causing the fine hairs to stand on end. "Uh-oh. Stop tempting me. If you don't get back to work, Harry will throw me off the premises."

"We can't have that." Dex mocked Harry's pompous tone. "You belong at my side…or under me. Or over me, I believe in equal opportunities." He grinned and pulled her close, his arms at her waist. "But there's just time for a goodnight kiss."

Closing her eyes, Jill felt his lips on her eyelids, her cheeks, the tip of her nose, and, at last, her mouth. The light kiss deepened, holding a promise. "It's been a fantastic day, *querida*," he murmured in her hair. "Thank goodness your divorce arrived when it did. Trying to keep away from you was destroying me." He nuzzled the tender spot below her ear, breathed in her unique fragrance.

"Me too." Jill pressed against him, her arms

circling his neck. "I wanted you so much."

"Bet you tell that to all the ceramic ethnoarchaeologists you know."

"Every single one." She turned him around and pinched his ass. "Go now, or I'll change my mind and keep you here all night."

"Well…"

"Then Harry will shoot me and strangle you."

"You're right, as usual. Dream of me tonight." He planted a big noisy kiss on her mouth and left.

Jill rubbed her tongue along her lips until his taste disappeared. As she undressed, she heard a crackling in her pocket, remembered the paper the ear spools had been wrapped in. She had shoved it in her pocket when she'd hurried to show Dex. Pulling it out, she examined the weird marks drawn on it. What did they stand for?

She turned it in all directions, but saw only doodles. Odd…they appeared to stand for something. Though she stared at the paper for a long time, her brain had shut down for the night. She shoved it under her pillow and blew out the kerosene lamp. Tomorrow she'd try again.

Jill awoke smiling, but her joy faded as she spotted Poppy's doll in the corner. In its dilapidated condition, stuffing hastily shoved in and leaking out the crack, the doll seemed to reproach her. She glanced at its feet. Both were covered, though she didn't know how. One bootee was still in her pocket, so who found another and put it back on the doll? Had anyone gone through Frank's things since her visit? She should check, make sure the *guayabera* shirt was still packed with her special fold.

Throwing on a bright yellow T-shirt and cutoff

jeans, Jill hurried to Frank's room. The duffel was where she had left it. Zipping it open, she saw the dirty underwear, but the *guayabera* was no longer on top. If whoever moved the black satin shirt to the bottom looked in the pocket, he would have found it empty. Now there were three bootees to account for...

Curiouser and curiouser. Jill emptied the duffel once more and shook each garment, wrinkling her nose at the stale, sweaty odor. Nothing more fell out. No pink bootees, no feathered gold earrings. As she re-zipped the bag, her gaze skimmed the dresser top. The silver mirror was gone, and it was valuable. She hoped some poor family would eat better for a little while.

Back in her room, Jill suddenly recalled the wrapping she had hidden beneath her pillow. She slid her hand under and felt around, then lifted the pillow and shook it. The paper with the strange markings had disappeared!

Panicking, she pulled back the covers, ran her hands over the sheet, yanked at a corner sticking out. The paper lay between the tucked-in sheet and the mattress. She must have really thrashed around last night. Sighing with relief, she dropped down on the bed to catch her breath.

After a moment, Jill worked the paper loose, careful not to tear it. She checked it once more. In the upper left corner, a tiny stick figure had been drawn with a triangle body and small squares on its head and feet. Could it represent the doll?

Rows of wavy lines ran across the bottom of the page. A large square, with a smaller box beside it, filled the lower right corner. Something was marked on the bigger square. She tilted the paper into the light, but couldn't make out the scribble.

In the center of the sheet, a zigzagging line shaped like an inverted "u" had been drawn. Underneath it was a matching smaller "u." What on earth could it mean? Maybe Dex would know. Returning the paper to her shorts pocket, Jill headed for breakfast. Yesterday's activities had left her with a raging appetite. She'd polished off three *sopapillas* spread with honey, and had drunk enough coffee to keep her hopping all day, when Dex finally walked in. He caught her licking honey off her fingers, and his eyes opened wide.

"How are you today?" he asked. "Still recovering from yesterday? Any sore spots you'd like me to massage?"

With a smirk, she kept licking the honey from her fingers. Jill saw the stirring of desire in his eyes. He reached for her, but she nudged his arm away. "We're not alone," she whispered.

His quick laugh annoyed her. "Always thinking of the proprieties, Madam X?" She pouted, and he gave her ponytail a yank, then poured a mug of coffee and grabbed a *sopapilla*.

She couldn't wait until he finished. "I've made a discovery," she said, eyes sparkling. "Can you spare a few minutes before starting work?"

"Only a few, I'm afraid." He bolted down the rest of his food, then walked with her down the path until no one was in sight. "Tell me quick."

Reaching into her shorts pocket, Jill pulled out the piece of paper. "This was wrapped around the ear spools I found." She handed it to him. "I would have shown it to you yesterday, but in my excitement, I forgot all about it."

He peered at the paper. "What do you think it is? Some kind of map?"

"I've been poring over it since last night. It's a symbols cipher, crudely drawn, but that may be deliberate. Look at this little toothpick figure in the corner. Could it be a vague drawing of the doll?"

Bringing the paper closer to his eyes, Dex inspected it. "You may be right. It's not too different from an early Indian petroglyph. But what are the squiggly lines?"

"That's what we have to figure out. Maybe it's a map leading to the hidden loot. But how would Frank have it? I don't think he's working with the bandits."

"No. They wouldn't trust a gringo."

"He may have followed them without their knowledge. Frank can be a sneaky bastard."

"We mustn't jump to conclusions. We don't know for sure who put the ear spools inside the doll."

"If it wasn't Frank, why was the doll's bootee in his *guayabera*? Now there are three bootees popping in and out of this case."

"Huh. The mystery deepens."

"I still think Frank gave the doll to Poppy. It's like him to offer that gift to a teenager with an overdeveloped body and an underdeveloped brain."

"Uh, Poppy isn't exactly like that," Dex said.

Jill's bright mood evaporated.

"She's flaky, full of woo-woo ideas, but she graduated from Bennington at a pretty young age, so there must be some smarts up there. The body, however, doesn't compare to that of a certain EXecutive I know. Poppy's only a slip of a girl. I can't see Frank choosing her over a real woman like you."

179

Why did those words make her feel so good? She should be beyond that, but… "Flattery will get you everywhere." Jill laughed to cover her chagrin.

He beamed. "Ain't it the truth! Let's work on deciphering the paper tonight, and have something concrete to give to the *policía*. I'll come to your room after the generator goes off at nine. I'll bring a flashlight and a map of the area. With a little luck, our combined brains should be able to solve this puzzle."

"Good idea! I feel like Sherlock Holmes."

"You do? I imagined you as Watson."

"Wrong answer."

"Have I got your dander up?" His lips quirked as he left.

The day passed quickly. Jill spent a few hours compiling data for the computer, then gave up for good. Grabbing a *cerveza* from the chow hall, she waited for night to fall. Between sips of beer, she brushed a strand of hair back and forth across her lips, recalling Dex's kisses as she fed him cherries. She'd never be able to eat cherries again without thinking of him. Her lover would always be there, his tongue licking the trail of dribbling juice as he sent the pit rolling into her mouth.

Jill's toes began to curl as her tipsy brain envisioned everything that happened behind the dunes…and all the things that could be in her future. For a while, she let her fluttering thoughts wander where they would.

She had never before considered living anywhere other than New York, but office work was accomplished electronically these days. Even if her life changed, even if she moved out of Manhattan, she could still edit and advise, still be a force in publishing.

She could do her job anywhere in the world. The knowledge was exhilarating. She lifted her beer and drained the bottle, but the boozy laugh that followed was rueful. She was getting ahead of herself. Her dreams were based on nothing more than a winter fling.

Picking up the wrapping paper, Jill studied the queer symbols drawn on it. There was something familiar about those jagged lines, but the awareness was too vague to place. Perhaps Dex would recognize them.

Staring at the doodles without actually seeing them, Jill relived the incredible day she had spent with her golden god. Everything about Dex was remarkable—his sharp brain, capable of such tenderness—his buff, suntanned body. She pictured the silky hairs curling on his chest, those long powerful thighs, his wonderful stroking fingers... As her imagination traced him hungrily from torso to toes, the overhead light blinked out.

It was nine o'clock. Padding through the moonlight that lanced through her window, Jill felt for the kerosene lamp and matches. She had just gotten the wick to light when she heard a *rat-tat-tat*. "Come on in," she called.

Dex stood in the shadows. "You shouldn't open your door at night without asking who's outside."

"Why? Is anything wrong?"

He stepped in, pulled her close, and lifted her till they were eye to eye. "No. I just don't want anything to happen to you. You're pretty damn casual about your room having been broken into twice."

She gazed at him and smiled. "The only thing happening to me, now, happens to be quite pleasurable."

Laughing, he slid her slowly down his body. "Just be cautious, for my sake. I've waited a long time for you."

Her heart skipped a beat. Perhaps dreams could come true... Swallowing hard, Jill dragged the bridge chair over to the bed and laid the paper with the doodles on it. "Did you remember your flashlight?"

He turned it on. The light was so bright, she blinked three times.

"Watch where you aim that thing."

"Okay, but I like to look at you up close." Dropping a kiss on her nose, he sat down beside her on the bed and examined the paper. "These are rather primitive symbols. Do you think Frank sketched them?"

"Maybe. Someone tried to give away the least amount of information. Barely enough to let the brain make the connection."

"Yeah." He stared at it. "The stick figure does resemble the doll, now that I look at it closer. The triangle could be her body."

"Yes, and that peaked square on the head could be her bonnet. Those smaller squares at the feet are her bootees. Look, Dex, there's even a little dash here in the center of the triangle where I inserted my fingernail. I thought it might be a keyhole in the doll's back."

They slapped hands in a high five. "All right!" he exclaimed. "Not a keyhole but a key, perhaps, to this whole affair. I'll settle for that. This is the doll—the slit confirms it. Now what about the two boxes in the lower right corner?"

"The bigger one could be a building? With a shed, perhaps? Or a garage?"

"Hmm, a possibility. And the wavy lines?"

"Water? That's the way we used to draw it in grade school."

"You still remember?"

"I'm not that old!"

"Hey, no more of that." He tugged her ponytail. "We've already been through the age thing, and it doesn't compute."

"Aye aye, Captain." Good thing the flashlight was still directed on the paper. She felt her ears glowing.

"Those wavy lines could stand for water, we've plenty of that. The Pacific Ocean borders the entire coast of Peru. But this doesn't get us any closer to the gang's hideout. If we guessed right about this being a map to the bandits' lair, the solution must lie in those jagged horseshoes."

They concentrated on the diagram until a discouraged Dex opted for taking the paper to the police. "If those wavy lines indicate the ocean, there's bound to be some clue to the shoreline. Lieutenant Castillo knows the coast much better than we do."

Jill hated to give up. "Let's give it one more day. If we sleep on it, maybe something will come to us."

"Okay, Sherlock. One more try. And speaking of sleep," he drawled, "that reminds me of other things a bed is used for. Shall I draw you a different map?" He reached under her T-shirt and ran his fingernails down her back.

She wriggled at his touch. "I can figure out this map with my eyes closed, Watson. However, a demonstration won't hurt…" She undid the laces of the cotton shirt he had worn the day they met.

Much later, after Dex left, Jill fell into a dreamless sleep. She awoke at dawn, sniffing the intoxicating scent of their lovemaking on the sheets. Her yawn turned into a smile of satisfaction as she snuggled under the blanket and dozed off once more.

When she next awoke, the sun was shining brightly through the small window. The sky was a glorious blue. And she had the answer to the puzzle!

Jill grabbed the paper and stared at it. Incredible—she knew what the symbols meant. Her unconscious mind had been hard at work while her conscious mind slept. Staring at the jagged line of the larger "u," Jill conjured up a picture of the beach they had walked on the day before. *Yes!* Her hand shot up in a fist. The jagged points drawn on the "u" fit perfectly with her memory of the large rock she had noticed off shore. Then the smaller "u" inside must be the entrance to the cave. Mentally, Jill went over and over the lines. She had no doubts. They dovetailed.

And the two boxy structures drawn on the paper, the rectangle and the square? As Jill squinted at them, she could just make out the likeness of…could it be a sail? A fin? Yes, a crudely drawn fancy fish had been attempted on the larger of the two boxes. Of course! The café sign at *Los Mariscos*. Then the smaller box wasn't a shed or a garage—it was the patio where they'd eaten those scrumptious Peruvian pizzas.

She could hardly wait to tell Dex of her discovery. Throwing on a tank top and faded jeans with deep pockets, Jill hurried to the chow hall. As she passed his worktable, she noticed he wasn't there. Damn. She had definitely overslept.

Inside the building, Sam sat at the long table eating his way through a huge pile of pancakes. "Believe it or not, Dex is off again," he told her. "Ran out of the special epoxy he uses to glue the pot shards together. Harry needed a few things, too, so he sent him off to Trujillo."

"Oh no!" Jill slumped.

"What's the matter?"

"I need to see him right away."

"He left only a half hour ago." Sam hesitated, his concern showing. "I'd lend you my car…" Jill looked up eagerly, "…but not after that blow dart incident. I'd hold myself responsible if anything happened to you. And Dex would have my head on this platter."

She tapped her fingers nervously on the table. "I've something to tell him that he needs to relay to the police."

"Can't they wait another day?"

"The sooner, the better." Jill started to explain, then stopped, turned. "Do I hear an engine?"

"Must be the tortilla guy. He's late today."

"I could try to hitch a ride with him. Do you know where I can find Dex?"

"There's a wholesale supply place on Avenida Zacaton. I'll draw you a map, but you must promise to be careful."

She nodded vigorously.

Sam took a pencil from his breast pocket and grabbed a napkin to write on. "You should be able to catch him here if the tortilla guy is going straight back to town. He could drop you off."

"I'll ask him." Placing a kiss on Sam's bald spot, she picked up the napkin with the map and hurried out.

Ernesto, *Señor* "Tortilla Truck," was happy to oblige. Jill had made a conquest when she'd called him her hero after he'd rescued her from the blow-dart threat. While he delivered the day's tortillas to the kitchen, she hurried back to the room for her carryall, adding a tide table and the flashlight Dex had left behind the night before.

Once again Jill found herself rattling along the rutted road. Ernesto was content to drive without talking, and that suited her, too. She gazed out the window at the awesome desert. Everything she saw was brushed with strokes of tan and brown. There wouldn't be a touch of green in this landscape until they reached the small patches of garden on the outskirts of town.

The hypnotic rhythm of the jostling springs lulled her into a dreamy state. How surprised Dex would be to see her. They could greet Lieutenant Castillo together with the solution to the puzzle. Well, maybe not. Her tank top and torn jeans would be inappropriate. She sighed. It would never do.

As they turned into the Avenida Zacaton, her excitement grew. Dex's red truck was parked halfway down the block. She thanked Ernesto and shook his hand. *Gracias* didn't seem enough, so she threw in, "*Feliz Año Nuevo*," since they were close to the year's end. With equal seriousness and a twinkle in his eye, he offered, "*Muchas Felicidades*."

Jill jumped down, waved, then walked over to Dex's truck. The cab was empty. Deflated, she leaned against the door and waited.

Minutes passed. Glancing at her watch, Jill unfolded the tide schedule she'd stuffed into her carryall. Low tide was at two p.m. If Dex showed up soon, they'd just have time to make it. They could check out the cave, determine if her guess was right, then return for the police. She had to be sure this time, not make a fool of herself in front of the arrogant lieutenant with his bedroom eyes.

Another fifteen minutes limped by. Jill grew more and more restless. They would miss the tide. Even though the warehouse was huge, she'd have to hunt for him. She headed inside and peered down the aisles. Asking for help would only delay her. At last, at the far end of an aisle, she spotted Dex watching a man high up on a ladder shifting cartons, one by one.

"It has to be here," the man called down.

"Keep looking." Dex sounded resigned. He turned. "Jill! What are you doing here?"

"Hi." She stopped to catch her breath. "Dex, I've solved the puzzle! The hiding place is the cave we saw off the beach at *Los Mariscos*. We've got to check it out now, while the tide is out." She pulled at his arm, but he didn't budge.

"That's great, Sherlock, but I've got to get this epoxy today. I'll be with you as soon as I can."

"But the tide!"

"We'll just have to hope for the best. First things first."

"I'm too antsy to wait. There's a taxi stand at the corner. Why don't I go ahead and scout the place? I'll meet you near the boulders by the entrance."

"Not a good idea." He shook his head. "It's too dangerous."

She scowled.

"Go ahead if you must, but wait for me at the restaurant." He looked up at the man on the ladder and shrugged. "I should be only a few minutes behind you."

"Okay, if I can see the cave entrance from there I'll sit on the patio. But if I can't, I'll hide behind the boulders outside. There's plenty of cover. All I'll do is watch for anyone going in or out, so we'll know if it's safe to enter. I promise to stay hidden. But hurry!"

Blowing Dex a kiss, she headed out.

Chapter 15

The taxi pulled into the empty parking lot at *Los Mariscos*. The café was closed until dinner today. Jill paid the driver, stepped out and peered along the beach. She couldn't see the cave opening, so hurried down to the water's edge. There she'd be able to run faster through the packed sand.

In the distance, Jill spotted the towering black rock, and as she grew closer, its gaping entrance. The last of the sea was oozing out, small waves lapping at the shore as the tide ebbed. The gulls swept by in lazy arcs.

As she reached the nearest sheltering boulder, she stopped, glanced around, and listened. Nothing moved except the waves. No human sounds caught her attention.

Heart pounding louder than the shushing of the sea, she ducked behind a group of rocks. Five minutes passed without a sign of life. She grew calmer, shifted to a more comfortable position, and waited some more. Just as she decided it was safe to rise, voices reached her ears.

Hurriedly, Jill crouched down again and peered through a crack between the boulders. Four men, pant legs rolled up, stepped out of the cave carrying their shoes and gesticulating. Their arms flapped wildly. One man shouted and pointed behind him toward the sea as the others headed for shore. His words were carried away by the wind. Loping clumsily through the receding water, he tried to catch up.

The four disappeared behind a large dune tufted with sea grass. Moments later, Jill heard the roar of their motorcycles. As they raced by, she shrank farther into the wedge between the boulders.

Again she waited, steadier now. Four men—the number she and Dex had seen ride by the other day. Was that all of them? Five more minutes passed. No one returned. Water trickling over rocks was the only sound coming from the direction of the cave.

She returned her gaze to the tide—it was no longer receding. They were going to lose their opportunity. Where was Dex? He should have left the warehouse by now. Should she keep waiting? Or should she sneak in and take a fast peek, see if the loot was there? She'd come right out again, but at least they would *know*. This might be their only chance.

Cautiously, Jill emerged from her hiding place. Still no sign of Dex. She strained to listen for motorcycle engines. Their roar carried a great distance, but all was peaceful. Taking off her sneakers, she hid them behind the boulders and headed for the cave.

****

Dex had been pacing ever since Jill waved goodbye. He thought he'd grown accustomed to the south-of-the-border definition of time, knowing there was no way he could hasten the procedure. Today, however, he was uneasy. When he finally acquired his supplies, he left the warehouse at a run. He jumped into his truck, jammed the key into the ignition, and ground down on the pedal. With a growl, the vehicle leaped forward.

He drove recklessly through the clogged streets of the city, pounding on the horn like a native, cutting in and out of traffic. He might be crazy about the woman, but he didn't trust her to wait for him. In his imagination he saw Jill's face, pale as the moon, her green eyes turning black with fright. He imagined a cutthroat yanking on her silky hair, pictured her lying on the cold stone floor of the cave—bound, bruised, raped! A vision of the Moche priestess on his pot flashed through his mind, her arms broken, blood dripping relentlessly from the vessels in her hands. The ancient goddess had Jill's face.

Why was he letting his thoughts run wild like this? It wasn't his MO. He was a scientist. But he had seen photos of the victims after guerrillas had pillaged their mountain villages, and he shuddered.

Get a grip, he told himself as he exited the city. Jill was Madam X, his keen, intelligent executive, and she spoke their language. She was smart enough to wait for him. But if, somehow, they had caught her, she would not succumb. She would beguile them with her enticing voice, seduce them with her lemon blossom scent.

Wishful thinking… Dex stifled a sigh as he drove swiftly along the highway. Surely, she was too wily to be caught. He would find her hiding behind the nearby rocks, watching the cave entrance.

Pulling into the restaurant parking lot, he leaped from the truck, scanned the shore. He saw nothing beyond the windswept waves, tiny whitecaps glistening in the sun. No squealing children. No sunbathing lovers. And no Jill. High in the sky, the sun beat down. The wheeling gulls swooped and screeched. Far and wide, the beach was deserted.

Dex began to run.

****

The damp pebbles at the cave entrance were slippery. After one skid, Jill slipped the carryall strap over her head. It hugged her body and left her hands free. Pressing them against the back wall, she moved sideways, sliding along the stone until she spied the entrance to a narrow passageway.

She poked her head in, saw nothing but blackness. Only her own quick breaths broke the eerie silence. Taking Dex's heavy flashlight from her carryall, she turned it on to view an uphill passage stretching ahead. High tide had left a deposit of salt on the wall, so she followed the chalky band, climbing higher as the line dropped lower until it disappeared.

When she reached the entrance to an inner cavern, Jill hesitated, listening once more. All was silent. She waited for her breathing to slow, then stepped through and flashed her light around the room. She gulped, swallowing an astonished gasp.

The cavern was huge, bigger than her college auditorium, with a high, jagged ceiling. From its contents, it could have been a museum storeroom. Stacks of pottery lined an uneven ledge along the back wall. Bulging burlap sacks littered the cave floor. In one nook lay a heap of naked dolls. A bunch of pink organdy dresses, bonnets, and bootees had been tossed aside and trampled on, leaving muddy footprints.

As she ran over to the sacks, her foot kicked an object. She looked down at a silver-edged comb. What was Frank's comb doing here? Was he part of the gang, or could Frank have been trying to rob the robbers?

She'd think about it later. Slipping the comb into her pocket, she opened a sack. One peek and she would leave.

The gleam of gold reflected in the flashlight's beam. Jill freaked, forgetting her vow to leave. Reaching in, she pulled out handful after handful of precious objects. A necklace in spun gold. An intricate nosepiece of electrum—she was beginning to recognize that odd amalgam of gold and silver. A huge chunk of rock crystal dangling from a heavy silver chain. Ear spools. Pendants. Bracelets. She was breathing so hard she had to sit down.

Legs spread out on the cold rock, forgetful of danger, Jill took piece after piece of fine metalwork out of the sack. How collectors would covet these works of art! Well, she had her answer. She had to get out of here. It was too dangerous to hang around any longer. With a deep sigh, she picked up her flashlight and got to her feet.

Suddenly, a noise.

A footstep.

Terrified, Jill glanced wildly about. The sacks weren't tall enough to hide behind. The evidence of her presence was strewn upon the ground. There was no place to conceal herself.

She had only one chance. As the footsteps came closer, she switched off the flashlight and loped over to the tunnel entrance, skidding to a stop at its side. Arm raised, she held the flashlight high, ready to strike.

The beam of a tiny keychain flashlight lit a small area in front of the passageway. As she started to swing her weapon, a familiar figure stepped into the room. Dex! With a squeal of relief, she threw herself into his arms, knocking the wind out of him. He staggered.

"Jill!" With a hoarse cry Dex closed his arms around her, the little light still held in one hand. The Swiss army knife he'd carried ever since their picnic was in the other, with its largest blade open.

"Stand still before I prick you. I've got to close this knife."

"Thank God you're here." She breathed the words into his chest.

"Rescuing you is getting to be a habit." He looked down at the trembling form clinging to him. "You don't follow orders well, do you? I like the end result, but we haven't the time." Taking his big flashlight from her clenched fingers, he shone it around the room. "Holy shit!"

Knees wobbly, Jill turned around, digging her fingers into his belt. "I think we've found the looters' storeroom," she whispered.

"More like Aladdin's cave." Pulling her along, Dex moved closer to the pile of precious objects she had spread out on the floor. Then he glanced up at the shelf of ceramic pots, and his eyes widened. "Good Lord, what a field day I could have in here!"

Turning away with obvious regret, he looked at Jill. "We've got to put it all back, *querida*, and get out of here. Coming here alone was not one of your smarter executive moves."

She bristled. "I saw the looters ride off on their motorcycles—all four of them. It was our one chance to get in when the tide was out."

"We'll talk about it later." He reached down and began to put the jewelry back in the sack. "The water has already begun to rise. We've got to get out of here fast…before the men return."

As she kneeled down to help him, Jill saw his gaze flash longingly on the pots.

"Dex, I've got my camera. I'll take a few fast shots of the pots while you put this stuff back."

"Okay, but be quick."

She took out her tiny camera and moved over to the ledge, gaping at some of the erotic poses of the clay figures, similar to the ones on the airport poster. As her gaze raked a series of extremely graphic pots, she giggled nervously. Was there an intimate position the Moche hadn't thought of? She didn't think so. And the huge phalluses! Male boasting certainly had a long history.

She photographed a duck, a jaguar, and, with a shudder, a man who was half flesh, half skeleton. She came next to a kneeling prisoner with his hands tied behind him. As she looked closer Jill winced, for the rope ran between his legs and was tied to his penis.

A painted vessel of a fisherman in a reed boat sat atop a woolen cloth with row upon row of helmeted figures woven into the design. Each soldier held a decapitated trophy head by the hair. Gritting her teeth, Jill snapped it, as well as an Inca vessel with a geometric design resting its pointed bottom in a ring of woven straw. The sparkle of an elaborate breastplate of interlocking golden leaves studded with turquoise caught her eye next. "This cavern must be the thieves' main storehouse," she called out. "We've found the pot of gold at the end of the rainbow."

"Move." He came up behind her. "You've taken enough photos for the police. Let's get out of here." Switching off the flashlight, he grabbed his knife.

"Oh, all right." In the darkness, she slipped the camera into her carryall. "But I did see all four men ride off."

"Ah, *pero* you not know, *señora,* we are *cinco,* five of us," a gravelly voice said in broken English. Light entered the cavern. "Drop the knife, *señor.*"

With a gasp, Jill grabbed Dex's arm.

Standing at the tunnel entrance, a burly man set down a smuggler's lantern but kept his pistol aimed at Dex. "I no have the 'og, so left behind to guard. But *el hombre* must eat and shit." Eyes narrowed, he watched as the army knife slipped to the floor.

The og? Oh, the motorcycle... Jill held back a hysterical laugh.

The bandit let out a loud belch. The odor of garlic wafted toward them, but the hand holding the pistol did not waver. His gaze raked Jill. "Move away from him, *señora."* With a leer, the looter switched to a stream of Spanish, his free hand grabbing his genitals as he described his plans for her once he got rid of the man.

Jill closed her eyes in horror, but they flew open immediately. The bandit's gun never left Dex, whose face had tightened into a grim mask. "If you let us go we can come to terms," he said. "I have many *soles.* You can have them all."

"No *señor,* I get them from you anyway. Afterwards."

The air grew thick with silence. Jill's mind raced. What could she do? The tide would be coming in stronger now. Soon it would be impossible to escape. And then the others would show up.

They needed a diversion. Switching to Spanish, she looked beseechingly at the bandit, letting her eyelashes flutter. "Such beautiful jewelry." She sighed and nodded toward the sacks. "I may never see anything like this again. May I look just once more?" She let her shoulders droop, and her tank top gaped wide.

The man's gaze roamed greedily over her body, pausing longest at her breasts. "It will put you in mood good for me, *sí*? Quick, then, one look."

"Gracias, señor." Jill simpered over the courtesy title. She managed a quick glance at Dex and caught a barely noticeable tensing of his frame.

Going to the sack she had opened before, she reached inside. Her fingers scrambled for the large rock crystal pendant hanging from the thick silver chain. "Look at this gorgeous piece, Dex." Hiding the pendant within both palms, she started to move toward him.

"Stay back!" For a breath, the gun shifted between the two prisoners.

At that instant, Dex threw the big flashlight at the man's head while Jill swung the heavy pendant by its chain. The bandit ducked the flashlight just as the chunk of crystal hit his gun arm. Dex was on him in an instant, grappling for the weapon.

The guerrilla was vicious but slow, no match for Dex's size and strength. Fueled by rage, he smashed his fist into the man's face. Jill heard bone crack as the bandit hit the stone floor. He was out cold.

Grabbing the pistol and his flashlight, Dex pushed Jill in front of him. They ran down the passage, chests heaving. As they neared the cave entrance, they heard water flowing in a rush over the pebbles. Waves splashed against the back wall.

In the pauses between the ebb and flow of the waves, barely audible, came the dip of oars.

Chapter 16

"Follow me!"

In a flash, Dex jumped into the water lapping at the cave floor and pulled Jill in after him. The sea had risen above her ankles, and the shock of cold water notched up her fright to near panic. She clung to Dex as they moved to the farthest corner of the cave's mouth.

"When I touch your back, step farther out and duck," he whispered. "It's dark under here, and their eyes will still be adjusted to the light from their lantern. With luck they won't notice us."

"Got it." She let out a tiny yelp when her shoulder bumped against a jutting ledge. Her carryall swung back, and Jill heard a thud. Her camera! She had to keep it dry. Hastily removing it from her carryall, she shoved it as far back as she could on the high ledge. It was small and black—no one would notice it. She stuffed her wallet and passport into her pockets and got ready to jettison the rest.

By now, the water had risen halfway to her knees. Wet sand sucked at her soggy socks as the tide came in. She scrunched her toes to keep from slipping. The sound of the oars grew louder.

Dex tensed beside her. "One...two..." His fingers pressed into her shoulder. Stepping off the cave floor, she ducked under the water. A moment later, one of the ancient reed boats glided into the cave.

Swiftly, the men beached it near the tunnel entrance. Their voices died. Unable to hold her breath any longer, Jill lifted her head till her nose was out of the water. No one was in sight.

Dex had risen too. He looked ruefully at his big flashlight. Water dripped from the battery compartment, and he let it slip from his fingers into the sea. Thrusting the gun into his pants pocket, he turned to Jill and put his lips to her ear. "Can you swim to shore?"

"No problema," she whispered, her voice shaky. "The ocean is calm." With regret, she watched her carryall sink slowly to the bottom.

He gave her shoulder a reassuring squeeze. As he dropped a quick kiss on the sensitive spot between her eyebrows, Jill's fear subsided. Her mind grew sharp. She felt him stiffen. Mouthing one, two, three, they dove under together and swam beyond the cave entrance, kicking underwater for as long as they could hold their breaths. When they surfaced, they were already near the shore.

With the tide giving them an extra push, Jill and Dex waded out of the surf and began running along the water's edge. Late afternoon fog had drifted in, veiling their figures. Farther out to sea, they could make out the misty outline of a small yacht. No lights showed. "The bandits will transfer the cave's loot to the larger vessel," Dex said, "but it will take four or five trips to move all the booty."

Taking deep breaths, they resumed running. Thank goodness the bandits were too occupied to hunt for them. She doubted they could outrun four armed desperadoes—five if the guard Dex punched had regained consciousness. If the thieves planned to transport everything, that might give them time to warn the police. What a coup it would be! Perhaps then the lieutenant would concentrate on finding Frank.

In the distance, the restaurant lights winked on, promising safety. Jill ran harder to keep up with Dex. When they reached the parking lot and stopped to catch their breaths, she began to shiver. Unlocking his truck, he picked up the picnic blanket and wrapped it around her shoulders. "You'll be warm inside the cab." He helped her up, giving her ass a boost. She looked back at him, and he winked.

****

"Wait here. I'll phone from the café." Dex raced across the beach and rushed inside. His luck held, for Castillo was still at his office.

"*Señor* Conroy," the policeman sounded tired and strained, "I was on my way out. This had better be worth holding up my dinner."

"Lieutenant, we found the looters' hiding place and all the stolen goods. You've gotta come quick!"

Castillo's languor disappeared. "Talk slower, *señor*. Where are you?"

"At Huanchaco. I'm calling from the restaurant *Los Mariscos*."

"*Sí sí,* I know where it is."

"Near here is a cave with a flooded entrance at high tide, but it's accessible at low. We found the loot inside. What a haul! You won't believe your eyes."

"You were actually inside the hideaway?"

"Yeah, and were almost caught, but we got away. The men have one of the larger reed boats. They're moving the artifacts now to a yacht anchored off shore.

You'll have to hurry to catch them."

"Caracho! I will take the police cruiser. We'll arrive faster by sea."

"Do you need us to wait, Lieutenant? We're soaking wet. The tide came in and we had to swim out."

"Who is 'we'?"

"Ms. Flanders is with me."

"Aah… It is still twenty-seven degrees Celsius, Conroy. That is over eighty degrees on your Fahrenheit scale. Wait for me. You won't freeze."

"Well, okay, but make it snappy." Dex hung up the phone, annoyed that he had given in to that last remark, but worried about Jill. When he reached the truck, she was still in the passenger seat, wrapped in the blanket.

"I'm c-cold, Dex." Her teeth were chattering.

"I'll warm you up, *querida.*" He slid beside her into the driver's seat. "We have to wait for the police, but it'll take them some time to get here. I've got the perfect solution."

Turning on the truck's heater, he unwrapped the blanket and pulled up her tank top.

"Wh-what are you doing?"

"You can't stay in these wet clothes, so we'll lay them out in front of the heater. The fan will blow them dry long before Castillo and his men get here."

"But, you're wet, too!"

"Okay, we'll both strip."

"Here in the truck?"

"The moon hasn't risen yet, and the restaurant won't open for patrons for another hour. We're well away from any parked cars. Don't worry, no one will see us."

He had wriggled out of his shirt and jeans while he

spoke, and now finished undressing Jill. "Hurry," he muttered as she raised her hips so he could slide down her jeans and panties. "I want to hold you close and warm you up."

"I don't believe this." She watched him as he laid their clothing over the steering wheel and parts of the seat. "Undressing in a truck. I feel like a teenager!"

"So this is how you passed your misspent youth," he teased. "Good thing those jeans are worn. The holes made the swimming easier. What's in your pockets?"

"Uh-oh. My wallet and passport."

"We'll dry them, too." He spread the items on the dashboard, separating the bills. His eyes twinkled as he found a condom behind the *soles*. "Castillo will replace whatever is water damaged. He owes you."

"There isn't much money. The rest is plastic."

"That's what I like about the modern world. What happened to your camera?"

"I hid it in the far corner of the cave, high up on a ledge. It's black and won't show."

"Smart woman. Come, sit on me, honey. I'll make sure you're thoroughly warm by the time the *policía* get here." He pulled her onto his lap.

****

With a sigh, Jill leaned into him. "I'm warmer already."

"You're still shivering."

"But not from cold."

He laughed and hugged her. "Why not straddle me? You can get closer that way—much closer." Dex lifted her into position.

Jill could feel his hard cock, and she moaned, her body wanting to melt into his. God, but she loved this man!

"That's it," he whispered, caressing her as he slid deep. "Let me warm you throughout. *Mi cielo...*" His breath was a hot whisper against her skin. "My sweet entrance into heaven."

"Dex," she murmured, arching as he started moving gently and rhythmically within her. "Oh my..." She tried to speak again. "There was a...aah... Moche stirrup pot in the cave." She rocked against him. "The man and woman...sculpted on it...were in just this position..."

"You know the old saying," he whispered into her mouth. "There's nothing new under the sun. I'll show you a museum full of those erotic pots when we get to Lima." His tongue slid between her teeth in a searing kiss. Clamping his hands around her waist, he helped her ride him. Up and down. Faster and faster. It wasn't long before her joyous shriek and his exuberant shout joined the sound of the lapping waves, as they shattered into a thousand glittering stars.

It took several moments for Jill to find the strength to speak. "Are they dry yet?" Contented, not wanting to move, she stretched out her hand, feeling for her clothes.

Dex grabbed them first. "Mm hmm. This dry climate does a fast job." He set them down on the seat and, ever so slowly, lifted her off his lap.

"I don't want to stop," she purred.

"Nor do I, but the lieutenant might not understand the, uh, effects of adrenaline on the body." He dangled her panties from his fingertip.

"Oh. Right." Jill sat up and grabbed them. She reached for tank top, scrunched her jeans to take out the stiffness and worked her way into them. "I doubt if there's anything about this subject Castillo doesn't understand."

Laughing, Dex opened the doors. "Agreed. We've steamed up the windows. Better let in a little night air."

Jill fussed at the wild strands of hair lying messily on her shoulders. "Do I have time to clean up a bit in the restaurant's ladies room?" She reached into her pocket, felt the silver comb. Good thing she'd picked it up.

"Give it a try. I'll wait here."

****

As she raced across the sand, Dex stepped away from the truck and gazed up at the sky. Night had descended, and the moon rising over the mountains cast a silvery path upon the sea. He heard the sound of a motorboat, but saw nothing. Instead, the yacht suddenly stirred to a rumble and began to move.

"Damn," Dex swore. "They're getting away!"

Five minutes later, the police cruiser hove into sight. The men came ashore in a rubber raft just as Jill returned, her wet hair falling in waves down her back. She had retrieved her sneakers, now tied by the laces over her shoulder.

Castillo barely glanced at her. "Where are the looters?" he shouted.

Dex pointed north and out to sea. "The yacht left about five minutes ago. You might still catch it."

With a curse the lieutenant signaled to the launch. It took off at once. "There are many hidden coves along the shore," he said. "If it is the yacht I suspect, it's a fast bugger."

He turned toward Jill, his eyes mere slits. "You

were told to keep out of police affairs."

****

Uh-oh, where's that bedroom gaze now? "There wasn't time, Lieutenant. When I found the map I…"

He interrupted her. "You found a map?"

"Well, not exactly." She looked helplessly at Dex.

"Why don't we go into the restaurant and discuss this over some hot coffee?" Dex suggested. "We did get a soaking, Lieutenant, and we're cold from water and shock."

Jill could barely suppress a giggle as Castillo's eyes lasered their dried bodies.

"First, guide my men to the cave. We'll take the raft. They may not have escaped with all the loot."

"Okay." He led the lieutenant toward the cave while Castillo's men followed them, carrying the rubber raft. When they reached the rock, Dex pointed to the entrance. "As the moon rises higher, you'll see it clearly. All the way in at the back, you'll find an opening. There's a dry area where the floor starts to rise, and you can beach the raft there."

"Oh, Lieutenant," Jill called to him. "I left my camera far back on a ledge opposite the passageway. I couldn't take a chance on getting it wet and fouling up the images."

"You took pictures?"

"Yes, as best I could."

The beginning of a smile lit his face. "Wait here." Castillo singled out a guard to stay with them as the others lowered the raft. He jumped in.

They stood beside the silent policeman, Dex holding Jill's hand. "Leaving the camera was a smart move. I'm amazed you remembered it at such a desperate moment."

"I felt the camera bump against me as we ran, and knew I had to keep it dry." She crossed her fingers. "I hope the water didn't rise as high as the shelf."

Several minutes passed. At last the raft could be seen heading back toward them.

Castillo wasn't happy. "A heap of dolls in a corner, and a few cracked jars from Chancay," he said in disgust as he handed Jill her camera. "Nothing left of the Moche."

"Blast." Dex's mouth thinned. "Not only Moche. There were pots from Nazca, and woven cloths from Paracas. They raided up and down the coast."

"Some Inca, too," Jill added. "And lots of jewelry, Spanish and Indian."

"We will go to the restaurant," Castillo said, "and you will tell me how you found the cave. Plus I want a list of everything you saw. The café owner will give us a private room, and we will look at your pictures."

"Over coffee?" Jill said hopefully. "And maybe tortillas?"

The lieutenant ignored her. *"Vamos."* He signaled the police guard standing by the raft to return and search for evidence. Briskly, the three crossed the sand toward *Los Mariscos.*

Although the restaurant was filling, the eager proprietor fawned over them. Soon Jill and Dex were seated at a candle-lit table in a private dining alcove. Steaming coffee, a platter of warm *sopapillas* tastier than those at the dig, and an earthenware jar of honey were laid in front of them before he discreetly vanished. In a few moments the lieutenant joined them.

Stirring three spoonfuls of pale brown sugar into

his coffee, Castillo stared at them. "You have disobeyed my orders."

"But, Lieutenant," Jill sputtered. Dex stepped on her foot under the table, silencing her.

"I know you found the looters' cache, but if you had come to me first, we might have retrieved it and caught the bandits as well. Now they have escaped with the artifacts, and we are back, as you Americans say, to square one. What would I have told the American embassy if I had two dead U.S. citizens on my hand, and one a woman!"

Jill bristled. What difference did her sex make? But she didn't comment. "Your men know the thieves' *modus operandi* now." She tried to sound knowledgeable. "Perhaps they'll catch the yacht. Or the Lima police will."

"That is not the issue. I intend to suggest to my superiors that you be 'requested' to leave the country."

Jill turned to Dex in horror. "I can't do that! We still don't know what happened to Frank. I came all this distance to find him." It was no longer necessary, but Castillo didn't know that. For once, Frank came in handy. His disappearance made a good excuse to stay longer with Dex.

The lieutenant thumped the table. "You'll do exactly as you are told. If you behave yourself and remain at the dig, I may let you stay for a few more days. It is possible the informer will try to search your room again, or try to get information from you directly, and we will be watching."

"Now, see here, Castillo." Dex started to rise. "I won't have you putting Jill in danger. She's been through enough in this charming country of yours."

"Sit down, Conroy. *Señora* Flanders will be guarded at all times. One of the maids is in my employ, as is one of your perimeter guards. They now know to be alert."

Frowning, Dex sat down. Castillo looked at them both, his face hard. Without another word, he took a small voice recorder from his pocket.

"Digame. Speak."

Shrugging, Jill and Dex looked at each other. "Shall I start?" she asked.

"Sí."

"About the map…I thought it was just a scrap of paper wrapped around the ear spools I found in the doll. I didn't notice there was anything written on it until after Dex delivered the jewelry to you. Truly."

The policeman continued to stare at her.

"When I found those gorgeous spools, I became so excited I shoved the wrapping into my pocket and forgot all about it. Much later, I fished it out and saw the funny markings. I took it to Dex, and we both tried to interpret them. We thought it might redeem our actions if we handed you the paper complete with an explanation. That seemed like the best idea, especially since we couldn't get back into Trujillo last night." Jill paused to drink her coffee.

"Dex and I decided it could be a secret code, or a map, but it was hard to decipher. I'll show you…just a minute."

Castillo's eyes opened wider as she licked some of the honey off her sticky fingers. Dex ran his tongue across his lips. Neither man could pull his gaze away from her mouth as she sucked each finger clean.

Biting her lip to hide her laughter at pushing the

two men's buttons, Jill wiped her hands and reached into the pocket of her jeans. She looked up in dismay. Frank's comb was there, but she wouldn't tell Castillo about finding it. She had no idea why she protected the bastard, but… Then her fingers touched the soggy piece of brown wrapping paper. It squished as she lifted it out. The paper hadn't disintegrated, but the soaking had obliterated most of the ink.

Grabbing it from her, the lieutenant glanced at the paper. His lips tightened as he peered at the smudges. "Tell me what was on it," he ordered.

Jill took the wrapping back and spread it out on the table. "You can just make out the wavy lines at the bottom," she pointed with a shiny red nail, "which we took to be the ocean. And in this corner is a little stick figure we decided was a doll. I'll trace it for you." She took the pen he offered, blotted the paper on a napkin, and outlined the faded figure. "See, there's the bonnet, the bootees, even the slit in the doll's back. We figured out the thieves used dolls to transport some of the smaller objects."

She looked up. The lieutenant nodded. "Go on."

"In the opposite corner are two boxlike shapes, and in between were these jagged lines shaped like horseshoes. We were too tired to figure out what they meant that night, but when I looked at the drawing in the morning, the explanation came to me at once."

Animated now, Jill rushed to explain her reasoning. "I made out the fancy fish on the rectangle," she pointed, "just like the one on the sign here at *Los Mariscos*. The smaller square had to be the patio. That gave me the direction toward the sea."

As Jill revealed her thought processes, her dark

hair dancing on her shoulders as she waved her hands about, she noticed Castillo's gaze soften.

"Once I knew the location and direction, I looked again at those horseshoe curves. The enormous rock we'd seen, with a U-shaped cave entrance, popped into my mind." She threw him a triumphant smile. "Pretty good guessing, yes?"

He did not respond. "What happened next?"

"I tried to find Dr. Conway, so he could decide what to do," Jill shrewdly deferred to the male ego. "But Dex had left for Trujillo on business for Harry, so I followed him. Since he had to wait for the supplies he'd ordered, I went on ahead to watch the cave entrance. I saw the looters leave. When the tide changed, I was afraid that would be our only chance to check out my theory, so I peeked in. Dex met me inside."

"You should have come to me first," the policeman rasped.

"Suppose I was wrong? I didn't think you would believe me. What if I had dragged you and your men here for nothing? And if you kept me waiting outside your office again, we'd lose the tide…" She dropped her gaze. "I didn't want to make a fool of myself in front of you."

Lips twitching, Castillo shook his head and waited for Dex to pick up the tale.

"I followed Jill about a half hour later. Broke the speed limit getting here." Dex winked. "Just in time, too. I found her in the cave with the loot. Almost got knocked out for my trouble!" He looked at her and grinned. "She had raised my heavy flashlight to use as a weapon and waited in the dark at the entrance. Luckily, she recognized me before she struck."

The lieutenant gazed at Jill again, his flirtatious eyes once more sending out signals. Then he sighed and listened to the rest—the roomful of loot, the thief who found them, Jill's ploy with the pendant, and their tricky escape. Taking out the bandit's pistol, Dex slid it across the table to Castillo and stopped talking. What happened afterward was private.

As the lieutenant looked down to examine the gun, Dex mimed a kiss to Jill. She winked back.

"So," Castillo pushed the "play" button on the recorder, "*Señora* Flanders hit *el bandito* with a rock crystal?"

"Yes," Jill replied. "It was huge, I've never seen one like it. I swung the chain by its heavy silver links, and that crystal flew."

"I suspect some Spaniard got hold of a Chimu pectoral stone and had it refashioned for his wife or mistress," Dex put in.

"Then some of the artifacts were *Nuevo España*?"

"I saw a conquistador's helmet, a dagger, a handful of gold coins. Most of the stuff was from the coastal Indian cultures, and there were some Inca artifacts, even a *quipu*." Dex turned to Jill. "That's the Inca counting device, those long strings with the knots in them." She nodded.

"I spotted a jaguar god with jade eyes mounted on the haft of a ceremonial knife. And a breastplate fashioned of overlapping gold leaves that was a knockout."

"There were woven cloths too," Jill chimed in, "with trophy head designs."

"Burial goods from Paracas, still rich in color."

"And linen," Jill exclaimed. "I was astonished at the quality."

The lieutenant puffed up with pride. "Our people were spinning fine weaves, creating great art, and traveling on paved roads while the Europeans were still walking on dirt."

Jill nodded. "Amazing skills for so long ago. Tell him about the pots we saw, Dex. That's your field of expertise."

Dex grinned at her, then turned back to the lieutenant. "A museum would give over a wing for that collection. Nazca pots with fanged heads, ollos from the Incas, black pottery from the Chimu." Dex let out a sigh. "But the most outstanding were the Moche stirrup pots. Animals. Fruit. Soldiers and scholars. The sick and the dead. And the erotic sculptures! They have to be seen to be believed."

Jill grew fidgety as Dex described the sexual positions on those pots. Both men were deriving immense enjoyment from the descriptions. She stood up abruptly. "I'm going to the ladies room." Male laughter trailed behind her.

Annoyed that she, too, was stimulated by visualizing the varied activities on the little pots, Jill spent several minutes holding her wrists under the faucet and splashing cold water on her face. When she emerged, the lieutenant was putting away the recorder.

"Did you take any pictures inside the cavern?" he asked.

"A few." She turned on her camera and looked in the view window. "They're blurred. I was nervous and in a big hurry, but you might get some idea of the scope of the haul."

Castillo held out his hand for the camera. "I will get it back to you. You may return to the dig now," he said to them both. "Remember, stay there for the next few days."

"Will you let us know if you catch up with the yacht?" Jill asked.

"I will keep in touch."

****

The drive back to the dig seemed endless. Jill dozed on Dex's shoulder, but was too tired, too overwrought, to sleep deeply. Her mind kept slipping back to the grubby bandit whose filthy leer pierced her skin as he described the sordid acts he had in store for her. His vicious face kept returning, jerking her awake every time they hit a pothole.

They finally arrived at the Pyramid of the Stars. Groggy, pushing wisps of hair from her eyes, Jill stepped out of the truck. She had no time to see who grabbed her before she was suddenly enveloped in a strangling hug.

"Sis!" Tim shouted. "Are you all right?"

Chapter 17

Tim's voice acted like a shot of adrenaline. With renewed energy, Jill hugged her kid brother. "So, *Abuelita* talked you into following me here? Not necessary, I'm doing fine…but it's good to see you." With another squeeze, she moved back, peered at him. "You look older."

"Law school ages a guy—and you look ti'ed, Jillie." The "r" in tired was lost in his newfound Boston drawl. "Any news of Frank?"

She stiffened. "No. We still don't know where he is or why he disappeared. I'm certain he's alive, though, following his own agenda. You know, the Indiana Jones thing."

"You're sure he wasn't kidnapped? That would be bad. Lots of horror stories on the Web about the guerrillas' treatment of captives."

"And I can guess who sent the stories to you." Tim grinned at Jill's sarcastic tone. "We haven't received any ransom notes. There's been no sign of a kidnapping, but we've called in the police."

"Okay, then, I'll work on my Christmas spirit. It's been a tough semester, and I can use a change of pace."

"Your Ba-aston accent needs some work, too."

He laughed. "There's a New Englander here who'll help me with it."

Jill looked him in the eye. "Is there something you're not telling me?"

"Nothing important. I had an interesting time traveling here. You'll get the details tomorrow."

"Okay. I've quite a story to tell, too. Dex and I found the looters' cave. You must meet him." Eyes shining, Jill called him over.

"Hi," he said, and held out his hand.

At the mention of Dex, a strange look crossed Tim's face. Jill couldn't imagine why he hesitated before shaking hands.

"Hi," he said, all warmth gone from his voice.

Dex raised an eyebrow but didn't comment. "Your sister and I have had quite an adventure," he told Tim. "Did you know she's a whiz at deciphering secret maps?"

"I didn't know that. We have some catching up to do." Tim turned away. "They've been holding dinner for you, Jillie, so go and get ready." He walked off with Sam Stern, who had been silently watching the scene.

Jill looked at Dex, bewildered. "What was that all about?"

He squeezed her hand. "Protective brother syndrome? He doesn't know about the divorce?"

"Uh-uh. Not that it's final."

"Don't worry, we'll get it straightened out." He tilted her chin up. "All will be well. Come on, I'll walk you to your room."

As they stood by the annex entrance, a thought struck her. "We still haven't solved the mystery of the informer."

"I've been chewing that over," he said. "You realize the snitch has had no trouble getting into your room each time he wanted to search. Or she. I'm beginning to suspect it must be a female to move so easily in the women's quarters. She could have ducked into another room the day I tried to chase her."

"But who could it be? Poppy comes to mind, but she hasn't been here."

"She would be my guess, too. There's definitely a connection between her and Frank through the doll. But Poppy couldn't be sneaking around without someone spotting her. She, uh, makes herself very visible."

"So I've gathered." Jill grimaced. "Still, I can't see how young Karen or Marge could have made contact with the thieves. They're new here, aren't they? A maid or a cook's helper, do you think?"

"Possible, but doubtful. It has to be someone who understands what he's seeing."

"Or she. There's our textile expert, Maria Topol," Jill went on when he nodded. "She has the room at the end of the hall."

"Topol wouldn't stoop so low. She's an important figure in her own field. Getting involved in something shady would ruin her reputation."

"But she's so unfriendly."

"That's just her manner. Not everyone is bewitched by your charms," Dex teased.

She pinched him. "So who's left?"

"If it's a male," he pondered, "the same goes for young Hank and Don—they'd have no contacts. This is the first year on the dig for them. It could be Harry, but I don't really suspect him. I've known him for so long, and his reputation is spotless."

"I know we considered him, but I can't believe it's Harry either. He's bossy, but not dishonest."

"Sam arrived at the dig too late. We haven't mentioned Luis Gomez, our Moche specialist, but being caught would certainly finish his career, too. He couldn't stand the disgrace."

"No. And he's such a sweet little man."

"You'd disqualify him for that reason?" Dex asked. "How many of the men here do you find sweet?" He stepped closer, stroked her arm.

"Only Luis," she said, mischief in her glance.

"I'm not sweet?"

"Nope, wrong adjective. Strong. Handsome. Protective. Sexy—definitely sexy, but not sweet. Although I'll admit you taste sweet." She licked her lips.

"Is that so? Works for you, too—sweet and buttery, like Scottish shortbread." He stepped nearer, bent his head and ran his tongue along her ear, nibbling on the lobe.

Jill shivered with pleasure. "Let's not lose track of our discussion. Who's left? A guard perhaps? But could one of them give accurate information to the bandits? Or to an accomplice?"

"Too complicated." He ran his fingers through her hair, curlier than usual after its saltwater bath. "If we start imagining more than one informer, we'll get lost in conspiracy theories."

"Well, there were those other incidents. You know, the stone that fell, the car that swiped us, the blow dart…"

"There has to be a simpler explanation."

"I suppose. All we can do is keep our eyes and ears open, hoping someone slips and gives us a clue."

"And consult with each other if we learn anything,

don't forget. No solo actions." Dex looked around. Seeing no one, he planted a quick kiss on Jill's mouth, his tongue running lightly along her lips. "Just a preview of what's to come," he murmured as she leaned into him. "Soon, I hope."

"Me, too." She gazed at him, her feelings revealed in her eyes. "The police are keen to get this mess cleaned up. I think they'll move quickly now." She stroked his cheek, then turned toward the entrance. "See you in a bit."

A smile still hovered as Jill hurried down the corridor to her room. It felt good to have both Dex and Tim here, though she didn't know why Tim had been so curt when she introduced them. Not like the well-mannered brother she knew. Well, she'd find out tomorrow.

As she reached for the handle, Jill halted. The door to her room was ajar. Could the wind have blown it open? Good Lord, she hoped the thief hadn't returned. Taking her hand off the knob, Jill stood still, biting her knuckle. Should she go in, or try to find Dex?

Stuff it. She'd been in such a hurry this morning, she had probably left it open. The wind did the rest. Taking a deep breath, Jill pushed the door wide—and stared.

The room wasn't empty. Grunting as she bent over, Maria Topol poked through the contents of Jill's chest of drawers.

Jill's mouth dropped open. "Dr. Topol?"

With an effort, the woman straightened and turned around, eyeing Jill with a malevolent glare. "You were not supposed to be back so soon." She spat the words.

Speechless, Jill contemplated the scene in front of

her. Maria huffed as she stood up, her slender ankles seeming too thin to support her large body. The sand on the floor where she had been crouching bore the stripes of her fringed shawl. Her face was red, and the bun in her jet-black hair dangled from her scalp at a crazy angle. It was so unlike the professor to appear disheveled.

"What are you doing in my room?" Jill demanded. "Why are you going through my drawers?"

"Why do you think?" Maria sneered. "I look for the map Francisco left."

"H-how do you know about the map?"

"You innocent fool. Francisco tell me. He tell me many things." Maria looked Jill up and down with contempt.

"Are you implying that it was you Frank was making out with, not Poppy?"

"Making out, no—making love! Poppy was, how you say, a decoy. I am the one Francisco loves, and will always love!" she cried out.

Taking a deep breath, Jill exhaled slowly. Boy, had she misjudged the woman. Who would have suspected a romantic side? "What have you to do with the map?" she asked.

Topol's eyes took on a peculiar shine. "You do not understand. Francisco tells me everything. We are life's true mates. *Francisco y Maria.*" She was breathing hard now, her eyes sending daggers at Jill. "It is the tragedy we have to wait so long to meet."

Despite her anger, Jill worried about the woman. Her flush was gone. Maria's skin had turned ashen except for two unnatural red patches below her cheekbones, delicate veins showing. She was beginning to gasp for breath.

Jill pulled her back to the bed and sat down beside her. "Where is Frank now?"

"He is escaping with our share of the treasure. Francisco has tricked the guerrillas. When he arrives at his destination, he will contact me, and I will join him."

"You'll give up everything?"

"Por supuesto. Not many are blessed to find their true mates."

Jill wouldn't argue with that. "How do you know Frank is safe?"

"Nothing has happened to him. I would feel it, here." She pressed a hand between her ample breasts. "He has a fine plan. Francisco is *muy* clever."

"I know that." Jill bit her lip. "I still can't believe you would sacrifice your professional standing to be a partner in something so illegal."

"Hah. It is no wonder Francisco found you—what did he say? *Pescado frio.* A cold fish. You do not understand *amor."*

"It's a cultural difference," Jill said, thinking furiously. "Why were you hunting for the map?"

"I…I do not know what the map signifies, but I catch him looking at it and feel in here." Her hands fluttered to her breasts again. "It is the place Francisco has gone. I go there myself, make sure he is not harmed." She pressed her lips together. "He has my trust *perfecto,* but many days pass since he left. It is a woman's lot to worry."

"That may be. I'm a worrier, too, but it won't help you to hunt for the map. I already discovered it and found the cave where the thieves kept the stolen artifacts."

"Usted?"

"You needn't sound so surprised. I can be *muy* clever, too."

Maria swallowed. "Did you see Francisco?"

"No, but he'd been there. I found this." Jill fished in her pocket and brought forth the silver-edged comb.

A long sigh escaped Maria's lips. "When I ask what he does, he makes love to me instead of answering. I…I prefer his kisses to answers, so I help him."

"How?"

"I tell him about the site's discoveries. And I take care of the doll for him. But you have destroyed that!" Her voice grew loud with rage.

"Please calm down." Jill reached out to touch Maria's hand. "The doll wasn't a good hiding place. If I hadn't found the earrings, Poppy would have." As Topol's breathing slowed, Jill said, "What will you do now?"

"Francisco promised us a wonderful life when he finishes this job," she muttered, then sat straighter, still defiant. "So I wait longer."

"We all will," Jill grumbled.

The woman hissed and started to rise, but Jill reached up and pulled Maria back. "Don't get so excited, Doctor Topol. Frank and I are divorced. I just found out the decree is final. He can run off with you, that's fine, but he owes me an explanation first, and Harry, too. Now the police are hunting for him."

"You called in the *guardía?* Why? What are you going to do?" Maria's voice rose in fear now. Her flush returned.

"The police had to be informed. Frank has been

missing for too long. You may not be aware of all *Francisco* has been up to, but knowing about the map will cause you trouble. Perhaps you, too, should contact the police, let them know you're not part of his scheme?"

"Never!" Topol started to rise, and this time Jill let her.

"If you hear from *Francisco,*" she said, poking Maria, "you had better tell me. If Frank has been caught by the guerrillas, his life may be in danger."

The woman paled once more, then ran out of the room.

Somehow, Jill didn't think Maria Topol would hear from *Francisco* again. The lady professor wasn't Frank's type. He might go for big boobs and the waist-long tresses that had fallen out of Maria's bun, but only on nubile young women he could train to suit him. Still, she'd bet Frank enjoyed running his fingers through all that satiny jet hair while he picked her brain.

She couldn't help feeling sorry for the woman. Dr. Topol had been used. She may have given Frank the information unwittingly, but not unwillingly. Maria must have known that what she was doing was illegal.

What would happen to the professor now?

Chapter 18

Manuel had a new job. He'd been hired to join the night security patrol at *Huaca de las Estrellas*. The mestizo's eyes gleamed as he circled the compound, his mind preoccupied not with spotting intruders, but with plotting intrusions.

He would have no problem sneaking into the women's quarters. No doors were locked in the old buildings. As for the woman *el patrón* wanted disposed of—Manuel looked around, determined no one was watching, and parted his dry lips in a garish grin. He had a small surprise to leave in the *señora's* bed…

****

No one commented on the textile expert's absence at dinner, pouncing on Dex instead to hear the details of his and Jill's adventure in the looters' cave. When he finished recounting the story, he clasped her hand and raised it high. The audience cheered.

Instead of joining in, Tim looked worried. "Sis, you sure know how to get into trouble. You shouldn't take such risks."

Jill patted his shoulder. "It's over now. I'm safe and sound."

"Well, maybe safe…" She pinched him. "Guess I'd better stick closer to you till we get back to the States."

"Protecting me now, are you? You needn't act like

Big Brother. I used to change your diapers."

Tim blushed. "Hell of a thing to remind me of. I'm twenty-one…almost."

"I know, and taller than I am now. But I'm still your older sister, so behave. I have to speak to Dex for a few minutes now that dinner is over, but wait and walk me back to the women's quarters. We need to talk."

Tim glowered, but acquiesced. "Okay, I could use another beer."

Beckoning to Dex, she headed for the bench under the awning. After leaning in for a quick, surreptitious kiss, Jill told him about Maria Topol. "What a scare I had when I walked into my room."

"So she knew about the map." He grew pensive. "It doesn't sound as if Maria partnered Frank in the thefts, but she must have known something. He asked for reports on the site, and she didn't blow the whistle on him. What people will do for—"

Jill interrupted. "I still can't believe she'd risk her reputation and her career for that womanizing—"

Dex cut back in. "Don't forget, you fell in love with Frank once." Annoyed at the flash of jealousy piercing him at the thought, he plodded on. "Men and women do strange things when they fall into Cupid's embrace."

Absentmindedly playing with his silver belt buckle, she sighed. "It's not so hard to understand why people take wild chances when they get lost in the L word." She ran her tongue over her lips, and he leaned over to kiss her again. Covering her hand on his buckle, he moved it lower.

"Mmph, stop tempting me. What shall we do, Dex?

Are you going to tell Harry?"

"We'll let the police do that. I'll see Lieutenant Castillo tomorrow. He's sure to have questions for Topol. You don't have to come. Spend some time showing your brother around."

He understood how she felt, saw from her smile that the knowledge was precious to her. She put her arms around his waist and rested her head on his broad chest.

He kissed her again and ran his fingers through her hair until she tingled. Looking up, Dex caught sight of Tim standing in the chow hall doorway, watching them. Cursing under his breath, he walked Jill back to her brother and said goodnight.

****

Lips tight, Tim eyed his sister and Dex.

"What's the matter?" she asked, noticing his scowl.

"I've heard nasty things about that man, Jillie. Aren't you getting a little too friendly? He's into more than one woman."

"What are you talking about, Tim? What nasty things?" She wondered if he realized the double meaning of his words. He was growing up so fast.

"Well...I met this girl on the plane. We sat next to each other from Miami to Lima. She's a fox."

"Yes? Go on."

"She told me she'd been working at this dig, but left because one of the older men was hitting on her. It disturbed her enough to make her leave for a while."

"Ah. Her name isn't Poppy, by any chance?"

"Yeah, how'd you guess?"

"There's been some talk about her—and Frank."

"Frank? Hell, no. She told me the guy's name was

Dex."

Jill stared at him. "You must have that wrong."

"I'm quite sure Dex is the name she said. That's why I keep giving him dirty looks."

"Where is Poppy now?"

"Staying in Trujillo with friends until tomorrow. She wants to surprise everyone—make a grand entrance. She's a bit of a drama queen, thought my arrival would take some of the focus off her."

Inwardly, Jill cringed. At least Tim saw through her to some extent. "Well, hon, let's wait till tomorrow to straighten matters out. I'm certain there's a mistake somewhere." She kissed him on the cheek. "You must be exhausted after all your traveling. I know I was when I finally arrived."

"Yeah. You'll meet Poppy tomorrow, Sis. You're gonna like her."

Jill watched him lope down the path. She entered her room and lit the kerosene lamp. Its flickering light cast shadows across her face, highlighting the worry lines between her brows. As she unbuttoned her blouse, she noticed the silver-edged comb was no longer on the chest. Topol must have taken it.

Poor woman. She shouldn't feel sorry for her. After all, as far as Maria knew, she was dealing with a married man. She must have suspected his shady morals. But Frank could be such a bastard. He didn't care who or what he destroyed in the pursuit of his own desires.

Her mind elsewhere as she undressed, Jill dropped her sweaty clothes and felt around for the oversized T-shirt she'd taken to sleeping in. Since Chimbote, her blue nightgown remained locked in her suitcase. She filled the basin and soaked her feet for a few minutes. After that, chilled and restless, she lay down on the bed and pulled the blankets up to her chin. Poppy must have made a mistake. The girl did have a thing for Dex, so using his name must have been wishful thinking on her part. But now that Tim had reinforced her own doubts, the conversation Jill heard in the shower shack kept playing over and over in her mind.

What if it were true?

The next morning she awoke with a start, her heart beating wildly as she tried to shake off the writhing tendrils of a bad dream. The images persisted in forming. She was back in the bandit's cave. Water trickling in from the passageway lapped at her feet. As she stood in front of the burlap sacks, now piled on top of each other to form a pyramid, the top sack rolled down from the pile. Jill picked it up, dipped her fingers in the opening and pulled aside the drawstring. She stared at Frank's severed head.

As dreams go, the apparition didn't frighten her. She continued to stare at the lascivious face. When a bloodshot eye winked at her lewdly, she pulled the drawstring closed and let the bag drop.

Another sack rolled down from the pile, splashing as it hit the water, which had now risen to her ankles. She opened this one to see a female head with glassy brown eyes staring sightlessly at her. Long, yellow hair fanned out in a crown around the girl's face and floated on the slowly rising water, the strands bunched into knotted strings like an Inca *quipu*. This one, she knew, counted scalps.

She closed the sack and let it slide from her fingers as a third came tumbling down. Shivering, she opened this one with great care. Before she had widened the hole more than a few inches, a familiar lock of sun-bleached hair fell out. With a cry, she dropped the sack and backed up, shoes sloshing as the water reached her shins. She kept stepping backward until the side of her head hit the wall of the cave.

Only it wasn't the cave wall, but the edge of the suitcase she was using as a night table. Jill's eyes flew open. Rubbing her head, she winced as her pulse slowly returned to normal.

This morning, Dex would tell Lieutenant Castillo about Maria Topol. On impulse, she decided to go with him. She swung her legs out of bed, stepped over the basin she had left on the floor after soaking her feet, and poured water from the pitcher to splash her face. As she rinsed off the last remnants of the dream, a mottled black scorpion crept out of her tangled sheets and fell into the basin. She stifled a scream as she watched it drown. Then, with a shudder, turned away.

Tim had said that Poppy would arrive today. The "fox" could keep him occupied. She pulled on her last clean pair of jeans, white ones with slits at the narrow ankles, then reached into the drawer for her red linen pirate blouse. Its full sleeves were slashed from shoulder to wrist.

****

Already at breakfast when Jill arrived, Dex licked his lips as he drank her in. "Super outfit," he declared. "The blouse brings out the red in your hair, and those jeans look like you've been poured into them. I like the candy-cane colors." He glanced around the room, checking that no one could overhear. "You look good enough to suck."

She grinned. "Candy canes are for Christmas."

"That's not far off. Are you all dressed up for Tim's benefit?"

"No. I've decided to come with you."

"The lieutenant will love that outfit. Stick close to me while we're in Trujillo. You'll need protection."

Jill laughed with pleasure. "When do we leave?"

"As soon as you've eaten. Better stoke up, lunch will be late."

She added a hard-boiled egg to her roll and coffee this morning, liberally dousing it with salsa.

"Missing your croissants and cappuccino?" he teased.

"Nope. A buttered bagel at my desk, and a mug of strong coffee, no sugar. That's my daily breakfast."

Dex grinned. "I can picture you, Madame Executive, bagel in one hand and manuscript in the other, dripping melted butter on a misspelled word!"

She threw her roll at him.

Catching it easily, Dex popped it into his mouth. His eyes gleamed as his tongue licked the bit of salsa about to drop off its edge.

"Cut it out," she groaned. "You're making it hard for me to digest this magnificent feast."

"You do the same to me..." At her look, he laughed. "Hurry up. I'd like to get away before anyone else shows up."

"Have you told Harry?"

"Yeah. Made up an excuse. He yelled at first, then bit the bullet. I promised to work around the clock when I returned."

"Does he know about Maria?"

"No, I couldn't tell him. Topol was his choice for

the dig. He won't believe she's betrayed him."

"I don't think Maria sees it as betrayal."

"Sure looks that way to me. Anyway, I need to put in a full afternoon on the pot."

"That's all right. I promised to show Tim around, although he'll probably have seen everything before I return. He may be young, but he's quite an operator."

"Unlike his sister."

Jill poked him. Grinning, Dex squeezed her hand.

When they reached the lieutenant's office, Dex let Jill describe her encounter with the dig's textile authority. Castillo listened closely, nothing but his narrowed eyelids revealing his impatience.

"Why did you not telephone me last night?" he asked.

"Would we have reached you?" Dex countered. "We didn't want to speak to anyone else and thought telling you in person would be the most effective way."

Relieved that he didn't announce they'd agreed to give Maria a chance to get away, Jill suspected the lieutenant guessed that was the case. There was no way the police could have reached the dig in time, even if a call had gotten through to Castillo the night before. It was a relief not to carry that particular burden of guilt, and rapturous love was an emotion they could empathize with.

"You have repeated everything *el profesor* said?" Castillo stressed the academic title with sarcasm.

As Jill nodded, he drummed his pencil. "I find it hard to believe. I attended a lecture Doctor Topol gave on the Paracas textiles. I am very interested in the trophy head cult, you see. The woman was so animated when she spoke of her subject. So forceful—a Valkyrie.

I listened for Wagner's music in the background."

Jill glanced at Dex, and he raised an eyebrow. There were more facets to this policeman than they had suspected.

"We will try to find the professor." Castillo sighed. "It seems, *Señora* Flanders, that we cannot keep you out of this case, no matter how hard we try."

Jill gave him a dazzling smile. "I'm happy to assist the law in my small way."

Dex watched their little byplay jealously. If he hadn't been standing so close to Jill, possessiveness oozing out of him, he'd bet the policeman would have responded differently. That red shirt and the tight white pants were *muy* provocative.

"Whew." Jill expelled a breath as they walked down the steps into the morning air. "I'm glad that's over with. I expected to be rebuked much more severely for not contacting Castillo earlier. At one point I thought I'd be eaten alive."

Dex shrugged. "Oh, he wanted to eat you, all right."

She giggled. "Do you really think so?"

"No doubt about it. I recognized the look. You'd be a very tasty morsel in that candy-cane outfit. Good for his 'digestion.'"

Her brows rose, and Dex chuckled. "The lieutenant has an eye for the women. He could devour you and lust after Topol at the same time, though he'd pick a mariachi band for you, rather than Wagner. Good thing I was there."

"What music would you choose?"

"For you? A blues guitar."

"Seems a better fit…are they calling you?"

"*Señor* Conroy…" They turned to see Dex being motioned back. Jill started to follow but was rebuffed. At the bottom of the stairs, she waited, tapping her foot.

Dex returned a few moments later. "Just some official stuff to report to Harry," he said. "Early renewal necessary for permission to dig next season."

He didn't look her in the eye. Instead, he took her arm and bought them ice cream cones from a vendor. They ate while driving. He kept darting glances at Jill, caught her licking the creamy cone, listened to her rumbles of pleasure. The moment they were out of the city, he pulled over to the side of the road and licked the chocolate from her sticky lips. Her tongue flicked out and licked the coconut flavor off his. With an aching growl, Dex forced himself to return to driving.

****

He dropped Jill off at the women's annex, and she complimented herself on her control—she'd refrained from asking questions he couldn't or wouldn't answer. She changed into khaki shorts and a green tank top. Small green pompoms on her anklets bobbled above her sneakers.

As she brushed her hair, a beam of sunlight flashed in the mirror, highlighting Poppy's astrology magazine. It brought to mind her conversation with Tim, and her uneasiness returned. She didn't believe the gossip, so why did his words grab at her gut?

Frank was gone, but he would show up eventually. Dex was here, and despite what Tim said and she'd overheard in the shower, she didn't think he was using her. He cared. Maybe not equally, for she had fallen in love with the man. She might as well admit that the feeling wasn't going away.

Poppy must be here by now. Perhaps she'd get some answers. The police would find Maria Topol, and the professor would lead them to Frank. Her Peruvian adventure was almost over.

She had to return to work, but Dex would spend another month at the dig to finish his research on the Moche priestess pot. What would he do after that, return to teaching for the spring semester? He'd told her he taught at U Penn, and Philadelphia was only a couple of hours from New York. Perhaps they would get together on weekends? So many things had been on their minds, they'd never discussed the future. Once she returned to Manhattan, would she ever see him again?

For several minutes, Jill stood in front of the little mirror, automatically brushing her dark hair until it gleamed. Finally, she twisted it into a ponytail and put on her straw hat. Glancing back at the basin as she left the room, Jill again noticed the shriveled scorpion drowned within. Well, the maid was sure to clean it up when she brought fresh towels. Putting it out of her mind, she headed down the path to the work area. With her energetic stride and tall, willowy figure, a passing stranger might guess she was a teenager—if no one came close enough to notice the worry lines etched between her brows.

As she walked by, Jill turned her gaze to the worktable under the awning. Next to it a young woman, blonde hair swinging below her shoulders, stood right behind Dex. Her arms were hugging his chest, and her cheek rested on his back.

Jill stopped short. *Poppy*. The girl was wrapped around Dex. Apparently, Poppy liked to dangle two men at once. He didn't move, obviously enjoying the attention. Without waiting to see more, Jill spun around and ran back to her room. Tears stung her eyes.

Slow down, she told herself. *Think!* Why did she react so strongly? All the miserable rejections of her youth, real and imagined, rose up to haunt her. She couldn't think. Something inside her tried to force its way through the noise in her head, but she refused to listen.

Reaching Poppy's room, Jill paused. The girl's aura haunted it. No escape here. Where should she go, just to be alone and think? Looking out across the desert, Jill made out the Pyramid of the Moon jutting through the shimmering heat waves. *That's it,* she decided. The walk would calm her nerves, give her room to contemplate. By the time she reached the *huaca*, perhaps she'd have made some sense out of her hopelessly negative, push-button reactions.

Resolutely, Jill headed out across the sand.

****

Dex was surrounded by white lilacs. He sneezed.

"So you're back, Poppy," he said. Without turning around, he reached for a handkerchief.

"You knew it was me!" Poppy squealed. "You're amazing."

"Anyone within a mile would know it was you, Poppet. But you'll have to find another bee to pollinate your flower. This one is allergic to your scent." He sneezed again.

"Ooh, you naughty man," she cooed, backing away. "Everyone else likes my perfume."

"Perhaps if you weren't drenched in it."

"I have this little atomizer, and I just squeeze the bulb. The perfume sprays over my entire naked body."

"Quit flirting, infant. Try it on someone your own age. I assure you, I am allergic."

"Spoilsport!"

"There's someone new here you can work your charms on. His name is Tim."

"I met him on the plane." Poppy licked her lips. "He's a hottie."

"I'm crushed—replaced already. Here he comes now."

Poppy turned and waved excitedly. As she sped away, Dex breathed a sigh of relief. Now he could concentrate on solving the mystery of his pot.

Chapter 19

Jill's walk was a long one. The dry air sucked all the moisture from her nose and mouth. She concentrated on the vision in the distance, blotting out all thoughts other than reaching the pyramid. The Poppy Problem would wait.

When she finally made it to the H*uaca de la Luna*, the sun was high in the sky. Panting, Jill looked for shade, but there was no escape from the scorching rays. Leaning against a broken wall, she sank to the ground and supported her head between raised knees. The brim of her Panama offered the only shade. Her eyes burned, too dry for tears. Closing them, she dozed in exhaustion.

Shadows gradually crept across the pyramid, offering respite. She awoke with a start. A hand shook her lightly, while a guttural voice whispered, *"Señora?"*

Startled, Jill looked up. A gnome of a man stood in front of her, shaking a head that seemed too large for his small body. He motioned for her to stand, and she rose, staggering. Pulling at her arm, he led her to a small adobe shack on the far side of the *huaca*. From his mixture of Spanish and Indian dialect, she recognized the words for fortress and guardian.

Inside, the hut was cool and dim. Jill dropped onto

a stool as the little man reached for a thermos and offered her some tepid water. She knew she shouldn't drink it, but her thirst was unbearable. Taking only a few sips, she spilled a little in her palm and ran it across her face and shoulders. The relief was painful.

"Usted tostado," he said, and she translated it as sunburned. Nodding grimly, Jill agreed. She felt like a slice of charred toast. How would she ever return to the dig?

"I'll rest awhile," she told him in Spanish, gesturing with her body to make sure he understood. He smiled, showing two blackened teeth and lots of gum. Then he left her alone.

The shadows lengthened. Jill became restless. She was about to get up and look for the little man when the door opened. He beckoned, and once more she followed him.

Walking over to the pyramid, he twisted his body into a cleft leading to the interior. Jill hesitated, suddenly afraid. They were alone at the ruin. Then she shrugged. If he had meant to harm her, he'd had plenty of opportunities. No need to take her inside the crumbling fortress.

She had followed him halfway around when he stopped and pointed to a pile of large stones. He lifted the rocks and moved them out of the way until the pyramid wall cleared. For his size and age, the man's strength was amazing.

Jill stared. Painted on the tightly fitting adobe bricks, a strange, oversized head stared back. The face had piercing eyes, a large nose, and an open mouth with teeth and long fangs. It was the jaguar god Dex had told her about, and he wore ear spools inset with shiny chips of obsidian. Black hair resembling snakes framed his face from the top of his head to the beard below—a frightening visage, even in its faded glory.

What a find! How excited Dex would be when she told him about the mural. Before she could phrase a question, however, the little man piled the stones back up, hiding the god from the sun's burning rays.

"Gracias," she said fervently, *"muchas gracias, señor."* She smiled through her cracked lips and shook his hand. His two-tooth grin reappeared.

The guardian offered her more water, but she took only enough to wet her dry mouth, then spat into her palms and splashed the liquid onto her face. Dusk had begun to darken the sky, and Jill decided to try for the road. A car or truck was sure to come along, and she would hitch a ride back to the dig.

"Adios," she called and headed for the sandy track shining pink in the last of the sun's rays. As she trudged down the road, Jill began to feel dizzy. Soon she grew nauseous. Her head was pounding. Everything began to blur. What was she doing on this deserted road in the middle of nowhere?

Her steps began to falter, but she stumbled on. There was no turning back—she had to hold herself together. Would anyone find her? The longing to sink to the ground was so overwhelming, only her fear of dying kept her moving.

The minutes crept by. Jill dragged one foot after the other, slower and slower. She had begun to slip to the ground when she caught the sound of an engine. A red truck came wavering out of the darkness. As its headlights fell on her, it skidded on the sand and rolled to a stop.

"Jill, my God!" The angry voice turned concerned as Dex leaped from the truck and ran to her side.

Jill's eyelids drooped. "Come to my rescue again, Superman?" She could barely whisper. Her eyes closed, and she began to sway.

****

Grabbing her, Dex lifted her into his arms and carried her to the truck. Without a word he sat her in the passenger seat, stripped off his T-shirt and wet it with water from his canteen. He removed her Panama hat and gently bathed her face with the wet cloth. Jill parted her lips, letting droplets from the shirt fall onto her cracked lips and into her mouth.

Holding her head, Dex dribbled a swallow of water from the canteen. Then he soaked the shirt once more, running it along her neck and arms, her thighs and calves. Wherever her skin had been exposed, the angry red of her sunburn slashed a line against pale skin.

He gazed at her. "No matter why you did this, you're going to be sorry tomorrow." Strapping her into the seat, he put the truck into gear and sped back to the dig. He parked and carried Jill through the office to a small room set aside as an infirmary.

"Water," Jill croaked as he laid her on the cot. A cone-shaped paper cupful was all he would give her. Holding her head once more, he stroked her hair as she swallowed.

He was rubbing burn ointment all over her skin when the door burst open. Tim barged in, followed by Harry and Sam.

"Sis!" Tim cried, rushing over to the bed. "What happened?"

"She's had too much sun, that's all," Dex said.

"My stomach," Jill moaned. "I'm going to throw up."

Dex hurried over with a basin. He held her head while she retched, but nothing came out. "Your stomach's empty. I'll bet you haven't eaten since the ice cream cone. Did you put anything in your mouth while you were gone?"

"Only two sips of water," she said, her voice so hoarse it was hard to decipher her words. "The guardian at the moon pyramid had a canteen." The men all looked at each other, Tim's eyes wide with alarm.

"She hasn't drunk enough to do much damage," Harry said, "but she's going to have a bad day tomorrow."

Turning, Tim looked accusingly at Dex. "She ran away. Why? What did you do?"

"Damned if I know." He dug his fingers through his sandy hair. "Jill, do you want to tell us why?"

"Don' wanna talk." Then she mumbled something, her eyes tightly closed.

Tim leaned over. "What, Sis?"

Wishing he were the one bending over her, Dex didn't move.

"Mural," she whispered. "At *Huaca de la Luna.* Hidden. Jaguar god. Tell Dex…"

Tim looked up, shrugging. "I can't make out what she's saying."

"It's okay, she'll tell us when she feels better." Dex stepped over to the cupboard and took out a bottle of pills. "Let's see if we can get some antibiotics down her before we take her back to her room to sleep it off." Shaking two pills into his palm, he got another cup of water.

Tim grabbed them from him. "I'll do it."

Helpless to control his anger, Dex shoved the paper cup at Tim, spilling a few drops.

He glanced at his wet shirt, gave Dex a dirty look. "Swallow these, Sis, then we'll take you back."

"Don't want room," Jill muttered, wincing as she shook her head. "Poppy's room."

Tim looked surprised. Dex raised an eyebrow. Harry and Sam exchanged knowing glances.

"Do you want to stay here in the infirmary?" Harry asked gently, but she was already asleep.

****

Jill slept for fourteen hours, awoke with a dry mouth, a pounding headache and a queasy stomach. As the day wore on she began to feel better, although the sunburn itch was driving her crazy. She lathered herself with burn cream, then stuck her hands under the pillow to prevent herself from scratching.

Later, she remembered the day only hazily. Someone had looked in on her every hour, fed her water and chicken soup. When she finally sat up in the early evening, she was given a small dish of rice and mashed banana to settle her stomach. Tim had poked his head in several times during the morning, but he'd disappeared for the afternoon. Dex had stopped by often but didn't step inside, and she'd been grateful. She wasn't up to facing him.

Unpleasant images kept tumbling around in her aching head. Poppy had looked so comfortable, so *familiar,* with her arms around Dex. Eighteen-year-old Poppy—slim, wrinkle-free, and blooming. Silky blonde hair. High rounded breasts and tight little ass. With this she had to compete. What a laugh.

Jill wanted to hide, to crawl under the desk in her Manhattan office. She would curl up on the rya rug, clutching her raku vase and her crystal telephone. She'd fall asleep staring at her bark paintings. Forget Peru and all that had happened here. When she awoke, she'd climb into her executive chair, ring for her secretary, and be in charge again. No more longings. No more beaches. To hell with love.

Wallowing in her pity party, hurting inside and out, Jill fell back to sleep.

****

Dex paced back and forth outside the infirmary. "It's all Frank's fault," he fumed. "If the sniveling coward hadn't run away from her, Jill would never have been placed in such danger." Of course, he wouldn't have met Jill if there hadn't been a mix-up with the divorce papers, but he wasn't feeling logical. He remembered only too well the message Lieutenant Castillo had told him privately.

According to one of the police informers, all the accidents—the falling rock, the blowgun, and God knows what else, had been instigated by Frank. The rat remained safely in hiding, while his cohorts did his bidding. Dex could hardly wait for the man to be caught, tried, and hung! Or better yet, given a life sentence in a Peruvian prison. He was in such a rage, he even blamed Frank for Jill's sunburn.

He had yet to figure out how to tell her what the lieutenant had said. His righteousness warred with his desire to protect her from more hurt. Hadn't she been traumatized enough? Although she wanted the divorce and hated the bastard, he was afraid she had a soft spot left for Frank. Didn't she say she hoped he'd be extradited and tried in the States?

He should warn her of Frank's perfidy, let her know what the man was capable of, but not after what she'd gone through today. Better to think about what to say, choose his words with care, and save them for a more appropriate moment. Now she had Tim watching her back, too. There was no rush.

Chapter 20

The woman must not have seen the scorpion, much less felt its poisonous sting. There had been no screams, no rush to get her to a hospital. Manuel had not even frightened her.

He had watched in disbelief as the maid emptied the water basin, using her toe to mash the drowned insect into the sand. Spitting on the ground, Manuel made the sign of the cross. *La señora* led a charmed life.

But he, Manuel, would find a way to carry out the balding man's instructions. It had become a matter of honor.

****

Poppy bunked in with Karen and Marge for the night. Leaving Marge sleeping, she and Karen headed out for breakfast. She couldn't wait to tell her *bff* about meeting Tim on the plane. "He's so good looking, with that come-to-me, come-*with*-me smile. Gran would call him a dreamboat."

"Well, I'm glad you're over Dex," Karen said. "I wonder if he and Jill have a thing going?"

"Oh, yeah, he and Tim's sister are getting it on, I can tell. I got myself into a stupid mess by telling Tim that Dex was my stalker."

"Poppy, you didn't! You're going to get into

trouble over that one."

"You're right. I'll own up. I fancy Tim and don't want to start a new relationship with a lie. I think he likes me, too. There haven't been any nasty cracks about dumb blondes majoring in no-brains art."

"That's a change."

"True. Tim's hot, and that's cool. Very Zen. I have to find out his birthday, see if he's compatible with a Pisces."

They sauntered down the path, passing the office just as Tim stepped out.

With a big smile he fell into step beside them. "Heading for some food?"

"Yeah, I need to boost my energy level. I dread getting back to the computer. Come have some breakfast."

"I've eaten, but I'll have a cup of coffee with you."

In the chow hall, Karen left them. Poppy took a taco, spooned on salsa and sprinkled extra hot sauce in the center.

As she took a large bite, Tim blinked. "That's your breakfast?"

"Sure. Great stuff! Really wakes you up." She ran her tongue over her upper lip, then all around her mouth where the salsa had stung. "I like hot things."

He stared at her roving tongue. "I'll be sure to remember that."

"When's your birthday?"

"February twenty-fourth. Why?"

"We're both Pisces. I'm intuitive and idealistic, and you're sensitive and spontaneous. We're a great combination."

"I won't forget that either." She took another bite,

and he waited for her to lick her lips again.

"Tim. There's something I've got to tell you."

"What's wrong?"

"Nothing, really, only I wasn't totally honest with you when I gave you my reason for leaving the dig."

"You hate skiing?"

"No, silly." She smacked his arm.

"It wasn't because a guy was coming on to you?"

"No, I meant that, too, but…it wasn't Dex. I didn't want to tell you the truth."

"Why not?"

"Because you're related to him."

"Do you mean Frank? That doesn't surprise me. He and my sister are getting divorced. My family's upset about it."

"Don't let it gross you out. Remember, each person should follow his bliss."

"Hell, I don't care what Frank does…as long as he didn't hurt you?"

"Oh no. Cool it, nothing like that. At first I liked the attention, you know, from an older guy. But then he started to get touchy-feely, and I began to squirm. I couldn't tell him to back off as long as we were both stuck here, so I packed my stuff. Leaving seemed the simplest way to handle it. I would get in a week of skiing, and give him time to find someone else." She grinned. "It worked just the way I thought."

"But you're not averse to being touched?"

"I love it when you talk 'lawyer.' No, not when the right person's doing it."

His eyes lit up. "You've made my day."

****

Awaking in the little infirmary the following

morning, Jill lay on the cot and mulled over the last few days. It had been humiliating to see Poppy and Dex together. What had she been thinking? She'd been every kind of fool to let a handsome face and gorgeous body get under her skin.

She sat up, pushed back her tangled hair. Where was the managing editor who took on authors, agents, contracts, and bent them all to her will? Where was the confident executive who was firm but feminine, secure in her success? What had happened to her sense of self?

Jill slumped. It was no use. Who was she kidding? She had betrayed herself by being a woman. By believing that ecstasy could last. By convincing herself that life gave one a second chance.

Frank could go to hell, although that weasel would probably talk the devil into making him a partner in the real estate. She had the papers, so there was no point to staying in Peru any longer. As soon as she ran into Tim, she would tell him to pack up and get ready to leave this godforsaken ruin. Dex and Poppy could have it to themselves.

With her decision made, Jill sniffed at her clothing, decided she could get away with wearing the sweaty stuff a few hours longer. She headed over to the men's quarters and knocked on Tim's door.

A sleepy voice invited her in. Tim must have been carousing quite late to be still in his room at this hour. Where could one carouse around here, she wondered. Poppy must have been with Dex, so who had kept him occupied?

Opening the door, Jill stepped inside. Tim was tying the laces of his sneakers. "Sis!" He straightened. "You're all better?"

"Yes." She walked over and hugged him. "Sorry if I smell ripe. I haven't been back to my room yet."

"You're nothing like the men's locker room, Jillie, even sweaty. Not to worry." He chucked her under the chin.

She stepped back and met his eyes. "Have you seen everything around here?"

"Guess so. It's a fascinating place, and the people are great."

"Tim, I want to go home."

"Now?"

"Today."

"But Jillie, it's too soon. And I've got things to tell you."

"You can tell me everything in the taxi. It's a long drive. I'll fill a couple of canteens, pack some sandwiches, call Trujillo, and order a cab for noon. By then, I'll have cleaned up and packed. Try and be ready by lunchtime, Tim. I can't wait to get away from this place."

In her depressed state, ugly pictures flitted through her mind. The skeleton with the broken arms. The naked doll with her stuffing hanging out. The deadly blowgun. The leering bandit aiming his pistol. She shuddered, recalling his lewd gestures. Violence was all around.

"It's not fair," Tim said sullenly. "I've only just arrived in Peru. Perhaps I'll stay on and let you go home alone."

"What would *Abuelita* say to that?" Jill caught his scowl, could see how much he wanted to shake her, but she was too wrought up to care. "You've seen enough of this barren place. We'll spend a few days in Lima.

There's a lot to experience there. Restaurants, museums—Tim, wait till you see the gold masks and jeweled knives. Then there are the carved pots that show men fighting, and fishing, and making music, and...and even making love. Did you see the poster at the airport—an erotica show!"

Before he could reply, Jill blew him a kiss and dashed out. Eager for a shower and clean clothes, she hurried toward the women's annex. As she passed the sorting table, Dex looked up and waved her over. She faked a smile and kept walking. Nothing he could say would alter her plans.

****

Dex watched her retreating figure, back stiff and straight. What had gotten into her? Was she trying to hide what was between them? Or was something really wrong? He kept his gaze on her until she was out of sight. Then, frowning, he went back to work.

It wasn't until the sun was high in the sky that Dex looked up again to see the taxi drive away, trailing a cloud of dust.

Chapter 21

Dropping the two shards he was fitting together, a stunned Dex stared at the swirling dust kicked up by the rapidly moving vehicle. When the horizon was empty of all but sand and sky, the taxi not even a dot in the distance, Dex finally snapped out of his trance. He jerked to his feet and rushed to the office.

Harry sat at his desk twiddling a black knight between his pudgy fingers.

"Was that Jill in the taxi?" Dex yelled.

Bewildered, Harry looked at him. "I don't know what's going on here, Dex. First Maria Topol disappears, then Jill Flanders drives off with her brother. She didn't say a word to me. What the hell is happening?"

Dex ignored Harry's question. "Did she take her luggage?"

"Yep. Left a note that she'd dumped Frank's things on his bed and taken the duffel for Tim. Then the two of them took off, lock, stock and duffel."

Running his fingers through his windblown hair, Dex dropped heavily into the camp chair. "I don't know what the hell is going on either, Harry. But I don't like it."

"Do you know anything about Maria?"

"Sadly, I do. She's the one who's been having an

affair with Frank. It wasn't Poppy after all."

"Topol? I don't believe it."

"It's true. Jill caught her pawing through her drawers a couple of nights ago, and Maria blurted out the whole story. I would have thought she'd be more professional, but… This morning I told the police, said that Topol knew about Frank's disappearance and the missing loot. They're on their way over to question her now—a bit late." He shrugged.

"Shit." Harry rose, paced over to the door and back. "I can't take it in. Topol is a recognized authority, with a hand-tailored government job. Honors at the university. Lectures all over the place. Why would she get mixed up with Frank? It'll ruin everything."

"Would you believe, for love?"

"Love?" Harry raised both arms into the air, then sat down again. "At her age? You've got to be kidding."

"Nope. There's no cutoff date for those feelings. You should know that. She told Jill she and *Francisco* were soul mates, and Frank had a scheme to pile up enough *soles* for them to run away together and live like royalty."

"Not hard to guess where the money's coming from. Topol and Flanders. Jesus. It boggles the imagination."

"Yeah. I choke on the visual, too."

The men were silent for a moment. "Did you know Poppy's back?" Dex asked.

"Sure, another complication. Still, we need all the help we can get to finish up the season."

"Poppy claims she left because Frank was hitting on her, and she couldn't handle it. She decided she'd give him time to cool off."

Harry raised an eyebrow. "So Frank was two-timing her, also. Well, that little blonde can handle anyone in pants. She'll probably be after you again, now he's gone."

"Come on, Harry, she's a kid. I don't take her seriously."

"Yeah? That's not what everyone else thinks. What was she doing draped all over you yesterday?"

"What? When? Oh, she sneaked up on me when she arrived, covered my eyes and asked me to guess who. Poppy loves to tease, but I had to get away. That lilac scent she wears makes me sneeze. Good Lord, you don't think Jill saw us and suspected…"

"I've no idea." Harry shrugged. "Do you really care?"

Dex sat up straighter. "Damn right, I do."

"I didn't realize you were that serious about Ms. Flanders. Watch your back, Dex. Frank may be lurking anywhere, and he's a conniving, vindictive bastard. Wouldn't appreciate your poaching on his territory, although, if he's really involved with Maria…" Harry shook his head again. "I still can't believe it."

"Frank and Jill are divorced. She just received the final papers from her lawyer, so you don't have to worry about me."

"Yeah, well, the point is moot, now. You'd better get back to work. Our deadline is getting closer and closer. I've made plane reservations for the end of January."

Dex rose reluctantly. "I haven't forgotten, but I've got to think this through. Something's not right."

Harry glowered.

"Okay, okay. I'll finish the pot I've started on first."

While part of his mind matched shards of broken pottery, another section functioned elsewhere, posing question after question. Why had Jill left without saying anything to him? Was their affair nothing but an exotic fling? Foreign country, different man? Pure lust? Were the heat and the longing for something more that he'd felt with her in his arms merely an adrenaline rush?

No, the passion was real. He knew in his bones that Jill felt it as deeply as he did. But the timing! Since that long ago romantic fiasco, short-term liaisons were all he had wanted. His summer affairs had all been sex on the hoof, mutually enjoyable but quickly forgotten when fall arrived. And now, just when he had begun to think that commitment might not be such a dirty word, Jill had run away.

Something serious must have happened, leaving her no time to say goodbye. Or…could she have seen Poppy wrapped around him and assumed more than it meant? Actually been jealous? Nonsense. A woman as intelligent as Jill wouldn't respond in that way. Jill was real, gutsy, level-headed. She'd know it was a childish trick of Poppy's.

Round and round his thoughts went, while his eyes sought and his fingers deftly fitted pottery shards together. Brush dipped into glue, shape took place in his hands. He hardly realized when the pot was finished.

"Hey, Sam," Dex called to the man seated at the far end of the table, "have you had any further ideas on our broken-armed female?"

"I've been going over photos of the murals we've

discovered," Sam replied. "It looks as if we can add the Moche to the tribes practicing human sacrifice."

"Yeah, life must have been a helluva lot scarier back then. I've often wondered how they explained Mother Nature's little bombshells—earthquakes and eclipses and meteor showers and the like."

"I'll tell you how," Sam answered. "I've never forgotten a quote from one of my anthropology books. The author said it all. 'There is nothing on earth or in heaven that cannot be explained by superstition.'"

Dex nodded. "I'll buy that. Still too much of it around today."

Sliding off the bench, Sam stood up. "If you've finished with that pot you've been working on in such a trance," he said, "let's go get a beer."

"Good idea." He and Sam strode over to the chow hall. "Did I really look like I was in a trance?" he asked.

"Let's say you were more than usually preoccupied."

"There's a reason. Did you see the taxi?"

"Mm hmm. Ms. Flanders left, I gather. And in quite a hurry. Did she tell you why?"

"She didn't tell me a damn thing, and it worries me. She just took off. Have you any idea why?"

"No. I thought you and Jill were dancing pretty well together. Did her brother's arrival make you miss a step?"

"I don't know. For some reason, Tim didn't like me when he first came. But last night the kid became friendly at dinner. Something happened to change his mind, and it wasn't Jill. She was still in the infirmary, in no shape to talk."

"Another mystery. This place is full of them." Sam

upended his beer, guzzled it down. "What are you going to do about it?"

"What can I do?" Dex tossed his beer bottle from hand to hand. "She's gone."

The older man raised an eyebrow.

Abruptly, the bottle came to rest. "I've just decided—first thing in the morning, I'll pay a visit to the police station."

"Why the police?"

"Have they caught the looters? Did they find Frank? Could his capture have been why Jill and Tim ran off so hastily? I need to find out what's happening."

"Hmm. I hadn't thought of that."

"The lieutenant and I have become friends, developed a rapport. He'll answer my questions. If I find out what's going on, perhaps I'll understand Jill's actions. There has to be a logical reason."

"Well, if Frank or Frank's body were discovered, that would require an immediate response from his family." Sam looked hopeful. "Let me know what happens. And good luck!"

"Thanks, old friend. I'll drink to that."

****

Early the next morning, Dex deposited the reconstructed pot on Harry's desk and left for Trujillo. For once Harry remained silent, waving Dex away.

At the police station, the lieutenant held a steaming mug. "Coffee? You look like you could use some."

"No thanks. I need the real thing, not sludge."

Castillo laughed. "You will get a better cup at the café on the corner. What brings you here this morning, *Señor* Conroy?"

Settling back in his seat, Dex rested an ankle on the

opposite knee. "I'd like an update on what's happening with the looters, the ones we found using the cave."

"Ah, yes. I expect word from Lima at any moment. Also on the whereabouts of *Señora* Topol."

"So she's still missing. What about Frank Flanders? Have you heard anything?"

"Unfortunately, he has vanished. But I do know there has been no contact between him and his assistant. The mestizo has not stopped hunting for you and Ms. Flanders, Conroy. Remain vigilant."

"Damn." Dex rose and began to pace. "Now I'm more worried than ever about Jill. I never told her what you found out about her 'almost accidents.' Would the man follow her if she left the dig?"

Castillo shrugged.

"So, it's still open season. Do you think Frank is alive?"

"Flanders would have to be very clever to invade the bandits' territory and get away unharmed."

"Cleverness seems to run in that family."

"You are referring to the lovely *señora*. How is she?"

"I wouldn't know. Jill has run away, too."

The lieutenant's eyes narrowed. "She has disappeared?"

"I saw her and her brother leave in a taxi yesterday. Since you didn't order her to come here and identify a body, I presume she's headed for Lima and a plane to New York."

Castillo regarded him closely. "So that is why you asked about her being followed. Her action does not please you?"

"No," Dex said in disgust. "She just found out her

divorce from Frank went through, though I don't believe she mentioned that to you."

"Why was she so secretive?"

"Jill was told she would be safer if the men she met in Latin America thought she was married."

"I see, she kept her true status a secret…but you penetrated her disguise?"

Dex was too absorbed in his misery to catch the innuendo. "I thought we really cared for each other."

"Then why let her go? I would put in extra effort for a woman like that."

Dex shifted uneasily. "You saw her qualities, too?"

"Cierto. One does not find a woman with such a body, and a spirit to match, every day of the week."

"I agree, but how do I find her? I'm not sure what my next move should be."

Before Castillo could offer a suggestion, the telephone rang. With a nod of apology, he picked it up. *"Allo. Castillo acqui."* Covering the phone he whispered, "Lima."

Dex could hear the rattle of rapid Spanish coming through the phone, but he couldn't make out the words. The lieutenant hung up with a satisfied smile.

"The bandits have been located," he turned back to Dex, "thanks to your tip about the yacht. One of our informers has learned they're heading for Lima airport. Too much loot to take away on a small plane, so a customs official has been bribed. He is one of our hidden men."

"You mean undercover?"

"Si. That is the word."

"Too bad we're so far away. I'd like to see them caught."

"I agree. I will arrange for a helicopter to fly me and a few of my men down. Then we can be, how you say, in at the kill. It could happen any day now."

Dex's eyes lit up. "Great! Can I come along? I can identify the bandit who held the gun on us. I'll also recognize Frank Flanders if he's with the gang."

"Fly with us in the helicopter? Ah…I see…it will get you to Lima ahead of the *señora*. Let me call the Talera Oilfields. They will lend me a military craft big enough for an extra passenger."

Edgy with anticipation, Dex waited while the lieutenant made the call. He sighed with relief when he saw Castillo nod.

"We'll be leaving in an hour. Can you make it?"

"I'm ready now. Just let me telephone Harry."

"*Excelente.* We will reach Lima before *Señora* Flanders."

At last he was doing something. Dex shook the lieutenant's hand, confidence returning full force. "I'm counting on it!"

****

For the first hour of their taxi ride, Jill and Tim were silent. Tim hadn't wanted to leave Poppy—things were bopping along with her, and he sulked.

Jill was withdrawn, lost in thought. Pictures flitted through her mind of the deserted beach at Huanchaco, the rocky cave, the treasure room. She recalled the terrifying bandit pointing his big black gun at Dex, and their watery escape in the dark sea and concealing fog.

The images faded into the Pyramid of the Moon, and the barefoot gnome lifting the heavy rocks to show her the mural of the jaguar god. Had Tim given Dex her message about the painting? Too late now.

Once again Jill saw Poppy leaning on Dex's back, her arms around him. Why had it upset her so? Her thoughts skipped about, and another picture developed of other arms winding around a man—small, skinny arms that didn't quite reach. She was five again, pleading with her father not to leave. He shook her off. She could feel his annoyance as he placed her little hand into the cold clasp of his mother.

"Enough of this behavior, Jillianne," her paternal grandmother's voice echoed through the years. "It's time you started to act like a properly brought-up young lady. Your parents will be back as soon as matters are straightened out." A maid was called, and Jill squirmed. The maid's starched white apron scratched her legs as she was lifted up and carried whimpering from the room.

Years passed before she understood why she had been abandoned that day. When the dictator, Juan Peron, had been called back from exile, her *abuelos* had felt obliged to return to Argentina. Relatives were endangered. Her mother insisted on accompanying her parents, so her father had gone along to protect them all. What they had thought could be settled in a matter of days had stretched into four weeks.

The month they were gone was an eternity to a five-year-old. She missed the warmth of her parents and the boisterous affection of her *abuelos*. She didn't understand the restrained attitude of the Boston household, knew nothing of more subtle ways to express love.

After her parents' return, Jill recalled clinging to her mother's skirts, crying when the bus stopped to pick her up for kindergarten. Those early feelings of rejection and fear had burrowed deep down, but never totally disappeared. They shaped her choices of friends, fostered her anxiety about not belonging. Later, they kept her clinging to an unhappy marriage. How peculiar the mind was.

Now, this strange interlude in Peru had brought the old childhood fears into consciousness once more. Jill suddenly understood why battered wives remained with abusive husbands. Weren't Frank's cruel comments and infidelities an emotional battering? She'd formed a shell around her professional life, but in her private life, insecurities had leaked through.

The divorce had been her first step in acting for herself. Here in this bouncing taxi, not exactly zooming toward Lima, the realization washed over Jill, calming her frazzled nerves. She could see the roots of her anxiety, and with that knowledge, that awareness, she would throw off the strangling ties to her past. A fresh, new sense of power filled her. She'd make her new life what she wanted.

But what an awkward moment to figure it out.

She sat up straighter, rubbing her back against the cab's upholstery to scratch the sunburn's itch. Her shoulders were tight, and her spine felt cramped. How she wished Dex were here. He would soothe her body as he had done after their escape from the bandits. He had a way of massaging each vertebra until she unraveled inch by inch. As her thoughts flew to those shivering moments in his truck, a curl of desire spiraled from between her legs all the way to her flushed face.

Forcing her mind away from satisfying sexual memories, she gazed out the window at the sand and sea and mountains, letting the stark beauty of the land soothe both body and brain. As they passed tortoise-shaped Tortuga Island, she heard the laughter of children playing on the beach. The joyful sound rolled through her, carrying hope. Her pity party was over. Indeed, her trip to Peru had served its purpose.

Jill turned to Tim. "Let's talk." Taking his hand, she rubbed her thumb nervously over the back of each finger. "What made you want to stay at the site longer?"

He slid his hand out from the pressure of her thumb and wagged a finger at her. "You haven't been listening in quite a while. Will you really pay attention now?"

She glanced around the cab. "I can't escape," she said. "Believe me, Bro, I'm all ears."

"That's a kinky visual!" They both giggled, and the tension lessened. "Okay." Tim settled back. "I'll take your word for it, but don't drift off again!"

"I won't. I promise."

"I told you I met this foxy girl on the plane to Lima, Jillie. We discovered we were both heading for the same dig, the *Huaca de Las Estrellas.* It was quite a coincidence."

Jill's stomach tightened. "Poppy! She likes you. You started to tell me before."

"Yeah, but you never gave me a chance to finish. We ended up taking the bus traveling north together, and had lots of time to talk. After that, I spent the hours you were recovering from your sun sickness with her, and we made plans to go into Trujillo and do the town. That's why I was so mad when you yanked me out."

"Then Poppy was no longer concerned about Dex hitting on her?" Jill held her breath.

"Nah. Turns out it wasn't Dex she meant." Tim

looked uncomfortable. "It was Frank. She thought it would upset me to know, since he's my brother-in-law, so she told a little white lie. But when she saw how close you and Dex were at the dig, Poppy figured she'd better confess the truth."

"What do you mean?"

"Well, you know. It was pretty clear you and Dex had a thing going, and she didn't want to spoil it."

So they had been that obvious. "Nice of her."

Tim missed the sarcasm. "She is nice, I'm telling you."

"Don't you find her a bit…quirky? I mean, astrology and crystals and Pyramid Power?" Facing him again, Jill raised her eyebrows.

"Poppy's a flake, but she's cool," he said, eager to explain. "Her mind is open to new experiences. That's one of the things I like about her. Before I started to pack this morning, I went looking for her. Told her I had to leave, though I didn't know why you were in such a f…darned hurry. She was so disappointed, I invited her to Cambridge for a basketball weekend."

"Sounds like you worked it out. Between now and then, you can e-mail and get to know each other better. I know you're too sensible to rush into things."

"Not like you and Frank…"

"Well, you're older than I was then, and smarter." She leaned over and hugged him. "The divorce has finally gone through, you know. The lawyer sent me the papers. It seems Frank left them with his mother, and she forgot to mail them."

"What a surprise." He grinned at her, understanding.

They gazed at the scenery in companionable

silence. Jill's thoughts were buzzing. She had been wrong about Dex and Poppy. What a throwback to her earlier self. She'd acted in haste, wondered how long she'd be repenting at leisure. Should she swallow her pride and call Dex from Lima? Too bad cell phones didn't work at the site. She might have to fax, but she would do it. It was time for her to act like a mensch.

Jill giggled inwardly at the New York slang, so politically incorrect but so right for emphasis. Cheered, she turned her mind to the future. What would be waiting for her at the office? She hoped she wasn't so far behind she'd have to work weekends to catch up. Francine was eager to progress beyond secretary. If she got her promoted to editorial assistant, Francine could pick up the slack, and she could have her weekends free for trips to Philadelphia.

Is that what Dex would want? As Jill heard herself doubting again, she laughed aloud. Hadn't she learned her lesson? She may be slow, but she was getting there. By the time Chimbote was reached, her mood had improved to such an extent, she introduced Tim to Pisco Sours. It brought back memories of her last visit, and melancholy slipped into her voice.

Tim picked up on it. "Care to tell me about you and Dex, Sis?" he asked.

"What's there to tell?" Jill sighed. "I walked out on him without a word today."

"Why did you do it?"

"I saw Poppy draped all over his back. He looked like he was enjoying it, and after what you'd told me…"

"Oh that. Hey, forget it. Poppy was having fun, whispering into his ear and asking Dex to guess who.

Didn't take him long, either."

"I guess not. I didn't wait to find out."

"Poppy wears this neat perfume, but it made Dex sneeze. If you had hung around a minute longer, you'd have seen her meet me."

"Wish I'd known earlier. I don't know what got into me, just felt I had to get away."

Tim squeezed her hand. "I can understand a feeling of rejection," he said, revealing all of his twenty-one years. "But it's time you admitted that Poppy and Dex as a couple was all in your mind. He's a good guy. Once I found out the truth, we talked a lot while you were busy upchucking."

"What a pretty picture."

"Sorry, but it's the truth. He didn't seem to mind nearly as much as you did. I think he really cares."

Her face broke into a radiant smile. "Thanks, Bro. You've cheered me up immensely. I'll try to straighten out the mess I created."

As they continued on to Lima the next day, Jill spotted a small crowd of tourists by the side of the road. "Look, Tim, the Quechua Indians have set up a stand. They're selling those incredibly soft alpaca throws. Let's stop and see." She leaned forward and tapped the driver's shoulder. *"Pare, por favor."*

They stepped out of the taxi. The sun was high, the sky blue, the day hot. As she heard the sound of a helicopter overhead, Jill looked up. *What a country of contrasts,* she thought. *Here are Quechua Indians living much as they did in ancient times, while up above the modern world flies noisily by.*

Shading her eyes, Jill watched the helicopter till it was out of sight. Where was Dex now? Missing her as much as she missed him?

She turned back to the handmade objects laid out on the crude wooden table. The silken hairs of the alpaca felt divine beneath her fingers. In a half hour she had bargained for a creamy white throw, a checkerboard rug, and incredibly soft scarves for Tim, her parents and *abuelos*, her best friend Jo, her secretary Francine, and a deep blue stunner to match Dex's eyes. Tim spent a few *soles* for a stuffed llama to remind him of Peru.

"We'll stop off at the airport on the way to the hotel," Jill said as they got back in the taxi. "We can mail the presents in the duffel and arrange for our tickets home at the same time."

Her brother had listened to Jill complain when Frank had brought the luggage home. "You're managing to get your own back on the duffel." He winked. "And arranging our tickets with your usual efficiency. Glad to see the old Jillie Adams back."

"I'm not sure if I like the new one better."

He smiled. "They're both you. Dex will love them equally."

"Hear, hear." Her eyes twinkled. "I can see you know how to plead a case, but I've got to find him first."

Chapter 22

A few hours earlier, Dex, the lieutenant, and a small squad of police, their ears bombarded by the rush and roar of agitated air, watched the helicopter land on the roof of Trujillo's newest hotel.

"Ever flown in one of these?" Castillo shouted, his jacket flapping wildly.

Dex read the lieutenant's lips. He shook his head.

While the chopper's engine was still running, Castillo motioned to the men. He pushed against the blast and climbed into the machine. Dex and the other officers scrambled in behind him.

Before he had settled into his seat the door closed, and Dex was in the air. The machine's vibrations shook him from his scalp to his toenails, while the deafening noise of the rotor blades wrapped around him, sealing him in a cocoon of sound.

His thoughts wandered. Here he was returning to Lima again, this time with a police escort. Strange not to see any wings outside the window. Weird to be flying at all, but a quick decision had been imperative. Would they catch the looters? How would it feel to be in at the kill? Surely dangerous. Probably violent. As his heart beat faster Dex grinned, counting on his friendship with the lieutenant to give him a piece of the action.

For once, he was relieved that Jill had left before him. She would have insisted on coming along on the raid, but he wanted her safe, nowhere near a firefight. When the bandits were captured, he would seek her out. By then he'd have a tale to tell. He'd bet a thousand *soles* she'd return to the hotel they had shared. Jill had a sentimental streak, and he would look for her there.

The helicopter shuddered, jerking his mind from the daydream. Once more he examined the events of the day before, his gaze trapped by the taxi's dust as it carried Jill away. Why had she left so abruptly? Had she run because of doubts about him? Was she back on that hobbyhorse of being too old to please him? He hoped not. Pubescent beauties were too shallow, too wrapped up in themselves, to interest him. He needed more. His desires ran deeper.

As Dex fantasized about just how deep he'd like to plunge with Jill, he twisted uncomfortably. Damn...he was growing hard. So much vibration in this blasted chopper! Adjusting his trousers, he concentrated on the priestess with the jaguar god on her chest. Envisioning all that blood pouring from her lotus-like vessels should cool him down. He closed his eyes and let his thoughts converge on the Moche puzzle he was trying to unravel.

It wasn't long before they landed at the Lima airport. The rotors stopped spinning, and his hearing returned to normal. Relieved, Dex waited as Castillo conferred with his colleagues already at the scene. He was primed to act.

The lieutenant returned annoyed, however. "It appears we will have a day to waste," he said. "The bandits and their loot are not expected until tomorrow night. Conroy, you can spend the afternoon hunting for

Señora Flanders."

Dex blinked, smiled, reoriented himself to the change of plans. "I'll try the Hotel Balboa," he said. "Will you call for me there when you're ready to head out?"

"Por cierto." Castillo offered him a ride in one of the police cars returning to town. "I have some news," he said, leaning on the door as Dex stepped inside. "We have received word that Frank Flanders has been captured by the bandits."

"Great! If they bring him along, we can kill two birds with one stone…that is, if he's still alive."

"My informant tells me they are keeping him with them, in case they need a bargaining chip."

"I can hardly wait to tell Jill the bastard's been found."

"Be sure to claim your reward for bringing her the news." Castillo winked, shook hands. As the police car drove away, the lieutenant's smile turned grim.

"Something wrong?"

He turned toward the Lima police chief. "Flanders' confederate is still on the loose. I wonder if he was paid before his cheating boss was picked up by the bandits. If not, the man might be following the gang to Lima. There's too much gold at stake for him to walk away."

"More complications?"

Nodding, Castillo dropped his cigarette and ground it into the tarmac.

****

When Jill and Tim arrived at the airport, she told the taxi driver to wait. They ordered return flight tickets at LAN airlines, then walked down the passageway to a post office kiosk where they could mail the gift-filled duffel to New York. Standing in line, Jill and Tim heard a commotion outside. "What on earth is going on?" she asked, but no one answered. As the din grew louder, they faced each other with growing unease.

Their turn came, and they filled out the forms and sent off the package. As soon as they stepped outside, the two were pushed into a rubbernecking crowd. A helicopter had landed, and police poured out. Recalling her experience in customs on her arrival, Jill's apprehension grew.

Tim stood on tiptoe, trying to peer over the crowd. She tugged at him. "Tim, be careful. This could be dangerous!"

"We're far enough away, Sis." He patted her shoulder, still watching the action. "Nothing's happened yet. Why do you think they're here?"

"To catch smugglers, I would imagine." She began to jump up and down, trying to see over taller heads. "Say, that policeman over by the baggage cart looks like Lieutenant Castillo." Her mouth dropped open. "Good Lord, is that Dex?"

Tim spun about. "Where?"

"In among the policemen—the one who's a head taller than the rest."

"It does look like him." Tim's eyes narrowed. "But it couldn't be. What would he be doing in Lima? Harry would never allow him to take off again. It's too soon."

"I could swear it's Dex." Jill tried to push her way forward, but the crowd was too dense. She gave up, finally, and turned away. "I guess I've got him on the brain."

Tim squeezed her hand. "Nothing wrong with that."

"No." *But I'd rather have him on another part of me, or in...* Snickering at the direction her thoughts had taken, Jill turned to leave. "I hope whoever they're after gets caught. Let's go."

Before they reached the exit, a hand tugged at her arm. Irked, she turned around, couldn't believe her eyes. She was face to face with Maria Topol.

"What are *you* doing here, Maria?"

"You, you have ruined everything!" the woman screamed at her. "You called the *policia*, but Francisco escaped. Now he is captured by the bandits!" Eyes alight with fury, she grabbed Jill's shoulders and shook her.

"Hey!" Tim pulled the woman off his sister. "What the hell is going on?"

Jill moved back a step. "What are you telling me? Is Frank working with the bandits?"

"Not working—caught." Maria spat. "After Francisco evades the police, he is surrounded by the looters. My cousin who guides the tourists brings me the news."

"So...you were the go-between at the dig. Was it your cousin who carried the messages?"

"*Si*, he is the brother of Manuel, the one who finds the Moche pots for Professor Conroy. When he overhears Harry tell the others you are coming, he thinks—danger. He gives the news to Manuel, who informs his *patrón,* and Manuel is ordered to follow you from Lima."

"Then it was your cousin Manuel who dropped the rock? And scraped our truck?"

"That is not all he did. Francisco tells him to scare you good, make you go home. But you don't leave, so then I spy on you, catch you finding the ear spools in the doll. How did you know?"

"It's a long story. Why are you here? Do you expect Frank to show up?"

"I learn the gang comes here to ship the loot out of the country. Francisco will be with them. I get here first, wait to help him get away."

"You've been in the airport all night?"

"*Si, si.* I watch the police arrive, and it is you who sent them." Her face flushed dark with rage. "You are the one I blame! You have ruined my life," she yelled.

Pulling away from Tim, Maria grabbed a knife from her pocket. One glance at her raised arm, and Tim kicked. His toe caught her wrist. The knife flew from Maria's hand, and she swore. Grabbing her again, he twisted her arms behind her back and held tight.

"You're crazy!" he shouted. "Someone get the police!" Tim hung on to the raving woman as she kicked at him, twisted around and bit his arm. He yelled, but didn't let go. One man in the crowd rushed over to help. Another pulled out a cell phone and called for aid.

As Topol was subdued, Jill tried to control her somersaulting emotions. Anger raged with pity. Although her heart was still pounding, part of it went out to this miserable woman. "Maria, forget Frank." Jill raised her voice. "He won't be faithful to you—it isn't in him."

The professor's nostrils flared. Before she could scream again, Jill tried once more to reason with her. "Go back to the dig. Confess everything to Harry. He needs you. He'll talk to the police for you."

At Jill's words, Maria's shoulders slumped. She

stopped fighting. Tim loosened his grip but didn't let go.

Jill kept on prodding. "The chief of police in Trujillo admires you. He heard your lecture on the trophy head cult and said your speech was magnificent. If you swear you'll never again have dealings with the bandits, there's a chance he'll go easy on you. Especially if he captures the looters and gets the artifacts back."

Topol was still glaring when a policeman arrived. As the officer took over, Jill saw the expression in the woman's eyes. It had turned more calculating than angry. Had Maria finally realized her folly?

In the end, however, Topol wouldn't give in. *"Puta!"* She spat at Jill as she was dragged away.

"Poor deranged Maria." Jill sighed. "A case of love betrayed. The police will let her go as soon as she identifies herself, but then what?" She looked up at her kid brother. "Hey, Ninja, nice job you did defending me. Those kickboxing lessons paid off."

"All in a day's service, ma'am," Tim drawled. "When she pulled the knife on you, Jillie, it scared the shit out of me."

"Me too. But you took care of her before my heart skipped too many beats. Did she hurt you?"

He looked at his arm. "Teeth marks, but the skin isn't broken. I'll live."

"Good thing, or you'd need a rabies shot. The woman was going berserk." Jill reached over and gave him a quick hug. "My hero."

Still, Tim looked worried. "Do you think Frank was truly captured by the bandits? He's so wily, he could snake his way out of anything."

"I'm sure it's true. Maria wouldn't make a mistake like that. She's another of his conquests. But to think his henchman was behind the attacks on Dex and me. And Frank ordered them! After all the years we were married... I knew Frank was a scoundrel, but I didn't think he was so vicious. I'm still having trouble absorbing that."

"Don't weaken now, Sis. Your ex is going to get just what he deserves." Tim's face hardened. He looked older than when they'd arrived at the airport.

"I won't." She squeezed his hand. "Let's put it out of our minds for a while. At the hotel, they've got big old-fashioned tubs in the bathrooms. After our two-day drive and all this excitement, I could use a warm soak. Hope our cab is still waiting."

The taxi was there, the driver asleep at the wheel. He awoke as they climbed in talking non-stop. "Tim, could that *really* have been Dex in the midst of those policemen?"

"As they say, *¡Quien sabe!*" His eyes twinkled now.

Jill blushed. Her kid brother had grown up. It felt good to share without needing to explain or apologize. She leaned forward and tapped the driver's shoulder. "Hotel Balboa," she called out.

Then Jill turned toward Tim, who nodded. Giggling together, they mouthed the words of a favorite TV rerun.

"And step on it!"

Chapter 23

The Hotel Balboa looked different by daylight. It stood stolidly on the square, softened by the sun but still haughty—an aging Madonna attempting to hide the years.

Peddlers hung out not far from the entrance, offering crude woodcarvings, toy blowguns, yarn-made llamas, Machu Picchu snow globes, and the ever popular alpaca rugs. Some men wore the brightly striped woolen hats of the Quechua Indians, their earflaps down even on this warm day.

One of the peddlers, cap pulled low, stepped in front of Jill and Tim. He held out a carved wooden ladle, thick enough to serve as a weapon. His impassive face belied the stormy look in his eyes and, instinctively, Jill cringed. Tim must have felt the vibes, too, for he pushed her toward the hotel entrance even as she shook her head.

The incident left her uneasy, but when she stepped into the familiar lobby, she put it behind her. At the front desk, the clerk smiled. "So happy to see you again, *Señora* Flanders. That will be two single rooms, yes?"

Surprised, Jill inspected the man. This was the desk clerk who had been here when she first arrived in Lima. He acted as though he were expecting them. Odd… She must have made an impression on her earlier visit, when she refused to settle for one room with the *cama matrimonial*. Remembering the small scene she had caused, her eyes brightened.

"Yes, two rooms will be fine," she said. "Are they connecting?"

"Lo siento, I do not have two rooms on the same floor. But I have very nice rooms on floors two and three."

Jill looked at Tim, who shrugged. *"No problema,"* she told the clerk.

On the second floor, Jill looked into the room and nodded. "This will be fine. Take it easy for a while, Bro. It's too late to do any sightseeing today, so grab a nap if you can. I'll meet you in the lobby at eight."

"I'm kinda hungry now," Tim hinted. "All that excitement at the airport gave me an appetite."

"Raid the mini-bar if you can't hold out. People dine late here. Lima's a sophisticated city. We'll ask the clerk to recommend a good Peruvian restaurant, broaden your education with gourmet native food. You never can tell when a law case will bring you down here." Blowing him a kiss, she followed the porter to the elevator.

Her room on the third floor was charming. The bed—and it was a *cama matrimonial* for her alone—was built of dark walnut, its headboard carved with birds and flowers. A large matching wardrobe stood against one wall, and an easy chair with plumped cushions, fanged jaguar heads as armrests, and paws sprouting from the legs, had been placed beside the window.

Its closed wooden shutters kept the room cool, but

gave it a gloomy cast. She hurried to open them halfway. Sunshine streamed in, highlighting a porcelain fruit bowl atop the narrow table at the foot of the bed. The sweet scent of ripe mangoes wafted to her nostrils, and her nose twitched. Such a beguiling aroma. The two pieces of fruit, their leaves still attached, seemed posed for a still life.

Closing her eyes, Jill smiled, remembering the mangoes she and Dex had shared at their picnic by the ruins of Paramonga. That had been the beginning…

Perhaps she could try calling him now. As she walked over to the room's telephone, it rang. She picked up the receiver. *"Allo."*

A muffled voice spoke. "Pardon, *señora,* but did the maid leave a peeling knife in the bowl with the mangoes?"

"Why, no," she replied, looking more closely at the fruit.

"Room service will deliver *al instante, señora*, all you need to eat the mango."

"Gracias." Putting down the phone, Jill decided to hold off calling Dex until she got rid of the waiter. She hung her jacket in the wardrobe, moved the bowl, and set her suitcase on the table. As she unzipped it and searched for fresh underwear, a knock sounded at the door.

"Adelante," she called.

The door opened. "For the *señora,"* a voice said softly. "One knife to peel the mango, one tongue to lick the juice."

"Dex!" Dropping a pile of panties, Jill spun around and ran into his arms.

****

A huge wave of relief washed over Dex. The problem, whatever it had been, was in the past. Smiling, he kissed her, keeping his lips tender but possessive. She opened her mouth beneath his, and the kiss grew more intense. Hugging her tightly, he lifted her to him. She swung her legs around his waist while their tongues engaged in a mating dance that left them both breathless.

Dex fell on the bed, tumbling Jill on top of him. She reached out to undo his shirt buttons, tearing one off in her frenzy. His hands moved as fast, sliding under her skirt and peeling off her silk panties. Rolling her over, he pulled up her lacy tee and nuzzled her breasts. Half laughing, half gasping, Jill wriggled out of her skirt, then undid the belt and zipper of his jeans. His nimble fingers unhooked her bra. Slipping the straps off her shoulder, Dex held her still. "Let me look at you."

Jill shared his hungry gaze, her own eyes dark with passion.

"You're so beautiful, so pink and perfect—and you smell wonderful. God, I missed you!" He bent down and nuzzled her neck.

"After two days…?" Words died as his tongue moved lower to circle her breast. Her breathing quickened. A puckered nipple thrust forward.

Grazing it lightly with his teeth, Dex felt her body respond to him. He could barely tease the other nipple erect before his own response had him kicking off his jeans. How silky smooth she was! Touching her was like stroking a rose.

"Do you know," he said, parting her legs and feeling the warm honey of her arousal, "this is the first time we've ever made love on a proper bed. That narrow cot at the dig doesn't count."

Jill moaned, too breathless to reply. Pausing for only a moment, he put on a condom.

"Look at me," he whispered, his hand caressing her cheek. Slowly, he slid into her, withdrew even more slowly, and then stopped, staring at her as he let their tension build. The moment she quivered beneath him, he thrust deliciously forward.

"Open your eyes, *querida*. See what you do to me."

Raising heavy lids, Jill clutched at him. He lifted her legs onto his shoulders, watching her dazed eyes follow his movements in and out. Plunging deep, he rocked inside her. As she began to twist and tremble beneath him, he touched the sensitive bud at the heart of her desire. With a shriek, she convulsed around him, pulling him with her into wave after wave of pleasure.

Sometime later, Jill lay snuggled in his arms. "I've always wondered about the word 'rapture,'" she whispered into his chest. "Now I know what it means."

Curling ringlets of her dark satiny hair around his finger, he smiled. "If any word can describe our feelings, that comes closest."

She ran her fingernails down his chest until his stomach quivered. "I know you saw to it that the mangoes were placed in my room," she teased, "but did you also arrange for Tim to be on a different floor?"

"Well, I didn't know how noisy you would be. Those screams of passion…" He winked, and she threw a pillow at him.

Unwinding the curl from his finger, Dex looked deep into her eyes. "Why did you run away from me?"

She hesitated, mumbled, "I saw Poppy with her arms wrapped around you."

"And you were jealous?" Taking her hand, he trailed nipping kisses from her wrist to the inside of her elbow. "My brilliant, clever Madam Executive? Did you really believe there could be any other woman once you got your claws into me?"

"Claws?" Jill turned her head to see him grinning at her. "I'm innocent, boss!" She giggled. "Those are the claws of the jaguar god. He cast a spell on both of us. I'm just a bouquet of catnip."

"Mmm." He munched on her fingers. "I've been meaning to ask. When you were sick with sunburn, did you mumble something about the jaguar god?"

"Yes! I'd almost forgotten. The guardian at the Moon Pyramid moved some heavy stones away from a wall to show me a fantastic mural of the jaguar god. The head was painted, but real obsidian was inlaid in his earplugs. Did you know about it? I wanted to be sure you knew."

From Jill's radiant smile, he was sure she felt the warmth of his gaze. "I did know," he said, "but I'm amazed that even when you were so sick, and so angry at me, you still wanted to help my career. You're a remarkable woman, Jill ex-Flanders, Adams."

"It's about time you realized it." Leaning over him, she swung her head back and forth. Her nose and lips nuzzled him while her dark hair fanned out to swish across his chest, brushing the blond hairs curling there. His muscles tightened.

"Am I tickling you?" she teased.

"Yes you are, witch." He laughed as she swept her head from side to side. His hand moved down her back until his finger glided along the crack in her butt, reaching a tender spot that made her quiver.

Jill's head stopped moving. She pressed her body even closer.

"Who's being tickled now? Fair's fair." He continued to slide his fingers around until neither could stand the delicious torture a moment longer. "There's still time," he murmured as he raised her above him and slid into her welcoming body.

"Oh, yes…please…" They soared higher and higher, climbed over the clouds, and flew into the rainbow.

****

At eight that evening the elevator doors opened, and Jill stepped out with Dex beside her.

"Look what room service delivered to me," she called to her brother who waited in the lobby.

The men shook hands. "Great to see you again, Dr. Conroy."

"Dex, please."

"Sure. What are you doing here?"

Jill turned to Dex, startled. "I forgot to ask you that!"

He returned the look and wiggled his eyebrows. "We had other things to talk about."

Her face warmed, and she caught Tim stifling a smile.

"I came down on the police helicopter," Dex told them. "Lieutenant Castillo has learned that the bandits plan to ship out their loot by air. The customs official they bribed is an undercover cop. We expected them today, but the latest word is, they'll arrive tomorrow evening."

As if on cue, his cell phone rang. "Excuse me." Dex took it from his jacket, spoke briefly, and turned back. "The bandits aren't due to arrive until late tomorrow. I'll be picked up at seven p.m., so we'll have all day to see the sights. There's a particular museum exhibit I promised to show you, Jill."

She glared at him. "I caught that. You said '*I'll* be picked up,' not *we*."

"Now, Jill, the bandits will be armed. There's apt to be shooting. I'm sorry, but it won't be safe for you to come along."

"We'll see about that," she muttered.

They glowered at each other until Tim broke the impasse. "So, Dex, it was you Jillie spotted at the airport, after all. She thought she saw a tall head sticking out among the policemen, but we decided it was just wishful thinking."

Jill punched Tim's arm. "Did I ever tell you that you talk too much?"

Dex laughed. "I'm glad to hear it. Thanks, pal." He was still grinning as he suggested they leave for dinner. "I know a great place that specializes in meltingly tender steaks."

"It'll be a treat. We rarely eat red meat these days."

"These cows have grown plump on the Argentine pampas."

"Wait a minute," Jill protested. "We're in Peru. Shouldn't we eat the local dishes?"

"Everything else will be Peruvian—the best Peruvian, trust me. You can't believe the inventive ways the chefs have with potatoes. And peppers, and avocados. Even the shrimp to start the meal can make you swoon." He puckered his lips, and Jill giggled.

"But Argentina has the grasslands. All the good restaurants import their beef. The steaks will taste as sweet and juicy as ripe mangoes." He winked at Jill.

"Oh my, we never did get around to eating them."

"We will. I've got plans for those mangoes…later."

The restaurant filled the top floor of one of Lima's tallest buildings. The first patrons to arrive, they were seated at a window table overlooking the city lights. Tim's eyes sparkled as he peered out. "Now this is more like it."

Dex ordered for them all, and they sipped a delicious white wine as they waited for their first course, fresh seafood *ceviche*. In the quiet ambiance, a cell phone rang again. This time it was Tim's.

"Excuse me. I, uh, gave Poppy this number." He pushed back his chair and hurried out the door, his napkin slipping to the floor. The waiter swiftly picked it up and moved away.

Casting speculative glances, Jill and Dex waited. A few minutes later, Tim came bounding back to his seat, a broad smile lighting up his face. "I've lucked out. Poppy's aunt called her from Trujillo. She's on a buying trip, and Poppy talked her into flying down to Lima for a day. They'll be here around nine tomorrow morning, and Poppy wants to show me her favorite places. You know, 'Historic Downtown Lima' is a UNESCO World Heritage site."

"And after the cathedral and churches, don't forget to visit the *Museo Nacionale*."

"She mentioned that, too. You don't mind if I leave you with Dex, do you, Sis?"

"Not at all. Don't worry about rushing back. We'll be in Lima for a couple more days."

"What will you do while I'm gone?" Tim looked at Dex.

"A private museum I know has Pre-Columbian ceramics I want to show Jill. The *Larco* is a special place to ceramic ethnoarchaeologists."

"Then it's all set. I'll take a taxi in the morning and meet Poppy at the airport."

"Get away from there as early as you can," Dex suggested. Noticing Jill's troubled look, he added, "There's so much to see and do, you don't want to miss a minute of it."

"Okay. And Poppy's got a special club in mind for the evening."

"No doubt it's part of Historical Downtown Lima?"

"Oh yeah." Tim grinned.

****

With their morning free, Jill and Dex visited the special exhibit of erotic art from around the world. China had sent jade carvings of the "peach" and the "stem," as well as graphic images of couples enjoying copulating. The Japanese offered prints from training books of sexual pleasure. Copies of temple sculptures and illustrations for the Kama Sutra came from India. Dionysian offerings from Greece and Rome were included, as well as paintings, sketches and sculptures from the Western world.

These ageless examples from different cultures introduced the exhibit, but the real heart of the show was the erotic pottery from Peru the *Larco* museum had contributed. They saved that for after a lunch of grilled *panini queso*, accompanied by a young red wine, at the museum café. They talked of the art they had seen, comparing cultures. Both were unwilling to spoil the day by mentioning the raid that night. After eating, they walked over to the special exhibit's inner room.

Try as she might to be blasé, Jill stared. On shelves and pedestals stood the most amazing representations of erotic art she had ever seen. Men and women were on their backs, on their sides, standing, kneeling, crouching, pleasing themselves, as a couple, as a threesome. She moved slowly around the room, examining each pot and immersing herself in the artist's vision, convinced that every sexual position known to humankind was portrayed.

The men wore headdresses and occasionally a loincloth, the nude women were sometimes adorned with beads. Their facial expressions were bland, indifferent, although on one or two, Jill thought she detected a tiny smile of pleasure or just a hint of lust. Was this a cultural bias, or were the artists simply uninterested in faces? Their body positions were flagrantly erotic.

One stirrup pot in particular caught her attention. It showed a kneeling man at one end of the stirrup, a kneeling woman at the other. Her left hand reached over to caress his penis, while his right hand was raised to his forehead in a salute.

"Dex, who do you think the man is saluting?"

"He's not saluting," came the whispered retort. "He's looking out for her husband."

Jill covered her mouth to hide a giggle. She moved away from a grouping of huge phalluses, heading for the plaque dedicated to this portion of the exhibit. "In 1664," she read softly to Dex, "Fernando de la Carrera, a vicar, compiled a dictionary of the Moche language. He claimed the Moche word for love is, *Checan.*"

"*Checan,*" Jill repeated. "I like the crisp sound. I'll

remember that word, just as I'll never forget these pots. You know, they call to mind two lines from a love poem by John Donne that I've always been stirred by. It's called, 'To His Mistress, Going to Bed.'"

"Catchy title. Can you quote the lines?"

"Oh, yes. I remember them well. *'License my roving hands and let them go/ Before, behind, beneath, above, below.'"*

His mouth curved in a devilish grin. "Memorable, indeed. Didn't Donne become the dean of some cathedral?"

"Yes, and he wrote moving religious poetry, too, later on in life. But it's his love poems that really grab me. And reciting them here, in this room, truly convinces me of the universality of our sensual dreams and desires."

He traced her lips with his finger. "You'll have to read all the love poems to me. In the proper setting, of course."

"One of these days." Her answering smile was wistful. "What's the scholar's opinion of Moche pottery? Why do they think the Moche represented sex so frequently, and so vividly?"

"Some attribute a religious significance to these vessels, since most were found buried in graves. There are tribes today with similar religious practices. After all, we are dealing with life's origins here. I suspect the Moche recognized the connection."

"Hmmm."

"Not only life, but death, too. Did you notice that one of the pots shows a woman copulating with a skeleton? Despite his bony appearance, his sexual organ is upstanding and engorged."

Jill laughed. "I couldn't help but notice. It suggests a fascinating view of the afterlife."

"Indeed. Must make it easier to let go."

"More appealing than a boring heaven or a scary hell, I imagine. And the other interpretation?"

"That the Moche were a lusty people, full of life, with a natural enjoyment of its physical side."

"I can empathize with that. I don't see any signs of shame or prudery in these sculptures, just hearty appetites. They're erotic, but not pornographic. Only a brainwashed few would add prurience to the vision."

As Jill looked away, another pot caught her eye. It featured a woman on her back, a man at her side with a hand on her breast and a leg draped over her. She examined it intently. "That position looks possible," she murmured, "although I can't say they all do."

"It's too bad photographs aren't allowed. Have you a good memory? We can try out the more interesting ones."

Heat rose in her cheeks. She'd bet her face matched the deep red of her pirate blouse. "I'll remember your offer," she said, "when my insides settle." She caught him sneaking a glance at his watch. "I agree, it is time to go. This room may be air-conditioned, but it certainly raised my temperature."

Before they left, despite the people all around, Dex pulled her behind a tall pedestal for a stolen kiss.

Chapter 24

When they returned to the hotel, Dex and Jill headed directly to their room. They came together in a teasing mood, all set for slow, kinky pleasure, laughing as they tried out some of the more outrageous positions they had seen. The erotic art exhibit had been an aphrodisiac.

Dex lay back and let Jill ride him, soaking up her purrs and pants. Hands behind his head, he let her decide whatever she wanted to do with him—and to him. She'd been quite inventive. It wasn't until later that she realized he'd had an agenda.

By 6:45 p.m., she was asleep, a satisfied smile on her face he would never forget. He sneaked out of bed, grabbed his clothes, and tiptoed into the bathroom to dress. When the police car came for him at seven p.m., he was waiting outside the hotel.

****

Jill felt his light kiss on her hair, but kept her eyes closed as he slipped out of the room. She dozed off again, satiated and delightfully tired. A few minutes later, she jerked awake. Why, the rat bastard, he was sneaking out on her! He had deliberately worn her out, so that he could go off with the police on his own. Still, being in charge sexually had been fun. What a delicious way to lose an argument!

But she wouldn't let him get away with it. Jumping up, Jill rushed to the window, saw Dex get into the police car and drive away. Her insides churned with anxiety and disappointment.

She paced the room, determined to do something. She had been involved in this case from the start. Well, almost. It was she who had deciphered the map to the bandits' loot and found the cave. She deserved to be in at the finish. Besides, the police would be busy with the looters. She would keep her distance, but watch Dex's back.

She couldn't follow him all the way to customs. It would be foolhardy to risk being caught, and it would put him in danger. Rather, she would wait in the cargo area—there were plenty of cartons and barrels to hide behind. She would be close enough to hear what was going down, maybe even get a peek at the action. And she could keep an eye on Dex.

Her mind made up, she changed into black slacks and a long-sleeved black tee. Only minutes after he had departed, she left the lobby of the Hotel Balboa and asked the doorman to hail a taxi. They were plentiful near the hotel. As the cab door shut, she tuned out the traffic noise and reviewed the steps she would take when they reached the airport.

The roar of a motorcycle starting up behind her faded from consciousness. She gazed out the window, but saw nothing to alarm her. She had seen the striped hats the Quechua Indians wore so frequently, they now served to camouflage the weather-beaten face of the motorcycle driver trailing her...

****

Dex sat beside Castillo in the speeding police car.

The lieutenant was passing on instructions via radio to his men in the squad car behind them, after conferring with the Lima police chief at the airport. The rapid-fire Spanish was beyond Dex's comprehension, but his pulse quickened as he felt the tension build.

When the conversation ended, the lieutenant turned to him. "The guerrillas have arrived at the pier and are shifting their cargo from the yacht to a lorry. We will arrive in ten minutes, well ahead of them, and join the Lima contingent at customs."

Dex tried hard to tamp down his excitement. Nodding, he turned away to gaze out the window at the busy port of Callao. He could make out the inns and shops along the waterfront, the ships and barges crowding the wharf. He spotted the turret of the old fort *Real Felipe* and, at last, the airport tower.

Castillo checked his gun, then turned to Dex. "Remember, *amigo*, you have promised to stay well behind. No pulling any daredevil *Americano* stunts."

"Who, me? I'll only tackle anyone who slips through the police line." Dex aimed a pretend punch at the lieutenant.

"Stay well in back. I mean it, Conroy. This is no place for amateurs."

"Only kidding. Hey, I'm an archaeologist. I'm into pots, not punches."

The entrance to the airport was ahead. The police cars followed the signs, passed the passenger terminals, and drove up to the electronic cargo gate. It had been left open for them. As they moved swiftly inside, no one remarked on the motorcycle that slipped in beside them before the bar went down.

The squad cars drove up the long cargo ramp to the

customs building. Castillo spoke briefly to the Lima police chief, and the men fanned out, finding places of concealment behind forklifts, barrels, and loaded pallets.

"We were told to expect the looters here," Castillo said. He waved at Dex and pointed. "See the stack of bales piled up in back, near the exit? Get behind them."

The tension in the air was palpable. "When do we move?" Dex bounced on his heels, primed for action.

"When the thieves arrive and finish unloading the lorry. Go now! Watch for the signal."

As if summoned, a large, muddy, tarp-covered van pulled into the airport, drove through the cargo doors, and headed up the long ramp to customs. A motorized luggage truck rolled over to it. Dex eyed the men who leaped out from under the tarp, scanning them swiftly. He drew back, startled.

For an instant, before the circle of men closed, he locked eyes with Frank Flanders.

Supervised by the burly, mustachioed, *el jefe,* the thieves wasted no time unloading their booty. When the last box and sack had been removed from the lorry and lifted onto the baggage cart, the Lima captain signaled. His men moved in.

An overeager rookie cop ran ahead. Catching the movement, the bandit leader turned sharply. "Back! It's a trap!" he yelled, reaching for his gun.

In an instant, all became a blur—police, bandits, and bodies, shouts, screams, and gunshots—chaos. Dex and Jill had witnessed a similar scene in customs a week ago, but this one was speeded up tenfold.

From behind the bales, he scanned the turmoil, adrenaline pumping. One of the bandits slipped through the cordon and fled toward him. Leaping out, he threw a body block and tackled the guy. They ended on the concrete, grappling for the thief's knife. Too furious to notice the gash on his arm, Dex stomped on the bandit's wrist. He held him down until an officer came to gather up the victim, giving him a thumb's up.

Looking around for Castillo, Dex observed one of the thieves squirming out of a policeman's grip. It was Frank, and the bandit leader saw him, too. "Gringo bastard!" *El jefe* yelled. "You have betrayed us!" He aimed his gun at Frank.

Without thinking, Dex ran forward and jumped on *el jefe,* knocking the gun from his hand. Two more cops were right behind him. They grabbed the furiously fighting leader, his fists flailing wildly as he tried in vain to shake loose.

Hidden by the melee, Frank veered sharply and wriggled through the men piling up around him. He grabbed a sack off the luggage cart and scrambled over the chain link fence separating the cargo area from the terminal.

Behind the bales once more, Dex gaped at Frank's escape. He watched the sack catch on a fence link and rip open. Its contents spilled out, glinting gold in the sun.

Taking off, Dex reached the fence and bent down to rescue the artifact—a golden pectoral surrounded by gleaming emeralds and polished pink shell. When he looked up, Frank was gone.

He let out a string of curses. Chest heaving, clothes bloodied, and eyes wild, he pocketed the gold pectoral dangling from his fingers and headed after Frank once more.

****

A rubbernecking crowd surged forward, following the ramp down toward the cargo doors. At the first sound of shots, Jill's head popped up from behind the barrel where she was hiding. She looked frantically around, saw people moving toward her beyond the fence. What was happening? Had they caught the criminals? She craned her neck, trying to see more.

Squatting behind a stack of cartons across from Jill, Manuel loaded his shortened blowgun.

Frank ran along the fence. From out of the milling crowd, Maria suddenly jumped forward. She yanked at Frank's sleeve, handed him his briefcase. Without stopping, he grabbed the handle and pushed her away. Maria fell to the ground.

My God! So the police hadn't detained the professor. "Don't you want the Vuitton duffel too, Frank?" Jill shrieked, incensed. She was close enough for him to hear her words above the tumult.

Frank stopped short. The police were gaining. He tossed the briefcase over the fence to Jill just as Manuel mouthed the blowgun. The dart flew straight into the briefcase Jill had caught a second before.

Dex came running round the bend. The air from the flying dart whished past him. With a howl, he leaped over suitcases and tackled Manuel. The two went down hard. Dex pummeled the mestizo over and over, fists crashing into the man's jaw, into his gut, a knee ramming his genitals. A policeman had to pull Dex off before dragging a barely conscious Manuel away.

Her heart pounding, Jill watched, helpless. At last she saw Dex was safe. As she turned away, she glimpsed two policemen capture Frank near the parking lot. They handcuffed him behind his back and led him up the ramp, where he caught Jill's eye.

Frank let out a bitter laugh. "So, you were my downfall, after all—the oh-so-smart daughter of college professors. How they'll rejoice!" He spat at her as the cops pushed him forward.

****

Nearby, Dex brushed the dirt from his pants. He could no longer see Jill in the cheering crowd, but located the lieutenant and walked over to say goodbye. Handing over the jewelry he had salvaged, he asked, "Did you round them all up?"

"Flanders got away, but we caught him in the end…thanks in part to you and Ms. F." Castillo sounded sheepish. "We gathered up all the others, even that blackguard *el jefe*—at last." Satisfaction leaked out of his smile.

"Well done." Dex shook his hand. *"Adios, Raul, y gracias."*

The lieutenant stared at the blood dripping from Dex's arm. "Not so fast, *amigo*. You should have that arm looked at. The first aid station is in the main terminal. Let a *medico* sew you up."

Glancing down, Dex winced. "It's nothing, just a scratch."

Castillo put a hand on his other arm. "Believe me, the *señora* will not like it if you drip blood on her pretty blouse."

With a laugh, Dex nodded. He looked around again for Jill, but the crowd had finally been cordoned off by the police and was dispersing. Pressing the tail of his shirt against his wound to slow the dripping blood, he hurried over to first aid.

As his arm was disinfected, stitched and bandaged, his mind raced through the events leading to the showdown with the thieves. Why had he gone after the jeweled pectoral Frank dropped and let the man get away? Should he have saved the artifact first? Did he subconsciously let Frank escape for Jill's sake? Thank goodness the police caught him. Dex hoped they hanged the bastard. It was what he deserved for setting all those traps that almost got her killed. But a noose around Frank's neck would be hard on Jill. She still had some feelings for the scoundrel. For her sake, he'd settle for a long, long jail sentence—with Frank locked up in Peru.

Dex looked deep into himself and found he no longer felt the need for vengeance. It was time to move on.

****

As the crowd began to drift away, Jill sank down on a bench. She looked at the briefcase, still clutched in her hand. "How ironic." Her words bubbled out, the sounds lost in the airport's noise. "The luggage I objected to so strongly ended up saving my life." She tried to open the case, but it was locked.

Gazing around the huge terminal, her mind spinning, she kept talking to herself. "I feel I've been in the last act of a play. We're at the end, when all the actors come out to take their bows. It's a huge high while it's happening, but quite a letdown when it's over.

"The heroes and villains were all on stage for the final curtain. Dex and I, along with the lieutenant, played the good guys. Maria, Frank, and Manuel acted the villains. Even the props—the motorcycle, the blowgun, the fancy luggage—ended up here on the airport stage. The coincidences are surreal. Positively scary."

Then her face broke into a sly smile. "What we need is Poppy to interpret the event. She'll use her crystal to locate a vortex here. I've no doubt she'll find the answer in the stars."

With a nervous giggle, Jill rose and headed for the taxi stand outside. She'd describe it that way to Tim. He would enjoy it. Weird, but she still felt charged up.

"Something tells me this night's excitement hasn't ended..."

Chapter 25

Too wired to sleep, Jill dropped off the briefcase in her room and took the elevator back down to the hotel bar. She ordered a Pisco Sour—probably the last one she would ever drink. Tim still hadn't returned. *Poppy must be showing him all the sites in Lima that rocked.*

She had begun to feel the effects of the strong brandy when her cell phone rang. "I'm at your door." Dex sounded tired. "Where are you?"

"In the hotel bar. Come join me." Jill sipped her second drink slowly. The Pisco's sweetness hid its kick, and she needed only one to get a buzz on. A few minutes later, Dex walked into the bar. His eyes lit up when he spotted her. Even rumpled and tired, he exuded buckets of golden sexiness. As she stared at him, he stared back—checking her out to make sure she was all in one piece?

"You took a dangerous chance, following me to the airport," he scolded. The bartender placed another Pisco in front of him. Sliding it over to Jill, he ordered a *cerveza*. "Pilsen Callao," Dex called out, "and keep them coming. I'm thirsty enough to drink the case."

Ignoring the glass, he picked up the bottle and took a long swig. As he lifted his arm, Jill noticed the bandage. She gasped. "You've been hurt! What happened?" Her buzz disappeared as anxiety took its place.

"It's nothing." Dex guzzled the rest of his beer. "One of the bandits got through the police cordon and came at me with a knife. The blade caught me by surprise before I wrestled it away." He smirked. "The s.o.b. got in a shallow cut, but I placed a solid right to his jaw before another cop pulled me off him. Felt great! It was worth it to be in on the action."

She gripped his arm, ran a hand over the bandage. "A stab wound was worth it? You men are all crazy!"

Dex grinned at her. "Afterwards, a medic in the first aid station sewed it up. Took only a few stitches."

"I had no idea you were hurt!" Jill wanted to hug him to her, berate him and kiss him all at the same time. Being in public restrained her. "I'm not sure I believe you. Let's go up to my room. I'll check out your wound to my satisfaction."

He arched one eyebrow and winked. As they finished their drinks and slipped off their stools, however, Tim walked into the bar. "I just heard about the big blowup at the airport," he said. "Wow! I'm sorry I missed that. You gotta tell me all about it."

"Dex has been hurt," Jill said. "One of the bandits pulled a knife. He needs to be in bed."

Dex rolled his eyes, and Tim chuckled. "Sis is quite accomplished at kissing booboos and making them better."

"I'll give her a chance later, I promise." He tweaked a strand of her dark hair. "Since we're all still keyed up, why don't we move to one of the padded booths and tell you about it. Your sister managed to get in on the action, too, despite my warnings."

"Jill doesn't take orders well."

"I've noticed."

"Stop all that sarcasm, you two. Look at who got hurt." As they sat down, Jill reached out and gripped his bandaged arm. Dex winced. "You took such dangerous chances," she admonished. "Are you sure you aren't seriously injured?"

"You'll have an opportunity to test all my parts," he teased. "I guarantee you'll discover they're in excellent working order."

This time Tim rolled his eyes. "So... Tell me all."

With waving arms and lots of interruptions, Jill and Dex described—drum roll—"The Shootout at Lima-Callao International Airport." When all the details were filled in, and Frank's capture recounted, Jill turned to Dex. "How did you get in on the raid, anyway?"

"I was upset when I saw you drive away from the dig," he began. "Really troubled." She grimaced. Looked down at her hands.

"Couldn't think of what else to do, so I went to the police. That's when I found out the raid was planned. Castillo said I could hitch a ride in the police helicopter, and joining the raid was the only way I could get to Lima in time to catch you." A finger under her chin, he pulled her gaze to his. "Have I caught you, Jill?"

She sputtered, coughed, couldn't find the words.

"Uh-oh, time for me to leave." Tim started to rise.

"Not yet," Dex said, his gaze still on Jill. "Let's have some dessert—to round out the evening. Dinner got lost, somehow, in today's agenda. But there's always room for dessert, and the hotel restaurant makes a cake you'll dream about. It's soaked in Pisco and has layers of fresh fruit and *flan*, something like an English trifle. You can't leave Lima without trying it."

"I am a little hungry." Tim sat down again.

"You're always hungry." Jill laughed. "Didn't Poppy take you to a swinging place to eat?"

"That was a couple of hours ago."

Chuckling, Dex called over a waiter. "This dessert goes very well with champagne, the perfect complement to a celebration."

"Yes, we can celebrate capturing the bandits."

"I've a better idea, I hope." For a moment Dex sounded unsure. "You didn't answer my question before. Have I caught you, Jill? I know you've lassoed me. We may not have known each other for long, but the time has been so intense. We've shared so much. It's brought us closer than I've ever been with another person." His eyes searched hers. "Would you like that closeness for a lifetime?"

"Uh-oh, I'm definitely leaving."

"No, Tim." Jill grabbed his shirt and pushed him back in the seat. "Stay as my witness, so he can't back out! I love you, too, Dex." She glowed with happiness. "The day I arrived, something clicked the moment you held me in your arms and protected me. The Lima airport is among my top ten favorite places in the whole world. So you see, your 'little bit o' luck' must have run out, because my answer is, 'Yes.'"

Reaching out, Jill took his hand in her right one, Tim's hand in her left. Warmth flowed in both directions. She turned and gave her lips to Dex. His kiss was long and tender, an offer and a promise in one.

Waiter," Tim called, as the two lingered over their kiss. "Time to open the champagne."

****

It was still chilly in Sands Point during Spring

Break that year, but the revelers under the wedding tent on the Adams' lawn didn't mind. Despite wearing no more than humongous sombreros, embroidered blouses, peasant skirts, or jeans and striped serapes, they warmed from inside out on the spicy *empañadas* and other hot Latin dishes that kept being served, one delicacy after another. The waiters wore fringed pink ponchos. The mouthwatering food was accompanied by the music of a Mariachi band winding among the tables and romancing the guests.

Champagne flowed as well as beer, and bawdy tales were told about the bride and groom. Jill's parents smiled serenely, while her exuberant *abuelos* called for toast after toast. Even Dex's father was caught smiling. The wedding may not have been traditional, but it set a new level for hilarity and joy.

Jill's best friend, Josefina, served as her maid of honor. When she'd first met Dex, Jo had whispered to Jill, "The guy's a hottie. Once you broke out of that rut you were in, you sure knew how to pick 'em."

"You betcha!" Grinning, the women slapped a high five.

The wedding cake—a surprise dreamed up by best man Sam, with help from Harry and Tim—was a gorgeous iced coffee-colored model of the dig, surrounded by mountains coated with dark chocolate ganache and topped by clouds of whipped cream. Cutting the cake was followed by more dancing, until the couple finally slipped away for a short, secret honeymoon where rolling waves rocked them to sleep…eventually.

And at the end of the semester, they packed to head back to Peru. The police had returned the laptop Frank had stolen, much to Jill's delight. Enough manuscripts had been downloaded to keep her busy editing for months. She didn't need New York.

As they took their suitcases out of storage, Jill discovered Frank's briefcase in the back of a closet. "Dex, look!" she called. "I forgot all about this." They were examining the case, battered by rough handling but still firmly locked, when the doorbell rang.

"I'll get it." Jill opened their apartment door and received a special delivery letter. She turned it over, checking for a return address. There was none. Wrinkling her nose, she sniffed. "Smells dank. Could Frank have sent it from prison? It's his handwriting."

"Maybe he's sending us wedding congratulations," Dex joked, laughing when it turned out he was right.

Jill read the note aloud. "My dearest Jillianne, I heard through the grapevine about your marriage. Can't seem to get your fill of archaeologists, can you?"

"He's right, I can't." Jill giggled, then returned to reading.

"I have a wedding present for you, the one piece I managed to get away with. Or, I should say, that you got away for me." Puzzled, Jill looked up, but Dex only shrugged.

"It's really more for Conroy. I'm sure you'll lead him around by the nose, just as you did me, so this will give him a handle on yours. Your ever lovin' ex, Francisco."

Scotch taped to the bottom of the letter was a tiny brass key. Jill peeled off the sticky tape and handed it to Dex. "I think it's the key to his briefcase."

"One way to find out." Picking up the case, he laid it on the table. He handed back the key with a flourish.

"For you, Madam Conroy."

With shaking hands, Jill aimed the key at the lock, missed, tried again, and this time inserted it into the keyhole and twisted. She lifted the lid and drew in a long breath. Dex moved over and glanced in, too.

Sealed in bubble wrap lay a golden Moche nosepiece. Its half-moon curved lower edge was lined with a row of tiny, filigreed bells. When she picked it up, the delicate bells tinkled with a sound so soft, it could have been the murmuring of baby birds.

"The piece is gorgeous," Jill muttered. "Frank must have decided he'd never get it back, so he might as well use it for a joke. I'm sure he sent the note and key for the irony of giving you a nosepiece to lead me by, not because of any lingering feelings."

Dex agreed. "It's the kind of gesture Frank would make."

"I guess we'll have to give it back?" She looked longingly at the stunning golden jewelry.

"To whom? It has no provenance. I wouldn't want you to part with your last remembrance from your ex-husband, Jill. Besides, it'll make a great after-dinner topic for our parties."

She giggled. "I feel like writing and telling him we're too busy trying out all the positions in the Moche pot exhibit to do any leading and following."

His wicked grin was back. "Go ahead. But if you want to lead me, I've got a better handle."

Licking her lips, Jill leaned forward, patting him down. "Where would that be?"

"You're the expert at finding things. Got to uphold your reputation."

"O-kay!"

Dex groaned softly. Lifting her hand with a reluctant sigh, he said, "We haven't finished packing."

"So?"

"Well, if that's the way you feel, how about trying on the nosepiece?"

Impishly, Jill plucked it from its bubble wrap and put it on. As she breathed lightly, the bells tinkled. "Sexy, huh?"

"Damned if it isn't a turn on. Come here, wife." He grabbed her and set her on his lap. In a minute they were half undressed, and she was straddling him. Jill threw her head back with a moan of pleasure, and the bells tinkled wildly.

"I'm entering the temple of *checan*," Dex's husky voice crooned. "Watch, *mi cielo. Te amo*. I love you."

Caught up in ecstasy, Jill looked down, mistily observing him glide in and out of her, all wet and hard and glistening. Deeper and deeper he slid inside, and she rocked with him, responding to every movement. The bells tinkled, faster and faster. *Checan!* She breathed the word into the atmosphere. Golden bells, echoing the rhythm of the universe, the music of the spheres. Ringing of joy and love. Ringing forever.

A word from the author...

I've bounced from East Coast to West Coast with many stops in between, now live in Arizona with my artist husband. Love to travel, read, write, walk with a book on my I-phone while I gaze at the scenery, attend concerts and watch lots of movies. Like to pal around with friends, especially writers and readers, and look forward to hearing from readers of my books.

You can find out more about me on my website, http://evedewcrook.com or e-mail me at
evedewcrook@gmail.com.

~*~

Oh, yes, I also like to write poems.
Here's "The Song of the Lovesick Siren":
I love you, I love you, I love you so madly,
If I tried to tell you I'd do it so badly.
I love you for will be, for was, and for is,
If I were a soda, I'd give you my fizz.

—

I love how you think, and I love how you feel,
I love you for promise, I love you for real.
I love you for touching, I find you enticing,
If I were a cupcake, you'd lick off my icing.

—

I love you for dreaming, for taking and giving,
I love what you put into warm-blooded living.
I love you completely, I'm out of control.
If I were a doughnut, I'd give you my whole.

~*~

Other Eve Dew Crook titles
available from The Wild Rose Press, Inc.:
TAKING THE TUMBLE